the WATER *of* POSSIBILITY

IN THE SAME BOAT

the WATER *of* POSSIBILITY

HIROMI GOTO

COTEAU BOOKS
WWW.COTEAUBOOKS.COM

This novel is a work of fiction. Names, characters, places, and incidents either are the product of the author's imagination or are used fictitiously. Any resemblance to actual persons, living or dead, is coincidental.

Editor for the Series, Barbara Sapergia.
Edited by Barbara Sapergia.
Cover painting and interior illustrations by Aries Cheung.
Gourd illustration by Hiromi Goto.
Cover and book design by Duncan Campbell.
"In The Same Boat" logo designed by Tania Wolk, Magpie Design.
Typeset by Karen Steadman.
Printed and bound in Canada by Houghton-Boston, Saskatoon.

Canadian Cataloguing in Publication Data
Goto, Hiromi, 1966-
The water of possibility

ISBN 1-55050-183-6

1. Title.
PS8563.O8383W37 2001   JC813'.54   C2001-911105-3
PZ7.G6935WA 2001

10 9 8 7 6 5 4 3 2 1

COTEAU BOOKS
401-2206 Dewdney Ave.
Regina, Saskatchewan
Canada   S4R 1H3

AVAILABLE IN THE US FROM
General Distrubution Services
4500 Witmer Industrial Estates
Niagara Falls, NY, 14305-1386

The publisher gratefully acknowledges the financial assistance of the Saskatchewan Arts Board, the Canada Council for the Arts, including the Millennium Arts Fund, the Government of Canada through the Book Publishing Industry Development Program (BPIDP), and the City of Regina Arts Commission, for its publishing program.

PREFACE

JANET LUNN

"Why aren't there are any stories about us?" has been a heartfelt cry of Canadian children not descended from either of our founding nations for too long. In recent years, writers like Paul Yee, Leo Yerxa, Shizuye Takashima, and William Kurelek have created beautiful picture books and retellings of folk tales from the cultures of their ancestors. But there have been almost no children's novels, no up-to-date stories with which these children might identify.

Not more than a generation ago, this was true for all Canadian children. All but a small handful of their books came from Great Britain, France, or the United States. That is certainly not true now. Canadian children can immerse themselves happily in stories set in their own towns and countrysides, identify with characters like themselves, and be comforted and bolstered by a shared experience. This is what children of Japanese or African or indigenous North American descent have been wanting to do.

This series, *In the Same Boat,* was motivated by the desire of Coteau Books to do something about this. What a good idea it was! In these first five books for readers in their middle years of childhood, five writers, from five different backgrounds, offer the children who share these backgrounds stories in which they can recognize themselves and the way they live. At the same time, they offer all children insights into these diverse cultures.

These are five good stories, strong works of fiction, but what is perhaps more important is that they are all told honestly and with the authority that is only given to writers who truly understand what they are writing about.

To Koji and Sae

1. LEAVING

THEY LEFT THE CITY. MAYBE NOT THE MOST GLAMOROUS city in the world, Sayuri supposed, but it had been her home all the same. Her favourite Vietnamese restaurant, the Memorial Park Library, the Lindsay Park pool. Her friends. Everything left behind, and for what? She glared out the window as the car whipped past field after endless field. Drying canola, sweet-smelling hay, small herds of black Angus, red-and-white Herefords. She sighed loudly, then sighed again. No one paid any attention.

Sayuri scrunched lower in her seat. The floor space was filled with boxes and backpacks. Shopping bags of games and laundry they'd forgotten to pack into the moving van cartons. Her seven-year-old brother turned his back and huddled furtively in the corner. Sayuri's lips turned down. She swung her runner into the back of Keiji's leg.

"Quit it!" she hissed. "Kimi! Keiji's picking his nose again!"

"Keijiiiii," Sayuri's mom moaned. "No one will want your kisses if you keep on eating your boogers!"

"Mucous and dust accumulate in your nostrils and are trapped by the hairs lining the inner membrane," their father, Jun, explained helpfully.

Sayuri rolled her eyes. Her dad was so sweet. But everything had to turn into a Health Issue! Meanwhile, Keiji had ignored everyone's comments and had eaten his snot. Ugh! He was such a disgusting little thing. Sayuri wished she was anywhere but here. This journey was worse than any Family Car Trip. At least you knew a car trip would end. No, the Katos were moving toward eternal boredom and prairie isolation. The Katos were moving to a small town!

Sayuri sighed loudly again. Kimi finally turned from the steering wheel and gave her a huge and hopeful grin. But she looked away.

There was a slight itching in her fingers. Sayuri looked at her hands, then rubbed her thumbs over the tips. The itching sank deeper and she dug thumbnails into her flesh to relieve the sensation. She frowned. Her fingers had started itching in the spring and sometimes it drove her mad, keeping her from sleeping long into the night. She'd told her dad about it because he was a nurse. He had raised his eyebrows and peered into her hands like he was reading her fortune.

"Well," Jun had said, "you're going through puberty... maybe it's a hormonal change?" He hadn't sounded too sure. "Maybe they've changed the chlorine content at your pool?" Jun had run his hand through his shiny hair.

"I don't care what it is." Sayuri had gritted her teeth, rubbing fingers up and down the outside of her coarse jeans. "Don't you have a cream to make it stop?!"

Sayuri reached into her backpack on the floor of the car. Her dad had finally given her a small tube of salve. Apply sparingly, Jun had warned.

Sayuri squeezed a thin worm of ointment on her forefinger. Rubbed her fingers with her thumbs. The itch dulled but didn't go away. She lifted her hands to her face and blew, hoping cool air would make a difference.

Welcome to Granola! A happy face sign whipped past the window. No, thought Sayuri, looking back again, not Granola. Ganola. Population: 5032. Sayuri blinked, to see if it was true. No, the town was bigger than a blink, and they continued to drive past a row of shops, small restaurants, a car and tractor dealership, and church after church. Baseball diamonds. People in Granola, Sayuri decided, must spend most of their time praying or playing ball. Sayuri turned away from the window and sank lower in the seat. This is all a mistake, she chanted in her mind. This is just a bubble in my reality and it will soon pop.

After wending through the main streets, Kimi turned east. She drove slowly on the pot-holed road, making wide swerves that had Keiji laughing uncontrollably. Sayuri stared sourly at her brother. The fool obviously didn't care where he lived. Didn't he know this was for keeps? Their mom pulled onto a long gravel drive. Dust plumed, spilling into the cracks of open windows.

"Close the windows," Jun called out.

"Don't worry, Jun," Keiji said. "I have my inhaler with me."

Sayuri stared at the back of Kimi's head. Her mom drove intently, hunched over the steering wheel so she wouldn't lose control over the washboard drive. She didn't seem to notice they were almost at the house until Jun yelped. Then Kimi stomped on the brakes. The car skidded on the loose gravel before it stopped.

"Pretty wild, don't you think?" Kimi jumped out of the car, flinging her hands toward the house. The wind whipped through the seams of the window, bringing dust and the smell of hay.

Sayuri watched her mother from inside the car. Kimi was short and her hair was cut close to her skull; practically a crew cut. Sayuri couldn't remember the last time she'd seen her mom without black eyeliner. Kimi wore jeans snug on her full butt and paraded T-shirts with logos that would be banned in any school. She sighed. Her mom was short and she spilled and bubbled everything. Her thoughts, her emotions, her laughter. Sayuri loved Kimi, but she wished her mom could be more, well, normal sometimes. How many moms wrote horror novels for a living?!

"Wild, all right," Sayuri glowered. Glared at everything she could see. The house was old. The paint was cracked and the windows covered with paper. The dry grass spread into mole-ish hills and the few spruce trees around the house were pointing their tips toward the ground. Maybe, Sayuri thought, they're looking for water. One enormous poplar tree grew too close to the house. Half of it was dead and the naked branches scraped against the attic window. Kimi strode here and there, arms gesturing enthusiastically at things Sayuri couldn't see from the car. She's probably talking to herself, Sayuri thought sourly. A gust of wind snatched her mother's silk scarf. The material jerked along the ground like it was being pulled by a string.

Keiji giggled as his mother ran after the light blue cloth. She teetered on bright red platform shoes.

Sayuri couldn't help herself. Even though she had sworn to herself she'd be mad all day, all week, all year! Her mom ran and crouched. Ran and crouched again. She looked like a silly city rabbit in the country for the first time. Sayuri laughed.

"You kids. Don't laugh at your mother!" But Jun was wiping his eyes with his fingertips, his shoulders shaking.

"Help!" Kimi cried faintly. "Someone help!"

Keiji gave a whoop and leapt from the vehicle. And after a pause, Sayuri tumbled after them, her short black hair flying in the wind.

"Watch out for gopher holes!" their father called out.

The scarf snagged on a rusty barbed-wire fence and Kimi trotted over, huffing. She bent over at the waist. Sucked at air around her knees.

"You puking, Kimi?" Keiji asked. Worried.

"No!" Kimi gasped, flapping her hand in front of her face. "Can't breathe. Okay soon."

Sayuri plucked the scarf carefully from the barbs. She frowned. "You really need to take better care of yourself. You should try swimming." Sayuri crossed her arms. She looked her mom up and down. She didn't look bad for a mom. Her hair was always stylish. She always had amazing shoes. But Sayuri couldn't remember the last time Kimi had done something like exercise. Walking back and forth in front of a computer didn't count as anything.

"Please!" Kimi still flapped her hand. Gasping. "Not you too! Besides. Swimming is boring. Up and down the lane! What for?"

Sayuri sighed. She'd tried explaining how the water felt, flowing past her body. How she pushed herself to the absolute limits and beyond. Then, how it felt like she could swim forever. But her mom didn't have a clue. Kimi dog-paddled if she really had to. Sayuri sighed. She'd forgotten. She was mad at her mom anyway. That was the thing about holding a grudge. You had to really work at it and not lose focus.

"Amazing scenery, don't you think?" Kimi gushed.

"It's flat," Keiji said. Shoved a finger in his left nostril.

"Ugh!" Sayuri stalked away.

"That's disgusting," Sayuri heard her mom saying. "I'm not kissing you until you brush your teeth. Sayuri! Sayuri!"

"What?!" Sayuri yelled. She wasn't yelling at her mom. Not really. The wind was loud, that was why she had to holler. She turned back to glare at her mother. Not, she thought grudgingly, that it was all Kimi's fault. They'd had to move because of Circumstances. But it still wasn't fair.

"Give this place a try. There's a lucky feeling here." Kimi wasn't looking at the house. Or at Sayuri. She was pressing her fingertips together, staring at the triangle of her hands. Sayuri rolled her eyes. Sometimes her mom did that. Lost contact.

"Lucky for you, maybe," Sayuri muttered. A hot wetness prickled her eyes and she angrily dragged her forearm across her face. She took quick steps, crunching dry grass beneath her runners. "No one asked me," she yelled over her shoulder.

Silence.

Great, thought Sayuri. Earth to Kimi!

But then her mother called back. "They have an advanced competitive swim club. Two Canadians who made it to the Olympics in Sydney started here!"

Sayuri stopped stomping across the broken grass. Wow, she thought, even though she wasn't really interested. Two people from one swim club. And such a small town! They must have an amazing coach.

"Can I join?" Keiji asked. "You said I could join!"

"Not until you stop picking your nose and eating it," Kimi said loftily.

Sayuri laughed.

Kimi beamed at her daughter. "The house is so much bigger than the one we had in the city. And all this fresh air! It'll be better for Keiji's asthma." Kimi looked up at the sky. Then sneezed.

Sayuri sighed. She knew how happy her dad had been about getting the job at the hospital. Nursing jobs were scarce in the city and Jun had been laid off four months ago. Kimi's advances and royalties were like Christmas. Not something that came every day. Sayuri wasn't stupid. She knew that things had been getting tight and they'd been eating a lot more curry rice and stews than they used to. But that didn't mean she'd like moving to the country.

"Hey, duckling." The wind was so loud Sayuri hadn't heard her father approaching. The tails of his cotton shirt flapped against his slim build. He kept his hair longer than Kimi's and the shiny length was pulled back in a low ponytail. The gusts that blew in from the mountains snapped his hair like a flag. Sayuri took after her dad and she was glad. If she was as short as Kimi, she'd never win at any of the swim meets.

Her dad's serious brown eyes looked a little sad.

Sayuri playfully punched Jun's arm as she dashed past him. "Quack! Quack! We better get satellite TV!" she threatened and ran back to the car.

2. THE NEW OLD HOUSE

T HE KATOS CREAKED UP THE DRY PORCH STEPS AND STOOD before the house. The wind had stopped and the silence rang like bells inside their ears. Kimi unlocked the door and Sayuri and Keiji huddled close behind her. Jun stood right behind them, and no one said a word as the door swung inward on old hinges.

The house was a mess. The furniture was gone and they could see where the couch and chair used to be, the only clean spaces on the hardwood. Dust covered everything else. Bits of paper, balls of pet hair, and shreds of newspaper littered the floor.

"A clean house was part of the deal!" Kimi moaned.

"Well," Jun said, "at least we have time to tidy up before the moving van brings the rest of our things."

They trooped to the kitchen, the thumps of their runners loud across the wood.

Whoever left the house had left it in a hurry. Not only was the linoleum filthy but there were boxes of cereal on the food-stained kitchen table. They'd even left four mismatched wooden chairs. Rusty cans of food remained in the few open cupboards and a large garbage bag, half-filled, sat in the middle of the floor. The fridge door was open but luckily it was empty. The stove was ringed with circles of soup and splatters of grease.

"Disgusting," Sayuri wrinkled her nose.

"Not much for cupboard space," Kimi murmured. "We'll have to build more."

"ChocoBalls!" Keiji gasped, peering into the open flaps. "Can I have some?"

Jun snatched the box out of his son's grasp and tossed it into the garbage. "Who knows how long it's been here? There might be hantavirus mouse droppings in it!"

"Huh?" Sayuri and Kimi asked.

"It's a virus that's carried by deer mice and it can be passed on to humans. It can be deadly and –"

"You said never grab things from people!" Keiji's chin jutted. His lower lip starting to tremble.

"I'm sorry, honey." Jun curved his arm around Keiji's shoulders. "That wasn't nice of me. I don't want you to get germs, that's all."

"We never buy ChocoBalls," Keiji muttered.

Sayuri rolled her eyes. Her brother was such a little baby. She was sure he was growing younger, not older.

"I'll buy you a jumbo box once we're all settled in!" Kimi announced.

Jun pursed his lips. Then smiled. "I suppose just once won't hurt."

"Yay!"

Sayuri started mincing out of the filthy room.

"Where are you going?" Kimi called out to her daughter.

"Upstairs." Sayuri leaned in the doorway. Arms crossed, she stared at the mess. "You sure these people are really gone, Kimi? Maybe they're going to come back home, any minute."

"Like the three bears!" Keiji whispered dramatically. "They had porridge on the table."

"No one's coming back. The family who lived here moved to Vancouver." Jun frowned. "But they were supposed to leave the house all ready for us to move in."

"Don't you think it's a little weird?" Kimi whispered overloud.

Jun laughed. "You and your imagination. Don't encourage Keiji. I'm sure they were just ordinary lazy people. We didn't leave our house the cleanest."

Sayuri wasn't sure at all. She rested her hand on the banister and looked toward the front door. Stepped slowly up the stairs. The first wooden board creaked and, for no good reason, her heart thumped in her chest. Dust shone in streams of sunlight. And although the air was hot, a prickle of shivers bumped along Sayuri's skin.

A damp hand touched her fingers on the banister.

"Eeeep!"

"Ahhh!" Keiji screamed.

"What's going on?" Kimi called from the kitchen.

"What are you doing?!" Sayuri hissed at her brother. "That's a creepy thing to do, you little –"

"Sayuri," Jun called out.

"Sorry!"

Keiji frowned. "I want to see upstairs too. I'm scared to go by myself. Will you hold my hand?"

Sayuri sighed. "All right, digger. But not your nose-picker." She gingerly held Keiji's right hand and they crept up the stairs. The second floor had three bedrooms and a separated bathtub room and toilet. The children peered from the windows. Stared at the spread of prairie cut by a distant wall of mountains. Across from the toilet room was another tiny flight of stairs. It was dark.

"What's at the very top?" Sayuri called down. Her voice didn't quaver.

"Attic!" Jun yelled from the living room.

"Oh," Keiji said in a small voice.

"Well!" Sayuri pretended she was her mother. Hands on her hips. The stairway was so narrow they had to climb single file. Keiji clung desperately to the back pockets of his sister's jeans.

"Don't pull!" she hissed. Sayuri marched upward, Keiji trailing behind her like poop on a goldfish.

"Tadaaaa!" Sayuri swung the door open on creaking hinges. A bright light fell upon them. And a fine sprinkling of dust. She watched as the motes bobbed and lifted, golden and bright. "How beautiful," she breathed.

"Beautiful," Keiji mouthed. Then he coughed.

Three skylights opened the sloped ceiling to the prairie sky. Soft mounds of white cloud passed from one window to the next like a movie on three separate screens.

"My room," Sayuri murmured.

"Not fair!" Keiji wailed.

"You know the rules. I said it first. Besides, you'd be scared going to the washroom at night."

Keiji glanced all around. The room was enormous.

"Look!" he squeaked. In the furthest corner was a wooden rocking chair. It was stained a deep red and on the seat sat a huge stuffed cat. Not a toy. It was a real cat that was dead and stuffed. One green glass eye. The other an empty socket. The cat was a dark purple and mauve, striped. Sayuri wondered if they'd dyed the fur.

"Gross!" Keiji admired. "I'm telling Jun!" He ran down the stairs, sneezing in the clouds of dust he created. "Jun!" he yelled. "Jun! There's a dead cat in Sayuri's room!"

Sayuri tilted her head slightly. The floor. The dust coated the wooden floor and she and Keiji hadn't entered the room, only stood in the doorway. But there were marks in the middle of the room.

Paw prints.

Starting from nowhere, just a set of prints, three, four, five, six, seven of them, leading to the rocking chair. As if the cat had appeared out of air in the middle of the room, then minced across the dusty floor to leap on to the chair.

Sayuri shuddered. Flicked her eyes to the stuffed cat. The cat. Everything was dusty. Not the cat....

"DON'T ANYONE TOUCH THE ANIMAL!" Sayuri heard Jun pounding up the first flight of stairs.

"I want to see!" her mom's voice huffed after him.

Sayuri thought fast.

Something was definitely going on.

Was it dangerous?

Uncertain.

Was she interested?

Yes.

Was she scared?

A little. Okay. Quite a bit.

How would her parents deal with the mysterious prints in the dust?

Jun: Contain all sources of germs. Throw out cat.

Kimi: Imaginative. Sell the house or call in a witch/priest/psychic.

Sayuri ran into the room, directly toward the cat, her arms outstretched to snatch the creature into her arms. And in a blink, the cat jumped off the chair, tail held high. Leapt into the wall like it was water. The empty rocking chair moved gently back and forth.

Sayuri's heart thumped in her chest. Purple cat. Not black. Liquid walls. No blood. Might not be evil. Okay? Breathe in, breathe out. Pulse tripping in her temples, Sayuri reached trembling fingertips to the spot in the wall where the cat had disappeared. Her skin tingled. Electric buzz. The hairs on her arm stood on end and a tickling crept up her arm, as if her cells were in faster motion....

"Sayuri!" Jun yelled.

"Ah!" she spun around. "You scared me!"

"Sorry. Where's the dead cat?" Jun had on yellow kitchen gloves. A green garbage bag in his hands.

Kimi crowded behind Jun's slender height. "Dead how?

Poor thing."

Sayuri crossed her fingers behind her back. A childish trick, she knew. But it always made her feel less guilty.

"There's no cat." Not a lie, really. It was gone, after all.

"Is so a cat!" Keiji yelled from between Jun's legs. "I seen it right there on the rocking chair!"

"Saw it, hon. Not seen," Kimi said automatically.

"Saw it! Saw it!"

Kimi and Jun looked all around the bright space. And Sayuri casually wiped out the paw prints with her feet.

Keji stared furiously at his sister. Eyes bright with the injustice. He dropped his mouth open to wail or yell, but Sayuri quickly formed her thumb and forefinger into a circle. Her parents thought it meant, "Okay," but it was a signal Sayuri had made up so her brother would keep his trap shut. She'd pay him a loonie later.

Keiji shut his trap. But his lips quivered with the indignity, his face bright red.

"What an incredible light!" Kimi glowed, easily distracted. "It's a lovely place for my study."

"I called dibs on it first!" Sayuri cried.

"We could negotiate...." Kimi began.

"What about this cat?!" Jun almost shouted. He rarely shouted.

"I guess," Keiji muttered, still looking at his sister's circled fingers. She circled the thumb and fingers of her left hand too. Two dollars!

"I guess I imagined it," Keiji choked.

"How wonderful!" Kimi praised.

"You people are impossible!" Jun exclaimed. "I'm going to straighten up the kitchen or there won't be any supper."

Sayuri breathed a sigh.

"We can negotiate the terms of the room at dinner, hmmm?" Kimi called as she carefully crept down the stairs.

"Where's the cat?!" Keiji hissed. "Did you hide it? You made me lie!"

"I didn't make you anything!" Sayuri sniffed.

"Where is it then? I saw it. And where's my money?"

"Ugh!" Sayuri reached into her back pocket for her vinyl wallet. "Here you go, capitalist!" She dropped two shiny loonies into his grubby palm.

"Hmmmm!" Keiji beamed.

"Now scram."

"No, really, what happened to the cat?"

"I don't know." It was the truth. Sayuri really didn't know.

Keiji's eyes widened. "It-it disappeared?" he breathed.

Sayuri nodded.

Keiji spun around and scrambled down the stairs, the money clenched in his fist.

Sayuri turned to face the wall. Crossed her arms and tilted her head. She marched to the spot where the feline had disappeared. But she wasn't exactly sure where the spot was. She cautiously reached out with her hand, palm extended. Stroked the surface with the flat of her fingers. But the wall felt like a wall. Slightly cool and smooth. There was no electric tingle. No static buzz.

Sayuri frowned in concentration. What had the cat done before it disappeared?

Sayuri took a small step backward. Another. Three, four more. She took a deep breath. Like the high diving board, she thought. Then sprinted toward the wall.

"Ahhhhh!" she yelled and leapt.

Thud! Bang! She bounced off the solid wall and fell onto the wooden floor.

"What's going on up there?!" she heard her mother's voice, faint from the living room.

Sayuri started to laugh.

3. THE BASEMENT

THE MOVING VAN ARRIVED BEFORE THE HOUSE WAS cleaned. Jun, in a panic, ran about with his yellow gloves on while Kimi wiped down the living room. The movers piled all their belongings on the front porch, then left. The dust rose and clouded so much that Keiji had an asthma attack and had to go lie down in the car, Jun by his side. So Sayuri lugged buckets of warm water around, slopping her pantlegs and muttering about the division of labour.

"You done upstairs yet?" Kimi yelled from the kitchen.

"Almost!" Sayuri hollered. There was only one mop that Kimi had called dibs on, so Sayuri was on her hands and knees, wiping up the wooden floors of the three bedrooms. At least, she puffed, her attic room was done first. It was shiny, spotless, and Kimi had burned incense so that the air would smell sweet. Sayuri had wiped the rocking chair. But she hadn't tried sitting in it.

Sweat trickled down Sayuri's face and stung her eyes. She finished up Keiji's room and dropped the rag into the pail.

She minced across the wet floor to open the window. The summer sun was still bright, though her watch pointed to five after eight. The evening was warm. She saw movement from the parked car. Jun was rhythmically tapping Keiji's back. He sure gets out of a lot of work, Sayuri thought, then instantly felt guilty. She grabbed the bucket and marched into the washroom to dump the water down the toilet.

Kimi creaked up the stairs holding two glasses of iced tea. Sayuri smiled thankfully and they slid down the wall of the hallway. They sat with legs sticking straight out and took a well-deserved rest. Sayuri's legs stuck out farther than Kimi's. But when she looked in her mother's face, they were eye to eye.

The iced tea was made from real tea and fresh lemons. Kimi must have made it the night before, knowing they'd get thirsty and tired, Sayuri thought. Kimi was like that. Making something special out of nothing. Sayuri watched as her mother swallowed her tea down in four large gulps, then set the glass next to her on the floor.

"When you were born," Kimi said slowly, "you came out of my body with the umbilical cord in your mouth. 'My,' Jun said, 'this one is a fighter. She's trying to break free!'"

Sayuri sipped from the icy sweet liquid and closed her eyes to the familiar story.

"When your brother was born, he was born holding tight, the umbilical cord in his hands. 'My,' Jun said, 'this one is a holder. He wants to stay forever.'"

Sayuri opened her eyes and saw that her mother's were closed. And as she watched, Kimi's hands seemed to move unconsciously into her lap. Forming a shape of a triangle with her fingers and thumbs.

Sayuri's fingers tingled and she hastily rubbed them against the rough grain of her jeans. Rubbed so quickly the friction made her skin hot. It must be the soap, she thought. Where'd I put my cream?

Kimi's hand reached out and stopped her sudden movement and Sayuri looked up. Her mother's eyes were far away.

"We're each born with our strengths and weaknesses. Lose one and the shape will collapse."

Sayuri could hear nothing. Not her watch. Not the wind. Just the thud of her blood, heavy and slow. She cleared her throat to break the stillness. "What are you talking about?"

Kimi shook her head and laughed loudly. "I have no idea! Come on. Let's order some pizza. I'm so hungry I could eat that cereal Jun threw out!" Kimi jumped up with the empty glasses and jogged down the stairs.

"The phone's not hooked up yet!" Sayuri called after her.

And her mom laughed loudly again.

Sayuri followed Kimi downstairs. The dust had been eradicated. The air was soft with the scent of lavender. Sayuri's mom had arranged the living room. The bookshelves were filled, the deep-blue carpet lay diagonally across the floor and the small couch and reading chair were close to the windows. The TV was in a corner on a stand. The paintings and photographs weren't hung but propped against the walls. Impressed, Sayuri checked the kitchen.

The boxes were flattened and tied up with string into several bundles, ready to be put away. The bite of pine cleanser lingered. And the dust was all gone, the cupboards wiped and filled with dishes and utensils, a few boxes of dried goods and canned fish, peanut butter. Kimi had even thrown the green tablecloth on the wooden table and the four chairs waited for the new family.

"Wow, Kimi," Sayuri's eyes were round. "You sure did a lot of work! How'd you lift the heavy stuff?"

Kimi pushed back her T-shirt sleeve and squeezed her hand into a fist, her biceps popping out. "I'm no pencil-pushing weakling," she bragged. "Keyboard punching, what-ever," she clarified. "All we have left to do is get the futons, desks, and dressers up into our rooms." Kimi popped her head out the kitchen door.

"Jun! It's safe for Keiji to come back in! I need your help with the furniture!"

Sayuri plunked into a chair holding a jar of peanut butter. She unscrewed the lid and began dipping her finger into the sticky depth. "I'm so hungry!" she moaned. She licked peanut butter until her throat started to get stuck. Then she ran to the sink to gulp water straight out of the tap. She sprayed her first mouthful back into the sink.

Kimi raised her eyebrows.

"Ugh! This water's rotten! It smells like a fart!" Sayuri clutched her stomach. "You think I'm a goner?"

Jun nudged past Kimi into the kitchen and poured some water into a glass. Sniffed. Took a small taste. "Sulfur," he proclaimed. "Maybe some iron. It's well water, that's all." He turned to his daughter. "But you'd be doing yourself a service smelling things first before eating and drinking, especially in unknown places. You have a nose for a reason." Jun sighed, then followed Kimi to the living room.

Keiji trudged into the kitchen and sank into a chair. Sayuri turned from the counter. Her brother's cheeks were flushed from coughing and blue smudges stood out beneath his eyes.

"You want to lick some peanut butter?" she offered, holding out the jar.

Keiji shook his head slowly, then rested his cheek on the table.

A loud thud came from the stairs. Sayuri could hear Kimi cursing. Jun giggled.

"Quit pushing!" Sayuri heard her mother hissing.

Sayuri smiled. Then frowned. If she was hungry, her mom must be starved. And when her mom was hungry she was "unfit company for beasts or humans." Sayuri jogged to the foot of the stairs and watched as her parents struggled to lift Keiji's futon up the steep stairs. The heavy bundle drooped sloppily over the banister as Kimi and Jun struggled to keep their grip.

"You need help?" she asked.

"No room," Jun puffed.

"Go – take – boxes," Kimi gasped. "Downstairs. Storage."

"There's a downstairs?" Sayuri frowned. Great. Another room they'd have to clean. "All right."

But her parents had manoeuvred the futon onto the second floor and disappeared into Keiji's room.

SAYURI GLANCED AROUND THE KITCHEN. She hadn't noticed before, but there were two small doors in opposite walls.

Keiji still drooped in his chair. The bony curve of his spine pressed against his T-shirt.

"He may grow out of it," Jun had answered when Sayuri had asked about her brother's asthma a long time ago. But her father's eyes had been sad.

Sayuri shook her head. Stared at the fragile curl of Keiji's back. She flourished her arm toward both doors, spoke nasally out of the corner of her mouth like a TV game show host. "And which door will you choose, my young man, Door Number One or Door Number Two?" She raised and lowered her eyebrows while she faked a tap dance on the floor.

Keiji giggled and pointed to the door closest to him.

"Okay, folks. He chose Door Number One. Are you absoluuuutely certain that's the one you want? You can't change your mind later, my boy."

Keiji smiled wide, revealing the spaces where his baby teeth had fallen out. He nodded eagerly.

"Tadaaaaa!" Sayuri flung it open.

The space was tall and thin. Not even a proper room. Just wide enough for the bucket and mop, the dustpan and broom hanging from a nail. Kimi had precariously piled the extra toilet paper rolls one on top of the other. Jun would definitely not approve. A waft of pine cleanser spilled into the room and Keiji sneezed.

"Congratulations!" Sayuri beamed. "You're the proud owner of useful household items! And let's see what's behind the door you didn't choose!"

As Sayuri reached to grab the knob, a slight tingling zipped from her itchy fingertips through her arms and up her shoulders. Shudder bumps spread across her back. She shook her head. A cold breeze from the basement, she thought, and flung open the door.

Darkness seemed to spill into the bright kitchen. Sayuri took a step backward, as if the darkness was a pool of ink spreading across the newly cleaned floor.

"Sh-shut the door," Keiji stammered.

"Silly duck!" Sayuri smiled to reassure both her brother and herself. "It's just dark. I'll find the light."

"Me don't want you to go downstairs," Keiji shook his head. His dark brown eyes round and shiny.

Sayuri didn't know if her brother talked like a baby on purpose or not. But she knew it meant he was Really Upset.

"I, not me," she chided. Like Kimi. She bravely stuck her head in the doorway and glanced around for the switch. The walls weren't covered at all. The outer layer had peeled away; only the bones of the two-by-fours remained, with the black plastic switch jutting from the cavity. Pursing her lips, Sayuri flicked the light on with cautious fingers.

A dull orange glow seeped from the bottom of the steep and dirty stairs. The stairs weren't properly made. Just old wood with no banister. Narrow wooden steps and open air dropped to the concrete floor far below.

"No one's going to be playing hide-and-seek down here!" Sayuri called out cheerfully, but the depth swallowed up the sound of her voice. She gulped.

"No go," Keiji managed. "Maybe cat's there," he whispered.

"The cat," Sayuri murmured. Blinking. "All right!" she said briskly. "It's just a basement. Kimi and Jun are right upstairs. I'm going to take these boxes." She marched to the bundles and wrapped her fingers around the string that held together the first stack. The flattened cardboard was awkward and heavy, the string cutting into the palm of her hand. She couldn't see in front of her. She'd have to be extra careful down those stairs, she thought.

The open side of the stairs felt like a vacuum, tugging at Sayuri's centre of gravity. She minced down the steps, toeing each one carefully. She couldn't see over top of the cardboard, so she looked down at her feet, glancing sideways now and then at the concrete floor far below. Dust rose.

"Me come with you!" Keiji squeaked from right behind her.

"No! There's too much dust. Get back upstairs. And quit talking like a baby. You're going to be in Grade Two!"

"Me don't care. Me coming."

"Oh, for – you better not get me into trouble!"

Keiji said nothing. Sayuri could feel his hot breath in the middle of her back.

They minced downward, Keiji's breath growing shorter and more ragged. Sayuri didn't know if it was from fear or asthma. The bottom came suddenly and Sayuri stumbled, thinking there was one more step left.

"Ugh!" she grunted, falling flat on her front, the wind knocked out of her lungs. Pain shot through her tender chest though the cardboard boxes cushioned most of the impact. But Keiji, too close behind her, fell with her momentum and landed smack on her back.

"Ugh!" Sayuri grunted again, the breath whooshing from

her lungs a second time. "Get off me –" she began, but broke out into giggles. Keiji giggled too. Then they were laughing, gasping, wiping muddy tears from their eyes.

"Ooooh," Sayuri groaned. "Stop making me laugh. My stomach hurts." But the giggles spilled out again.

"Sorry, Sayuri," Keiji laughed. "I can't get up!"

"What's going on?" Jun called from the doorway.

"We've fallen and we can't get up!" Sayuri laughed.

"What?!" Jun pounded down the rickety steps and rushed to the children. He expertly and gently ran his hands over their skulls, their limbs, checking for broken bones and murmuring, "Just lie still. Don't move. Everything will be all right."

The children howled with laughter. Rolled on to their backs to clasp their arms over the sore muscles of their stomachs.

"Oh, Jun!" Kimi exclaimed, mincing down the steps. "They're perfectly fine!"

Jun stood and put his hands on his hips. He frowned, his lips turning downward. "Don't do that to me! My heart is pounding! Get off the floor, Keiji. You know better than to roll around in dust."

Jun stooped and scooped Keiji into his arms.

Kimi extended her hand and helped Sayuri to her feet. The children were white with dust and the parents started laughing too.

"At least there'll be plenty of hot water for your baths," Jun said, catching sight of two hot water tanks.

Kimi started poking around the room. The concrete walls were pockmarked with crumbling holes. And instead of one large room with smaller ones attached, each room was a tiny warren that opened up into another tiny concrete room, like a maze or a cloister. The concrete rooms seemed too small for the spread of the house.

"The walls must be at least half a metre thick!" Kimi observed. "How very odd."

Sayuri glanced at her mom. Kimi surprised her sometimes. She seemed so in her own world, but her bubbling mind noticed things.

"Why, do you suppose?" Sayuri asked. "Is this the way they used to make houses a long time ago?"

"I'm not sure," Kimi shook her head. "But we could try doing a search on the Internet to find out. Or go over old architectural plans in the town archives. What do you think, Jun?"

They meandered in and out of rooms, flicking on lights as they went. Some of them still worked, but a few were burnt out. Sayuri couldn't say if they were under the kitchen anymore or if they were under the living room.

"I have no idea," Jun raised his eyebrows. "Maybe the last owner was a bit of an eccentric?"

"A messy one," Sayuri muttered.

"Me want to go upstairs," Keiji squirmed. Jun lowered him to the ground.

"Look!" Kimi pointed. They were in the last of the rooms. In it were two wooden chairs with broken legs and an old box of vinyl records. Kimi wasn't pointing at the objects. She pointed at a door in the middle of the wall, a door so low that Jun would never get inside without bending.

The door was different than the rest of the house. The wood was hewn out of thick timber and left without being planed or painted. Age had darkened the colour, and black metal hinges were nailed into the surface. Instead of a door-knob, there was a black latch handle.

Sayuri's fingertips buzzed in a frenzy of sensation and she rubbed them against her jeans. The buzz rose along her arms, across her shoulders, to settle into the back of her neck.

Kimi turned to look at her daughter's face. Sayuri stared back into Kimi's eyes. Her dark pupils were round and deep. Sayuri felt as if she stared into a long hallway. "What?" she breathed.

Kimi shook her head. Smiled. "This house feels like an adventure!" And she opened the door.

Moist dank air rolled into the room, lapped at their feet like a wave. Earth, rich and moist with growing things, the sweet thickness of rotting leaves. The air was cool and wet and their heated skin shivered.

"Oooooh," gasped Keiji.

They peered into the cool space and Jun caught sight of a string, dangling from the ceiling. He stretched out a long arm and pulled.

A dim and naked light bulb cast a tiny orange glow.

The walls. The walls.

Not walls at all, but dirt.

It was a room that wasn't, a hole burrowing outward from their house, carved directly into soil. Gnarly roots spread through the dirt and poked out long thin fingers. The tree, Sayuri thought. That huge poplar tree, we must be right under-neath it. She shuddered and pressed closer to her mother.

"How quaint!" Kimi said excitedly.

"Quaint?! I call it Major League Creepy!" Sayuri burst out. She glanced at her brother, but he was incapable of saying "Me anything." His eyes were squeezed shut, his arms wrapped around Jun's thigh.

"What is this hole?" Sayuri asked. Wanting a name for it.

"I think," Jun paused, "I think this must be a root cellar."

"No wonder!" Sayuri shuddered again. "It's made out of roots."

Kimi laughed. "How clever," she beamed. Laughed again. "They used to have root cellars in the olden days to store their vegetables. Vegetables that would keep a long time in a dark cool place, like carrots and potatoes and turnips. See those bins?" She pointed at four large wooden boxes. "Apples keep a long time too," she mused. "We could store a lot of food down here!"

Now that Kimi mentioned it, Sayuri could catch a faint scent of sweet apples. Autumn. That was what the room smelled like!

"I wonder if mice can get in?" Jun murmured.

"Well, if you store food down here, Keiji and I won't be coming to get it for you!" Sayuri warned.

Keiji nodded emphatically and tugged Jun backward. Jun scooped her brother up again and pressed his face into Keiji's stomach. Keiji bubbled into giggles as Jun jogged back toward the stairs. "Time for a bath!"

"Come on, Mom," Sayuri tugged Kimi's hand. She hadn't held hands with her mother for ages.

Kimi cupped her palm against her daughter's. "Let's go into town to pick up a pizza!"

4. THE NIGHT

THE FAMILY GORGED ON THE CHEESY SLICES. WELL PAST suppertime, the night pressed against the kitchen windows. But inside was warm and filled with laughter.

Keiji started yawning halfway through his third slice of plain cheese pizza.

"Come on, button. Let's get you to bed." Kimi grabbed the tip of his nose.

"Honk! Honk!" Keiji kidded. Then yawned again. As they creaked up the stairs, Sayuri heard her brother asking if he could sleep with Kimi for the first night.

Not a bad idea, Sayuri thought. When they were all together, everything seemed so safe and cosy. But the thought of her huge attic room made her heart pang with something. What if the cat came back at night...?

"You okay, duckling?"

Sayuri gulped. Nodded.

"It's a little strange, moving, isn't it?" Jun said. "Once we have memories in this house, it'll feel more like home."

"You think?" Sayuri asked dubiously.

"You want me to sleep in your room tonight?" Jun smiled with his eyes.

"Would you?"

"I bet you have the greatest view of the stars."

Oh! The skylight! She had forgotten all about it. She could watch the moon flying through the night!

Laughter trickled down the stairs. Keiji was squealing and there was a roar of water running in the tub.

"Your butt!" they heard Kimi holler. "Your face, neck, pits, butt, and feet! Even if you're too tired to take a proper bath, you gotta wash those parts at the very least. That's what my grandmother always said!"

Sayuri glanced at her father and laughed, rolling her eyes. "Kimi's really weird." She shook her head.

Jun grinned. "I suppose so. I suppose that's why I fell in love with her."

"Please!" Sayuri quickly crunched through the last bit of crust. "I'd rather not hear the gory details!" She stacked dishes, cups, then put them in the sink. Jun nudged Sayuri over to help her wash up. Smiled. Didn't say anything else. They left the dishes to dry in the rack.

Sayuri jogged up the creaky stairs, a small shudder running down her spine at the creepy noise. She stuck her head in the biggest bedroom.

Keiji was tucked into Kimi's futon, reading out loud from *Where The Wild Things Are*. Kimi lay beside him, her mouth slightly parted. She snored softly.

Sayuri paused, Keiji murmuring about a forest growing inside Max's room.

Kimi rolled over, rubbing her hands on the blanket.

Sayuri backed thoughtfully into the washroom.

The sink was ceramic and more of a bowl than anything else. The faucets looked like something found in a garden. But it was shiny clean. Jun must have gone through here, she thought. The tub stood on strangely-bent legs and, if she squeezed her eyes to look at them through the blur of her lashes, the brass legs looked like lions.

"Stop it!" Sayuri said aloud.

No one answered.

Sayuri blinked at her reflection in the small rectangular mirror. Her hair was cut bluntly along her jawline. Thick and straight. But the constant exposure to chlorine had tinted some of the black into a brittle reddish auburn.

"Not fair!" Mika, her best friend at Japanese school, had moaned. "That colour is sooo in right now! But my mom'll never let me dye my hair. Not in a million years, she said!"

"I think my hair looks dead," Sayuri had answered. "If you join Compet, though, your hair'll turn this colour without dyeing."

Mika had shaken her head. "Hate swimming," she sighed.

Sayuri grinned at the thought of her friend. A hot surge of tears burned her eyes and she blinked. Rubbed the back of her hand over her closed lids. Stupid.

Sweat had dried on her neck and the dust had creased darkly into the skin. Her armpits felt sticky, and it didn't seem right to sleep in her new room when she was so dirty.

"Face, neck, pits, butt, feet," Sayuri muttered. She filled the tub, dropping her dusty clothes in a circle at her feet. Dirt caked between her toes.

When she sank into the steaming liquid, a long sigh seeped from deep inside her lungs. So hot. Water. She loved it. Couldn't get enough of the way it touched her body, the way it embraced without holding. Water a touch that was also movement. Sayuri dreamily stared down at her body. Two little nubbins of flesh poked out of the smooth surface of water. Ugh! She flipped over so she didn't have to see the evidence.

Not that she didn't want to grow up.

"Love your body, love yourself!" Kimi often chanted. Sayuri snorted bubbles.

Mika already wore a bra. But Sayuri would be happy if she never had to. Breasts were bound to affect her efficiency in the water. And her nipples had started to hurt. What with her itchy fingers and tender chest, her body was spilling out of control! When she'd asked Jun about the pain, he'd smiled and said it was perfectly normal during puberty.

Puberty! She didn't like the sound of the word. Puberty. Pubic hair. Puking. Putrid.

Having a mom who was a horror writer did have a plus, Sayuri mused. She knew more adjectives than any kid in her class. And her mom never complained about her marks in

Language Arts. "Hmph," she'd sniff. "What a meaningless assignment. And your teacher spelled 'perceive' wrong."

Sayuri giggled bubbles into the tub. Kimi was irreverent and Jun was practical. He'd given her a book called *What's Happening To My Body Book for Girls*. Kimi had a different approach.

"This is where you're going to be living, no matter where you go. Learn your body. And respect it. You should love your body more than anyone else!" Kimi had given Sayuri a small mirror. "Look at your body everywhere. It's not a mystery. It's a living work of art! Your body is your body is your body."

Sayuri had taken the mirror rather doubtfully. But after feeling embarrassed, she'd figured out she was embarrassed about what she imagined she thought of herself, and that didn't make any sense at all! So she'd looked everywhere, even between her legs. Her body was her body was her body. Made sense. But she still wasn't thrilled about the growing changes. Sayuri sighed. At least, she thought, at least I don't have my period yet. Mika had started a year ago, and Suyin, her best friend in Compet, had started two years ago! She had to use tampons when she swam! Sayuri could still remember when she was little. She had thought it was great fun to peel the backing off the adhesive strip from her mom's napkins. What a nut! Her brother still thought it was fun.

Sayuri rose from the cooling water. Looked around.

"Towel please!" she called in a whispered shout. Though she doubted that Kimi would wake up now. "Someone! I need a towel!"

She heard a soft pad, pad, pad of feet.

Animal, Sayuri thought. Cat....

The doorknob turned and Keiji's face peered inside. He thrust his arm straight out, a huge towel dragging on the floor.

"Thanks, digger," Sayuri said affectionately. He was a considerate little boy. Not like Suyin's brothers.

"Your boobies are growing," Keiji pointed.

"Ugh!" Sayuri shoved her brother out of the way and shut the door in his face.

Keiji banged the panels. "Let me in! I want some water!"

"What's the matter?" Sayuri heard her father's gentle voice.

"She won't let me in," her brother whimpered. Sayuri rolled her eyes.

"I need some privacy, Jun! You know."

"Come on, button. I can get you some water in the kitchen." Sayuri heard them go downstairs.

Sayuri briskly dried her body, careful to pat the towel over her tender nipples. Sighing. She brushed her teeth, watching the muscles in her arm. She had to do more push-ups. She filled a mug with water and brought it to her lips. Paused. If she drank too much now, she'd wake up during the middle of the night and have to creep down the stairs in the darkness. Sayuri pursed her lips and took two tiny sips. Dumped the rest back.

The floorboards were cold beneath her heated feet and Sayuri could hear the wind whistling through cracks in the old house. She shuddered. She jogged up the attic stairs and burst through the door. Before she could change her mind and give up the room to Kimi.

The lamp glowed orange on the small table next to her futon. Her fluffy quilt was pulled back. The rocking chair had been draped with an afghan and a small pillow. It was placed next to her bookshelf. Sayuri tipped her head and gazed at the windows opening up the roof into an eternal sky. The moon was a pale persimmon drifting down the milky river of stars. She sighed. She thought she heard the sound of purring. Looked around. But it was gone.

Sayuri heard Jun coming up the narrow steps. He shuffled into the room, carrying the small extra futon they kept for visitors. He flopped it down next to her bed.

"Tomorrow," he said, "we can go into town and see about connecting the phone. You can call your friends. And we'll go to the pool and talk to the swim coach."

Hot tears filled Sayuri's eyes so quickly she didn't notice until they streamed down her cheeks.

"Oh, honey." Jun tucked Sayuri's damp hair behind her ears. "Everything'll be all right."

"I don't know why I'm crying," she wavered. Hating the quiver in her voice.

"We've made a big change in our lives," Jun said. "And puberty also affects your hormones, which also affect your emotions. You'll be crying, then laughing the next minute."

"Aghhh!" Sayuri exclaimed. "Puberty this! Puberty that!" She flung her arms in the air. "I'm beginning to hate the putrid word!"

Kimi stuck her head through the door, dark eyes gleaming. She grinned mischievously and ran across the floor to bellyflop in the middle of Sayuri's bed.

"So give it another name," Kimi suggested. "Like, umm-mmmm, Prunella."

"Prunella?" Sayuri snickered. "How about Pubina?"

"Or Puberta?" Kimi snorted.

Sayuri laughed loudly, flopping on her bed beside her mother. Mother and daughter clung to each other, snorting gleefully.

"I rest my case," Jun uttered. And left the room with calm, dignified steps.

They laughed even louder.

IN THE DARKNESS, NIGHT'S COOL LIGHT CAST ODD SHADOWS. Sayuri snuggled deeper into the folds of her quilt and pressed her back against her mother. Kimi wrapped her arms around her daughter.

"My," she said, "I can't believe how much you've grown. Did you know that it's magic?"

"No," Sayuri murmured, "I didn't know."

"It's the best magic in this world."

Sayuri closed her eyes. "Can you tell me a story?"

Kimi cleared her throat. Her voice sank deeper, a mesmerizing chant that always carried Sayuri to distant lands.

"A long, long, very long time ago...."

5. FOLK STORY

"THERE LIVED A GREAT YAMANBA IN THE EVERGREEN forests of Aso mountain."

"Ass ho?" Sayuri giggled. "Are you serious? There's a mountain called 'Ass ho' in Japan?!"

"It's not only a mountain, it's a volcano," Kimi said loftily. "Your grandfather came from that area."

"A volcano called 'Aso'?!" Sayuri guffawed.

"Do you want to hear the story or what?" Kimi warned.

"Sorry," the girl giggled. "Please go on."

"Hmph! Where was I?"

"Aso mountain," Sayuri crowed. Pounding her pillow with her fist.

"I'm going now!" Kimi threatened.

"No! No! I'm kidding. I'll stop." Sayuri wiped tears from her eyes. Giggles erupting in her chest. Gulping. Return of Puberta, she thought. Almost burst out laughing again. "Please continue."

"The great giant mountain woman lived in the dark pine

forests, for she was the keeper of the fires in the volcano. Hers was a lonely job, but she knew that without a keeper, the volcano's hunger would surely consume the world. The people of the nearby village also knew this. Every autumn, they had a Festival of Fire to honour the Yamanba's great work. So this continued for many generations. Every few decades, the Yamanba would release the beast to feed, for all living creatures must eat. But then she would call the creature back, and so control the balance of life and death.

"The years passed. Generations came and went like the tides. And Yamanba continued her lonely work. But the people started to change. Instead of travelling on foot, connected to the magic of earth and water, human creatures created strange contraptions of metal. They whipped around in a noisy frenzy leaving stink and garbage in their wake. Yamanba, who had never felt the passing of eons, started curling brittle with age. Her spine creaked, her muscles dried, and she tended the volcano as best she could.

"'Ahhhh,' Yamanba sighed, 'this change has come uncalled. Who will mind the creature if I am to pass before my time?'

"For the people had forgotten that a Yamanba kept the world safe. They had forgotten they lived next to a living beast. Just as the creature had to eat, so, too, the Yamanba had to be honoured. The people had ceased performing the Festival of Fire by the time the village had grown into a city. The people had forgotten the old ways.

"So the great mountain woman shrank smaller and smaller. Her giant bones and muscles withered, her thick hair grew thin. Yamanba no longer, with the last of her strength, she built a high wall of timbers to contain the fire beast of Aso mountain. And when the wall was complete, Yamanba fell into dust and rejoined the forest that had birthed her.

"The people of the city went about their city ways, billowing smog and creating islands of garbage. The timbers that held the beast started to give. Until the walls finally broke and Aso erupted in a fury of flames and lava.

"The fire beast roared into the skies and ate everything that came in its path. For there was no one to control its hunger. The creature fed long and hard before it was sated, then crept back to its mountain lair.

"The city was laid to waste. From the embers, a few survivors crawled from their broken homes and wept with anger and sadness. 'What are we to do now?' they cried. 'We are lost. We are lost.'

"'Wait!' An aged woman hobbled from an ancient temple. Her head was shaved in the manner of priests and her voice rang strong across the smoke-filled air. 'We are lost because we have forgotten our ways. We have called this destruction upon ourselves, but it is never too late to change. We must perform the ancient Festival of Fire. This we have not done and we reap the consequences.'

"'Are you mad?' a young man shouted. 'A festival of fire? Everything is burned down already! The last thing we need to do is celebrate fire!'

"'Fool,' the old priest said. 'Fire is destruction and rebirth. Let the fire burn full circle and life will grow from the embers.'

"'Yes,' someone murmured, 'the Festival of Fire. My

grandfather told me of such a thing.'

"'Yes,' the people called. 'Yes!' So they gathered around the temple and looked to ancient scrolls. They lit torches, and the people wended through the ancient path that meandered up the side of the great mountain. The long row of flames flickered like a burning snake and girls pounded on ancient drums to awaken the dead. The people cried with a great voice. With mourning and jubilation.

"And from beneath the soil, there was movement. The earth heaved, shuddered, and a loud wail filled the night air. For a Yamanba had been born anew."

WHEN SAYURI WOKE UP, she wasn't sure if her mother had finished the story, or if she had dreamt the ending.

The sun was bright against the pale yellow walls of her room.

6. GRANOLA

SAYURI'S HEART THUDDED HEAVILY IN HER CHEST, HER palms damp, her throat dry. At least, she consoled herself, it wasn't the first day of school. She swallowed and her throat felt even drier. What could go wrong? She'd meet new kids who loved swimming as much as she did. They'd have something in common. She gulped.

Kimi glanced at her through the rear-view mirror.

Sayuri smiled wanly.

"You can drop me and Keiji at the grocery store. We need to stock up on fruits and vegetables," Jun said.

"And ChocoBalls! Remember? You said!" Keiji bounced up and down on the seat.

Jun rubbed the top of his son's head. "What a memory!"

"I need a lot of carbs," Sayuri reminded.

"Don't forget cranberry juice," Kimi added.

"Aiiiiii!" Jun groaned. "Have you people ever heard of a shopping list?" He shook a piece of paper at them. Keiji and Jun hopped out at the IGA and Sayuri jumped into the front seat.

"You okay?" Kimi asked.

"Hmmmm," Sayuri answered.

"Remember, you're one amazing girl. You kick butt if anyone gives you any trouble!"

"Kimiiiii!" Sayuri groaned. "I'm not like you. I don't go around kicking people's butt."

"Well, if anyone gives you trouble, you tell me. And *I'll* kick their butt."

"Don't you dare say anything embarrassing when we get there!" Sayuri warned. "Promise?"

"Have I ever embarrassed you?" Kimi raised her eyebrows.

Sayuri stared at the theatrical eyeliner and the bright pink T-shirt with a snail decal. "Eat My Slime!" was scrawled beneath it. Toes with black toenail polish peeped out of sparkly platform shoes. She sighed.

Kimi smiled. Lightly cuffed her daughter on the shoulder. "Your mom's no fool. Do you think I popped out of your grandmother's womb looking like this?!"

Sayuri laughed out loud.

"It took me a long time to be proud of who I am. You take your own path. But always be proud of who you are." Kimi's lips smiled, but her eyes were serious.

Sayuri absent-mindedly rubbed her itchy fingertips on the nubbly material of the car seat. She flipped down the visor and checked her face in the mirror. Tucked her hair behind her ears and bared her teeth to see if there was anything stuck between them.

"How do I look?" she asked nervously.

"You're so beautiful my heart aches," Kimi smiled. Her eyes slightly wet.

THE FAMILIAR WAFT OF CHLORINE made Sayuri's stomach clench with a surge of homesickness. Suyin would be working on butterfly, her weakest stroke, and Marta, their coach, would be shouting encouragement, pushing her to the limits.

"We'd like to speak with the swim coach," Kimi said at the front counter. A tanned teenaged boy gaped at Kimi's eyeliner, then lifted his eyes to stare at her closely cropped hair. Sayuri sighed.

"Pardon?" he managed.

"The coach," Kimi enunciated. "We would like to speak to the swim coach about joining the competitive team. Is there some sort of problem?"

"Uh, no! No. He's at the pool. You can go through there." The boy pointed to a door marked "Spectators."

"Very good," Kimi sniffed and marched through. Sayuri trailed after. Her ears felt hot.

The spectator's room wasn't separated from the pool area with a sheet of glass. There was only a small wooden fence. In fact, Sayuri thought dismally, the whole space was basically an outdoor pool! There was no ceiling, just concrete block walls that circled the space. The pool was tiny, too. Not Olympic-size; she'd have to double back for it to count as one "real" length. What a crock! What a little hick excuse for a swim team! What did they do for the winter? Ice skate?! And was that the coach? That middle-aged man with the melon stomach? He must be, he had a whistle and a stopwatch. About fifteen kids stood around him as he gestured earnestly, kids of all sizes. Some were tall, some short, and some of them weren't even fit! What kind of team was it?

"Kimi!" Sayuri hissed. "I can't train here –"

"Excuse me!" Kimi shouted, her voice echoing over the water and against the concrete walls, "I need to talk to the swim coach!"

Sayuri sunk behind her mother, scrunching her back to make herself smaller. Maybe, she hoped, the world would swallow her whole. Her ears burned, but she couldn't help peering around Kimi's shoulder.

Melon-ball man glanced back. He held up his palm toward them as he gave everyone their required lengths. The kids slipped into the water, some of them squealing with the cold. The melon-ball man strode toward them.

"How can I help you?"

Sayuri blinked. Melon-ball man, she noted, wasn't fazed by her mom's appearance at all. Sayuri was impressed.

"I'm Kimiko Kato and this is my daughter, Sayuri." Kimi shook the coach's hand firmly. "My daughter was in the Calgary Competitive Swim Club and we've just moved to Ganola. She'd like to continue training, of course, and I've heard that you have a very good club here."

"The name's Donovan. We're always looking for keen swimmers. Sayuri, you say?" He smiled.

He didn't stumble over her name, Sayuri noted, properly rolling the "r" halfway between an "l" and an "r". Wow. No one ever gets it right the first time, Sayuri thought. She smiled, nodded, and held out her hand. She shook Donovan's hand firmly, the way her mother had taught her.

"What level are you swimming at?" Donovan asked. "What's your strongest stroke?"

"I made Provincials last year in back," Sayuri answered. Kimi beamed.

Donovan whistled, eyebrows raised. "Great! Great! How old are you?"

"Twelve. Turning thirteen in September."

"Excellent!" Donovan clapped his hands. "Did you bring your gear?"

Sayuri shook her head.

"We train twice a day."

"Twice!" Sayuri gasped.

"Yup. 7:00 AM to 9:00, then again in the afternoon, 1:00 to 3:00 PM."

"How many times a week?" Sayuri asked.

"Monday to Friday," Donovan smiled.

"Aiiiii!" Kimi moaned. "How will I get up in the morning?"

Sayuri laughed, her heart skipping. Twice a day! These people were hard core! "I can ride my bike in. It'll make my legs stronger."

"Excellent!" Donovan nodded. "I like that kind of attitude. Well, you can see about the fees at the desk and then be ready to start tomorrow morning. Glad to have you on board." He gave a quick wave then turned back to the pool.

"What do they do in the winter, you know?" Sayuri asked her mom, watching the swimmers going through their lengths. One girl, tall, cut the water with clean strokes, a beauty of aquatic motion. Sayuri hoped the girl didn't do the backstroke as well as she did her front crawl.

"Some of the children don't swim during the off-season, but I understand the serious swimmers commute to White Buffalo to train at the indoor pool they've got."

"How far away is it?"

"About twenty minutes drive, south on the highway."

"You better hope they don't train every morning at 7:00!" Sayuri teased.

"Please!" Kimi grimaced. "It's enough to give me night-mares! Well, let's get going."

"I want to watch for a while," Sayuri said. "You go ahead. I'll jog home."

"Jog?" Kimi raised her eyebrows. "Do you know how to get back?"

"Uh-huh."

"Well, be careful then. You want my pepper spray?" Kimi tapped her carryall bag.

"Kimi!"

"All right!" Kimi strode toward the door on her sparkly shoes. "Training's over at 3:00, so I'll expect you home by, say, 3:30?"

"3:30," Sayuri called back.

THE CONCRETE WALLS KEPT THE PRAIRIE WIND OUTSIDE, cup-ping the summer heat. Sayuri's head burned hot and she wished she'd brought a hat. The children splashed up and down the lanes, Donovan shouting advice and encouragement to the ones who lagged. The tall girl's backstroke was better than her front. Sayuri bit her lip. Maybe she was in a different age group.

By three o'clock, the exhausted swimmers dragged their bodies out of the water and trudged to the changing rooms. The tall girl put her arm over a friend's shoulder and they chatted, laughing. When they passed by where Sayuri sat, the tall girl looked over and gave a quick smile. Sayuri grinned back, blushing. The friend smiled too, but her eyes were hard, her teeth a metallic jumble of braces.

Donovan jogged over. "Hey! Meet Sayuri," he called. "She's joined the club and she'll start tomorrow. Sayuri, this is Darryl," he gestured to the tall girl, "and Sidney. They're both in your age group."

"Hi," Sayuri managed. She didn't think of herself as shy, but this being a "new kid" was simply awful.

"Sah yer eee?" Sidney wrinkled her nose. Her voice was a hiss of scorn. Like she was talking through a mouthful of razor blades. "What kind of name is that?"

Sayuri's face burned painfully. A dry rock in her throat. Kick butt, she thought.

"I beg your pardon," Sayuri said icily. "Your accent is atrocious. It's Sa-yu-ri. Equal emphasis on all syllables. Roll the r."

Darryl smiled. "What a pretty name."

"Japanese Canadian, hey?" Donovan beamed.

Sayuri nodded. Staring at Sidney until Sidney looked away. This one's trouble, Sayuri thought.

"See you tomorrow morning, Sayuri," Darryl grinned. Sayuri watched her. Darryl's hair was cropped shorter than even Kimi's. And her long legs and arms were brown naturally, not tanned from sun. Sayuri sighed. If she were as tall as Darryl, she'd carve a good two or three seconds off her time for sure.

Sidney chased after Darryl and whispered fiercely, glancing back over her shoulder.

Donovan sighed. "Anyone give you trouble, you let me know, okay?"

Sayuri stared into Donovan's warm brown eyes. This one, she thought, this one's okay. And she smiled.

7. ALONE IN THE HOUSE

SAYURI WATCHED AS HER BROTHER RUBBED THE BACK OF his hand over his nose. Sniffed. Sniffed again. Sayuri reached into her jeans pocket and passed her brother a Kleenex.

"Is it used?" Keiji asked, eyebrows raised.

"No!" Sayuri snorted, giving her brother an affectionate shove. "What do you care, digger? You eat snot every day! Ugh. Speaking of eating, I'm starving! The lunch Kimi packed was too small and Donovan made us do extra lengths of butterfly."

"I have a snack left in my backpack," Keiji offered, balling up the used Kleenex and shoving it back into Sayuri's pocket.

"Get lost!" Sayuri jumped away. "Don't litter!"

Her brother sat on the side of the road. The fields were still and the sky loomed with heavy dark mounds of a summer storm.

"You shouldn't sit on the side of the road," Sayuri cautioned, as she looked up and down the gravel drive. She squinted at the growing clouds, amazed at how swiftly they covered the blue skies. She could see their house on the next rise. "Hurry, digger. It's going to break any minute!"

"Here," Keiji offered. He held up a marshmallow treat with one bite taken out of it.

"Thanks!" Sayuri bit into the chewy sweetness. "Why didn't you want it?"

"It was my second piece. Marion was crabby. Then she felt bad, so she made treats for us. Don't tell Jun, you how he is about sugar."

They trudged on, the gravel crunching beneath their runners.

"You doing okay at the summer camp place?" Sayuri glanced down. Keiji hadn't had an asthma attack since the day of the move, but he still had blue smudges beneath his eyes.

Keiji shrugged. "There's a nice girl named Sita and we play paleontology. Some of the guys are jerks."

"Yeah," Sayuri sighed. "There's always a couple of jerks, aren't there?" The swim club kids were all pretty friendly, but no one hung out with her after training. Sometimes Darryl'd give her an apologetic look, but then Sidney would grab her arm and drag her away to go get some fries. Fries were useless calories anyway, Sayuri told herself.

Keiji was looking up at her. He patted her arm with his grubby hand.

"That's funny," Sayuri said. Gazing down the road.

"What?"

"The car's not in the driveway." She glanced down at her

wrist to check the time. Ugh! She'd forgotten to put on her watch. They'd left Marion's place at 3:30. Maybe it was close to 4:00?

Keiji jumped up and down to get a better look. Eyes growing wide. "Me can't see! Maybe Kimi went to pick up Jun?"

"I dunno," Sayuri said, glancing down at her brother. His anxiety babytalk was so annoying. "But it's nothing to worry about. Dad was saying something about working extra hours tonight because a lot of people have colds. Maybe Kimi had to go out." Sayuri's stomach growled. The marshmallow treat had only made her crave more. If her mom had gone out, she hoped that Kimi had left a pot of special spaghetti. She'd even welcome a stew.

WHEN THEY GOT TO THE HOUSE, the curtains were closed and the never-locked front door was locked. A letter with Sayuri's name on it was taped to the small glass window. Sayuri slowly reached and opened it.

"What does it say?" Keiji demanded. He craned to see the words he couldn't read yet. The letter was written in Japanese so that no one else would be able to understand it and Sayuri smiled at her mother's childish writing. She read out loud:

Had a sudden call from my agent. Had to meet her in the city. Sorry, couldn't arrange for someone to be here for you. Marion was busy. Sayuri, I know you're careful and smart. You're in charge. Keiji, listen to your sister and be good. I didn't have time to leave some dinner. You'll have to fend for yourselves. There might be extra food in the root cellar. I'm out the door! I'll phone to let you know when I'll be back. Jun won't be home until 8:00 or 9:00.

Love, Kimi
PS. The key is under the ochre flower pot in the back.

Sayuri gulped. They'd been alone before. When they lived in the city, Jun would work his double shifts and Kimi would have meetings. So they'd be on their own. But in the city they knew that the Sorensons and the Farooqs were right next door. They could even yell really loudly and someone would hear them. But that was the city. In the country? Their nearest neighbour was at least half a kilometre away! Sometimes, when she was younger, Sayuri'd thought about how easy if would be for her mom and dad to sneak out after she and her brother had gone to sleep. And she'd tried to stay up in case they did.

She liked the idea of being in charge, but the countryside felt so empty. If Keiji got hurt, would it be her fault? Sayuri stuffed the note into her back pocket and crossed her arms.

Ouch! Stupid nipples! She dropped her arms.

"What's ochre?" Keiji asked, but Sayuri only grabbed her brother's hand and walked briskly to the backyard. She quickly found the key and unlocked the door.

"Yay!" Keiji shouted gleefully. "Let's watch TV. Let's drink some pop!"

Sayuri bustled her brother inside and locked the door and

the deadbolt. She breathed a sigh of relief.

"No pop until after supper," she said automatically, then laughed at the sound of her father in her voice.

"Tattle-tale!" Keiji groused. Sayuri didn't bother correcting his usage. "What's for supper?" her brother continued. "I want korrokke!"

"Korrokke? Hardly! You ever watch how long it takes Jun to make them?"

Sayuri's heart sank into the bottom of her stomach. Fine and dandy for Kimi to tell them to fend for themselves. If there was something to fend with. Jun had been on night shift for the past two weeks, so he'd been out of family commission. Kimi had been meeting a deadline. So the groceries had dwindled, Kimi exclaiming it was a great opportunity to use up all the dried goods so fresh stores could be bought. The past week had been suppers of pancakes and scrambled eggs, breakfasts of instant curry udon and celery sticks. Sayuri marched to the cupboards, opened them one after the other. She clasped her hands together beneath her chin and chanted like a nursery school child.

When she got there
The cupboard was bare
And so her poor dog had none.

Keiji scowled. "I'm not a dog!"

Sayuri laughed and mussed up the top of his head. "It's a nursery rhyme, digger. Don't you know it?"

"Kimi says most of the nursery rhymes are morbid."

Sayuri raised her eyebrows. Wow. She couldn't have used "morbid" in a sentence when she was seven. "Kimi's one to talk," she muttered.

A strange squealing sound ended in a series of gurgles. The hair on Sayuri's neck rose and shivers shuddered down her spine.

"Did you hear that?" she whispered. Eyes darting.

"It's my stomach," Keiji giggled.

"Ugh!" Sayuri exclaimed. She pounced on her brother and wrapped her arm around his neck in a loose headlock.

"Not my fault!" Keiji laughed and laughed.

"Hmph!" Sayuri sniffed. Releasing him. She turned to the fridge, though there had been nothing eatable there in the morning.

Jars of jam, chili sauce, oyster sauce, ketchup, fish sauce, tonkatsu sauce. A bottle with a centimetre of milk left in it. Three lemons. Two withered limbs of celery. A melty half-head of lettuce. Mayonnaise. Sighing, Sayuri checked the freezer. Dried-out ice cubes, a rectangle of frozen fish, ice cream gone chewy, and one rock-hard bagel.

"It doesn't look good," Keiji shook his head.

Sayuri glanced down. He was such a funny little old man sometimes.

"Well," Sayuri mused, "Kimi did say there might be extra food. In..."

"The root CELLAR!" they screamed and laughed simultaneously, like a silly movie, holding each other in terror.

"The Root Cell," Sayuri moaned. Normal dark wasn't a

problem. The terrors of a midnight washroom were banishable with a flick of a switch. And her bedroom was never completely dark with the ceiling windows. But the reaches of the basement – a tomb of a room in the darkness of earth! The root cellar was literally a hole in the ground, a ceiling held up with old wooden planks and the floor crumbling concrete. The walls all dirt. It could cave in any time. Animals could burrow through. The Root Cell, a penitentiary for imaginative children everywhere! The bars of the jail cell a twisting, choking mess of gnarled roots. Potatoes and withered carrots. Tins of oily fish with no can opener. Turnips long forgotten and gone maggoty. That was what the prisoners ate! A single light bulb and the string for a switch dangling in the centre of the room – you had to walk halfway across the cavern in pitch dark before you could turn it on. And the light so ghoulish dim, why even bother?! "How quaint!" her parents said. Were they nuts?! Sayuri shivered, though her stomach growled ferociously. Why store food in a dungeon that no child would even consider entering?

Outside, the wind began to gust against the windows. The sound of dust skittered on glass.

"Maybe," Keiji gulped, "Kimi home soon."

"Yeah." Sayuri nodded grimly. They could barely make it into the root cellar when their parents were there. It was too much to imagine trying it on their own.

SAYURI THAWED THE SINGLE BAGEL AND SPLIT IT IN HALF. Toasted the slices and added extra jam to kill the taste of freezer burn. She offered one of the wilty celery sticks to Keiji, but he furiously shook his head, so Sayuri ate both pieces with mayonnaise on top. She munched determinedly while they watched cartoons in the living room. Keiji was pressed right next to her side. Normally, she'd have pushed him off, but his small warm body was a comfort.

Comfort. Comfort food. Rice! She could make some rice, at least, she thought. But when she checked the big tin, there was only a handful of grains at the bottom.

"Boy," she said, "Kimi better remember to get more."

She returned to the TV, but the cartoons weren't that entertaining. Sayuri tried not to imagine that they'd get hungrier. But the more she tried not to imagine it, the hungrier she felt.

The phone rang. Sayuri jumped and Keiji gave a little yell. Then they dashed into the kitchen for the receiver.

"Hello," Keiji said in a low voice.

"You sound so grown-up!" Kimi yelled so enthusiastically that even Sayuri could hear her. "You kids doing all right?"

Sayuri grabbed the phone from her brother. "We're fine. Are you coming home soon?"

Keiji jumped up and down. "Not fair!" he howled. He dragged a footstool over so he could listen from the outside of the receiver.

"It's going to take close to three hours until I'm back. I have to pick up rice, the basics, greens, and tofu at the market. And I'm going to get caught in rush hour. You guys want me to see if Marion's free now?"

Keiji, who'd been listening, wrinkled his nose and made "X" marks with his fingers.

"It's okay," Sayuri sighed.

"You're sure, honey?"

"We're kinda worried about supper. Is there anything else we can eat other than stuff in The Root Cell?"

"Root Cell? Great imagination, honey! No, we've stored all the extras in the root cellar because it's the coolest room. You've been down there before, hmmm? Don't let your imagination get too carried away. You'll be okay."

"Uh, never mind," Sayuri answered. "Come home soon, though."

"I'll come as quickly as I can," Kimi said warmly. "If you feel like it, you can call Jun at work."

"Okay. I love you."

"Me love you!" Keiji called out. "Me love you and love you!"

"I love you both lots and lots!" they heard Kimi's enthusiastic voice and a great warm laugh.

When they hung up the phone, the room seemed quieter and somehow enormous. Outside, the heavy clouds split open with a huge CRACK! The children screamed. Hail pounded hard, drumming on the roof of their old house. The hail raged for a full three minutes, then was strangely silent.

"Me scared!" Keiji's bottom lip trembled. "Me hungry. Me want to phone Jun," he started to wail.

"Ugh! Don't talk like a baby! Stop crying. I'm hungry too!" Sayuri snapped. Feeling like crying herself. "Jun's helping sick people at the hospital, so let's phone him only if it's an emergency, okay?"

Keiji just stared at his sister with big wet eyes. The cartoons were over. A wind picked up and rattled the glass in the windows.

"Let's look for food in the root cellar!" Sayuri put her hands on her hips. "We can face it together and, once we do it, we won't have to be this scared again."

Keiji's eyes widened even further, mouth dropping open. "No way!"

"Come on," Sayuri pleaded. "I'll let you sleep with me in my room tonight!"

"Uh-uh," her brother shook his head. "Me not hungry enough to go down there."

"I'm going, either way. If you don't come, you'll have to wait upstairs for me all by yourself," Sayuri threatened, then took exaggerated thumping steps down the creaky stairs.

Keiji squeaked. "Okay! I'm coming!"

8. THE ROOT CELLAR

THE STEPS DOWNSTAIRS FELL INTO AN ENDLESSLY DARK abyss. Sayuri was annoyed when Keiji latched his arms around her waist, but the deeper they descended, the more it made sense. Sayuri's own arms clung around her grubby brother. His warmth was comforting. They shuffled awkwardly downwards. They giggled, the tension and fear breaking out of their bodies in gasping laughs, hands sweating, hearts pounding. They shuffled through the maze of warrens, flicking on lights in every room. Some of them turned on, but a few were burnt out, and they ran through those darker rooms like baby rabbits.

And the closer they walked toward the dreaded door, the farther away it seemed. Sayuri was sure she could hear sounds. But what they were, she couldn't say. She blinked her eyes in the dimness. Hadn't her parents heard of hundred-watt bulbs, for goodness sake?!

"Me want to go back," Keiji shuddered. "Me not hungry any more."

"I can't go back," Sayuri clenched her teeth. "I made a promise I'd do it, and now I have to!"

"Made a promise to who?!" Keiji hissed. "No one's here!" He cast about wildly, in case there was.

"Made a promise to myself."

"Not matter if you break a promise to yourself." Keiji choked.

"Kimi says it's the most important to be honest with yourself," Sayuri swallowed, as they continued shuffling into the deepest recesses of their home.

"Me scared. Honest!" Keiji giggled in terror.

"Did you crap your pants?" Sayuri asked.

"I'm no baby!"

"I did," Sayuri confided.

"No! I can't smell it," Keiji whispered.

"Just kidding!" Sayuri giggled.

THEY STOOD BEFORE THE DOOR. The moisture-dampened wood was stained and rippled. The rusty handle old and wet. Sayuri wanted to look over her shoulder in case something had followed them across the basement, but now she was too scared. If something was there, she didn't want to know.

"Open the door," Keiji nudged. "Hurry! Just do it!"

"I can't," Sayuri whispered. "My hand won't move. You do it."

"No way!"

"Let's do it together...."

Sayuri and Keiji stretched out, clasped cold metal and

pulled the door handle out, toward them, the hinges creaking, their hearts pounding.

A burst of dark erupted from the door, a flutter of wings, the rubbery flap-flap of bats, bats! The children squeaked, but the image disappeared, and it was nothing at all, only a wedge of greater darkness spilling from the room.

"Me not hungry anymore," Keiji wobbled. "It's not worth it."

"I can't stop now," Sayuri moaned. "If I don't make sure there's nothing on the other side of this room, how can I ever feel safe upstairs!" her voice ended somewhere between a squeak and a cry. "How could I ever go to sleep?!"

"Wuh, wuh, wuh," Keiji's lower lip wobbled, not able to say a word.

Sayuri wrapped her right arm around her little brother and Keiji clasped her around the middle again. His face pressed into her T-shirt. The children gripped tight to each other and took faltering steps into darkness.

9. INTO THE EARTH

THE DARK FOLDED AROUND THEM, A COOL ALMOST clammy grip. It was so dark that they saw the afterimage of light, like when eyes were held too tightly shut. Then even that disappeared.

"Keiji?"

"Wuh, wuh, wuh...."

"Say something, Keiji! Don't say 'wuh, wuh!' Anything could say that!" Sayuri snapped, gave her brother a little shake.

"Shut up!" her brother managed.

Sayuri crept forward. Toeing her runnered shoes on the cold hard cement. She slid her feet without lifting, in case there was something to trip over. The darkness spilled. Sayuri slowly, slowly stretched out one shaking hand. Reached for the light string in the centre of the room. The darkness seemed to clasp her entire arm. She didn't like the way her hand was so exposed. Anything could grab it! But how could she turn on the light if she didn't reach for the string?

Keiji's face still pressed against her side, Sayuri shuffled awkwardly. But hard to walk was far better than walking alone.

They crept, inched, tremored together, and the room stretched, darker, farther, until, until...something.

Barely discernable, but something....

Sayuri's arm hairs rose. An icy breath whispered against her neck, goosebumps sliding down her spine. Her fingers tingled madly. Beyond itching, almost pain. A small changing of air or sound. Smell. What was it?

The floor.

The floor, it felt less solid beneath her feet and there seemed to be a gentle give, not concrete-solid at all.... But there was no turning back, only the barely forward movement into the reaches of the darkest room on earth.

Then there seemed to be spots of light. Sayuri blinked eyes held too long open. Tears trickled to wet the dryness and the light seemed to grow. Sayuri's hand, still held ahead of her, brushed against something coarse, rough. Not string at all.

"AH!"

"Ya! Ya! Ya!" Keiji hollered, eyes tightly clenched. He kicked randomly around himself to fight off any unseen attacker.

"Ow!" Sayuri yelped, as her brother's foot came into contact with her knee.

"My sister!" Keiji yelled. "Don't touch my sister!" He flailed his arms in two windmills.

"Keiji!" Sayuri shouted. "Keiji!!"

"What?!" Keiji managed to open one eye.

"You're kicking me," Sayuri explained, and burst into giggles.

Stopped. Amazed. She could see her brother. See him, and she hadn't turned on the light.... Slowly, she turned around in a complete circle, her mouth opening in incredulous wonder.

They had walked into the middle of a great forest.

Tiny fragments of light gleamed pale between the mesh of thick branches, evening falling in the rich dense woods, and they stood on the cushy softness of moss. The silence was deeper than the forest itself, and the air fragrant with the sweet bite of pine, the perfume of cedar.

"Wow," Sayuri sighed.

"Wow! Where are we?!" Keiji exclaimed. "Wh-where's our house?"

Sayuri frowned. She pinched herself, then her brother.

"Ow! What did you do that for?"

"I don't think we're both dreaming," Sayuri murmured. "Or we've come to a living place of dreaming. This is Some Place Else. This is magic...."

"Magic is either tricks with mirrors or make-believe," Keiji said factually. "That's what Jun says!"

"Does it matter what we call it? We're here, aren't we?" Sayuri didn't know why she wasn't more frightened. But the forest reminded her of something. She couldn't say what. She'd never seen a forest like it, ever. But she was reminded not of something she'd seen, but maybe something she'd felt....

"Me don't believe in magic!" Keiji angrily muttered.

"What about *Where the Wild Things Are?* That's your favourite book in the world!"

"It's a *book,*" Keiji enunciated.

Sayuri stared down at her brother. Sometimes he seemed such a baby. Then he'd say old man things! "Come on." Sayuri tugged her brother's hand. "There's no point in arguing about magic or not. It's going to be dark soon. We have to find somewhere to go."

"Which way is my house?" Keiji whispered.

Sayuri looked all around. Every bit of the forest looked like the rest. There was no path or anything resembling the room they had entered. "I think we can't go back to the house the same way," she shuddered. "That's what usually happens in magic stories."

"They're going to come home and think someone took us away. They'll be sad and scared and call the police. And we'll never see them again!" Keiji started to wail.

"Shhhh," Sayuri soothed, anxiously patting her brother's shoulder. She looked all around. What if something unfriendly heard his bawling? "I'm here. We'll be okay." Though secretly she wondered. She didn't have a magic bone in her body either. For a time, after she'd read a book about psychic powers, she'd trained with a candle, trying to extinguish the flame with the power of her mind. But it'd only given her a headache and it was so boring, she'd given up. Now Sayuri was sorry she'd given up so quickly. If she'd learn how to put out a flame, she might have learned how to make one. And they'd need one soon. It was getting dark.

"COME ON." Sayuri put her arm around Keiji's shoulder. He finally stopped gulping and Sayuri dug for another Kleenex in her jeans pocket. Keiji wiped his tears and blew his nose.

Now it was dark.

"Great," Keiji sighed. "Dark in the cellar, dark in this forest! Dark, dark everywhere!"

"I don't know," Sayuri grinned. "Look! The moon is rising. It's not so bad."

The moon was full and round, a great orange gourd. Sayuri gulped.

The moon had been a crescent the previous night. She'd watched it cross her skylight windows. How could the moon be in a different phase? Sayuri glanced down at her watch. Ugh! She hadn't remembered to put it back on!

"The moon was skinny at my house," Keiji whispered. "Me want my mom. Me want my dad! Me want to go back to my house!"

"*My* mom!" Sayuri mimicked. Just as if they were back at home. "*My* dad. *My* house," Sayuri joked, to break the clutch of fear in their hearts. She gave her brother an affectionate shove.

"*My* house!" Keiji giggled, shoving back.

"*My* house!" Sayuri laughed.

"MY HOUSE!" an enormous voice bellowed.

"AHHHHHHHHHH!" Sayuri and Keiji screamed. They plunged into the deeps of the forest. Sayuri grabbed hold of her brother. The moss uneven with the deadfall, they stumbled. Low branches smacked at their upheld hands, held high to protect their faces. They ran, hearts pounding, muscles straining. Sayuri drew harder on her brother's wrist, pulling him faster than his short legs could move. Faster, she thought. Faster! The rasping hollow gasps of his breath. Oh, he was holding her back! She could run so much faster than this!

And behind them, the tramp of enormous feet. Louder than anything human. What horror lived in this dreamland forest?

Not fast enough, Sayuri panted in her mind. Her brother, so slow. The little asthmatic. What if she let go? What if she were to leave him behind...?

But she didn't. She gripped tighter and dragged her gasping brother deeper into the woods. Propelled by fear, like little squirrels they leapt, clambered, scurried. After a while, all Sayuri could hear was the thud of the blood in her chest, her head.

"Stop," Keiji managed to gasp. "Can't breathe."

Sayuri stopped and pushed her brother into a sitting position. She reached into the front pocket of his overalls and held his asthma inhaler to his lips. Keiji sucked in the medicine and held his breath. Slowly breathed out.

"Okay?" Sayuri asked.

Keiji nodded.

They sat in the chill damp. Sayuri gazed about her. Stars specked the sky through the breaks of branches. The moon shone a pale lemon. A bird cried, but a bird Sayuri didn't recognize. And maybe the "MY HOUSE!" creature was sneaking up on them this very instant. How could they run forever?

"What do you think it is?" Keiji squeaked.

"It sounded like it was a person. I mean, it talked. Maybe it's an oni? They live in the woods." Sayuri pictured the red and blue ogre demons from her Japanese folk tales book at home. Shuddered. "Maybe it's a tengu," she mused. "They live in tall pines and they're not necessarily bad...."

"Maybe it's Clown Face Man!" Keiji pressed his knuckles to his lips in terror.

Sayuri laughed out loud, imagining a circus smiley face with a squirting water daisy on the clown's hat.

Keiji jumped up, stamped his foot. "Clown Face Man is the scariest thing on earth! They aren't people! They smile, but they don't mean it! You don't know what they're thinking! Why do grown-ups invite them to kids' birthday parties?!"

"All right! All right!" Sayuri laughed.

"My House!" They heard from the distance. The purpling dark. The crunch of brittle branches. Sayuri leapt to her feet.

"Ohhhhhh!" Keiji covered his eyes.

Sayuri's heart thudded, pounded. Never make Keiji run farther than he can, Jun had once warned. It might kill him.

If he couldn't run, what should she do? Was abandoning him an option? Was it?

She glanced down at her brother. There were smudges on his cheeks and his face seemed to glow in the darkness. His breath still rough, his skinny chest wheezed in and out.

Little weakling, she thought. Sayuri turned her back to him and clasped her middle. Her feet wanted to run. Flee. Leave him, a tiny voice niggled from deep inside.

She shook her head. What was wrong with her? Something Kimi had once told her rang through her mind: If you think you have no choices, it's because of the limits you create for yourself.

Tears warmed Sayuri's eyes. Kimi and her ridiculous shoes! She'd be worse at running in this place than Keiji! Kimi would definitely have to use her head if she wanted out.

Use her head....

Sayuri relaxed her tensed-up shoulders and thought some more. "What if...?" she mused.

"Got to hide," Keiji gasped. "Can't run anymore."

"What if....?"

10. WHAT IF....

"WHAT IF WE THINK IT'S SCARY BECAUSE WE THINK IT'S scary?" Sayuri wondered aloud.

"What?!" Keiji stamped his foot.

"What if," Sayuri continued, "our fear makes a monster? What if our not-fear made it a friend?"

"What if it's really a monster and it eats you up while you wonder?!" Keiji hissed, tugging at his sister's hand.

"I'm not running or hiding," Sayuri stated.

"Don't," Keiji blinked. Tears dripped down his grubby cheeks. "I'm scared. I don't want to see."

"I want to see," Sayuri stated. Gulping a little, but certain in the deeps of her heart. "I'll boost you up into this tree, okay? You can climb up high and be safe there."

"Then we'll be separate," Keiji wailed. "And if you get eaten, I'll be stuck here all alone, forever and ever."

"I think we're going to be okay," Sayuri tipped her head slightly to the side.

"– my house," she heard.

"Listen!"

The tramp of footsteps came closer. The snap of branches beneath a heavy step. The sound echoed in the ringing forest and they heard a panting breath. Keiji stood behind his sister and wrapped his arms around her middle. Sayuri's heart warmed in his desperate hold.

Sayuri tilted her head to one side. She bravely faced the sounds coming closer, with fear in her heart, but also with an open curiosity.

"Come to my house!" A deep voice panted from behind the last stand of trees.

"Hello," Sayuri greeted.

"You shouldn't run in the forest," the low voice admonished. "It's dangerous. You might trip and fall." And an enormous woman in old-fashioned Japanese garb stepped before her. A patched samui spun from coarse cloth and short leggings cropped at the knees. Broad feet covered in woven sandals. The woman was so huge that Sayuri tipped her head back to see.

The giant woman smiled, and her teeth were flat with big gaps in between. Her white hair was wild around her head, but her eyes were crinkly from laughter, her face brown as leather from outdoor living. Her arms were as thick as Sayuri's waist and her thighs like pine logs. "You must not be forest people. Why don't you come to my house? It's too late for little ones to be out. The oni might make you dance until dawn."

"You're a yamanba!" Sayuri shouted joyfully.

Keiji peeked between fingers and saw the yamanba's

happy gentle face. Her brother laughed out loud and raised both hands to be picked up.

"Wa! Ha! Ha!" the mountain woman bellowed and the earth moved a little beneath their feet. She swooped down, fast and nimble despite her gigantic size, and swung both of the children upon her strong shoulders as if they were little squirrels.

"Funny human children! I haven't seen any for many forest lives. There is some mischief in the air."

The children barely listened, snuggling in the sweet hay smell of the yamanba's hair. They were suddenly exhausted after the fear.

"Sleep for now," the mountain woman rumbled softly, and the children, soothed by her gentle voice and secure in her strength, fell asleep.

11. LIVING EARTH

SAYURI WOKE TO THE WARM LIGHT ON HER BEDSTAND AND blinked sleepily, unsure whether it was morning or still evening. She'd forgotten to turn it off again and Kimi would be mad about wasted electricity.

The light moved. Not static, but a glowing dance. A loud snap! rang in the air and Sayuri started.

It wasn't her bedroom at all.

She was bundled on a futon next to an open firepit in the middle of a tatami-covered floor. An enormous black metal pot hung over the low flames and the smell of a rich, hearty miso broth filled the air. The pot was suspended from a hook. The hook, attached to a large metal piece shaped like a fish, was held by a line that rose up, up, into the dark beams above Sayuri's head. The ceiling was too dark to discern the depth, but Sayuri imagined she saw a glimmer of one green eye. When she blinked, it was gone.

The fire sparked, crackled orange and sometimes blue, the warmth a great comfort.

"You were sleeping forever!" Keiji said loudly. He barely managed to hold a stick over the red embers. He bit his lip in concentration, roasting a fat fish. The smell was exquisite, and Sayuri's mouth watered as the juices dripped off the fish to sizzle in the coals. She sat up. Folded up the futon the way she'd learned in her grandmother's house in Japan.

"Here," a gruff, kind voice offered. Yamanba held out some steaming broth, filled with pungent roots, tubers, and forest mushrooms.

Sayuri reached for the bowl with both hands. It was same size as Jun's largest mixing bowl, and she could barely lift it to her lips.

"Don't worry," Keiji whispered, "I'll eat the mushrooms for you."

But Sayuri was so ravenous that even the mushrooms tasted delicious. She gobbled them all up and finished every bit of her soup, ending with a great sigh.

Outside, the night was inkier than anything she'd ever seen. Not a light source in sight; there was only the howl of a rising wind and the creak of trees waking for the night.

Sayuri looked around the room for a clock. Shook her head. What a nut! Did she think she was in her own kitchen? Maybe there might be a giant hourglass like the Wicked Witch's in *The Wizard of Oz?* She shuddered.

"What is this place?" Sayuri asked, eyes round.

"The Mountain Women call this place Mother Forest." Yamanba sat, her great body on a flattened cushion next to the fire. She lit a long-handled pipe and a sweet smoke filled the cosy room. In her other hand, she held a huge earthenware jug of sake and she drank from it now and then, nodding with her words. She waved a large circle with the ember of her pipe, and for a moment, the orange circle of light lingered in the air.

"And this world, we call this Living Earth."

"Living Earth," Sayuri and Keiji repeated.

Sayuri glanced at her brother. He struggled to keep the heavy fish from the flames, but the weight was becoming too much for his skinny arms. Sayuri took the stick from her brother and he gave her a grateful smile.

"I think," Yamanba sucked from her pipe, "you children are not of this place."

Sayuri and Keiji looked at each other. Nodded.

"Are we in Japan?" Sayuri asked, frowning.

"What is Japan?"

"Nihon?" Sayuri translated.

"We are here," Yamanba took a sip from her jug.

"But you're a yamanba," Sayuri thought aloud. "Yamanba come from Japan, or that's where the story comes from...Kimi, my mother, said...folk legends come from real events, only the story gets bigger and bigger."

"Perhaps," the mountain giant mused, "perhaps the stories of our worlds spill into each other. For we tell stories of human children. And here you are."

Sayuri frowned in concentration. Turned the fish to brown on the other side. Yamanba reached into a bucket and tossed a pinch of salt over the roasting fish. The grains that tumbled into the fire made the flames leap and crackle.

"Remember," Keiji said thoughtfully, winding a dangling

THE WATER OF POSSIBILITY

string from his T-shirt around and around his index finger. "Kimi was telling Jun about otherworlds going on at the same time as us, kinda the same, but not?"

"Yeah," Sayuri frowned slightly. "Parallel dimensions...but somehow, Living Earth *feels* like – like a folk story caught between a dream and – I don't know. And how did we move from our home to here in the first place?"

"There are magic places on this earth. There are powers in the lines of life. Between death and life, dreams and myth. Perhaps there was a passageway where two lines lay very close together." Yamanba nodded, then slapped her knees, as if the discussion was over. "The fish is done. We shall eat of it."

The fish was the best Sayuri'd ever tasted.

WHEN THE BONES WERE PICKED CLEAN and the dishes carried to the washing area, Sayuri and Keiji sat close to each other by the fire. Now that they were full in their bellies, they started thinking of home...and how very far away it seemed. Sayuri's eyes burned and she blinked so nothing spilled over. Keiji gave her hand a little squeeze and she looked up, surprised.

"Can you help us find the way home?" Sayuri asked Yamanba.

The enormous woman grunted and tapped out the ashes from her pipe into the open firepit. She pulled out a small pouch from the inside of her sleeve and pressed new leaves into the now empty bowl. She lit her pipe with a stick from the fire. Yamanba puffed and small clouds rose into the darkness of the ceiling.

"I believe," she puffed, "I believe you hold that power within yourselves. For did you not cross over of your own accord?"

"But we don't know how," Keiji explained. "It was an accident."

There was a thud on the tatami next to Sayuri and she turned slowly to look at the hugest cat she'd ever seen. It was as big as a cougar and three times fatter. There was a low growling thrum and Sayuri's eyes lit up. Purring! Mauve and black stripes curled around the ample belly of the cat and it leaned forward, almost knocking Sayuri over when it rubbed against her.

"Momo!" Yamanba scolded, affectionately.

The purple cat had only one brilliantly green eye.

Sayuri gave a small cry of delight and threw her arms around the cat's dense neck. "It's you! You were in my room!"

"Don't forget your allergies," Keiji cautioned, so much like Jun.

Sayuri pushed her nose into the cat's fur. It smelled of seaweed and shiso, and the scent of home made her blink and blink. "Someone has to teach us magic," Sayuri whispered. "We can't wait for another accident to take us home."

Yamanba waved her pipe again, and in the darkening room, the orange circle of light left by the ember glowed long, faded slowly. "There are few true accidents, and somehow your being here does not seem to be one. As for magic, it is everywhere. Is there not the magic of your every breath?"

Sayuri watched as the last light of the orange ring faded into darkness. The fire had burned low. The night ripened.

The mountain woman sighed. "They are children, after all," she murmured, almost to herself. "They do not know the powers they hold."

"Come." The tatami creaked as she stood, the long-handled pipe still clamped between her lips. "I can but help you help yourselves." Yamanba lit a small oil lamp and held it, shoulder level. "Come."

12. WATER OF POSSIBILITY

SAYURI FOLLOWED AFTER YAMANBA, KEEPING A FIRM GRIP
on her brother's hand. The mountain woman led them to
a sliding door and they peered into a room, lower still than
the one they had left. The floor was uneven soil. The space
was empty except for a large earthenware basin in the centre
of the room. The light of the lamp flickered slightly and cast
shadows upon white plaster walls. And the basin. The basin
held a liquid that didn't reflect, but pulled light inwards.

A rich moist smell rose from the wetness. The scent of
decaying leaves, wet earth, and a tinge of sulphur...the smell
brought an almost-memory to Sayuri's thoughts, which vanished just as she thought she could name it.

"This," Yamanba nodded, "is the Water of Possibility."

Sayuri stared; something tugged her senses, almost hypnotic. She shook her head. "What's it for?"

"To make things possible." Yamanba beckoned for them
to come closer and they did. Stood next to the earthenware
basin to peer into liquid depths.

"What things?" Keiji asked, his mouth an "O" of wonder, for the scent of magic was heavy in the room.

"All things," Yamanba smiled.

"What's it doing here?" Sayuri frowned. "Where did it come from?"

"Iiiya, iiiya. A child who asks questions," Yamanba nodded approvingly, "a child who thinks. I don't know how the basin came to be here. I wandered to this mountain three forest lives ago and the basin was already in this very spot. I built this house around it."

"Mreow." The children looked back. The enormous cat, Momo, sat in the dirt by the entranceway. He stared back at them, the tip of his tail flicking, his body otherwise still. The lamp caught his emerald eye and it glowed brilliant.

"Yes, Momo," Yamanba laughed. "Of course I haven't forgotten you. Momo was here too, when I came to this place."

"The cat talks to you?" Sayuri gasped.

"I know what he says," Yamanba clarified. "Now, to answer your second question, I'm not certain where the basin came from, but the Waters, I suspect, come from the Old Baba Tanuki Mountains. There is a spring there called Source. Old Baba Tanuki was a great sorceress, but she disappeared long before my time. Some say she fell victim to the tricks of Great Uncle Mischief, the old fox Patriarch."

Keiji pulled his hand out of Sayuri's grasp and moved toward the giant cat. Sayuri frowned at her brother. He should be listening to important information!

Keiji started. Raised his hand to his mouth.

Yamanba turned to gaze at the cat and boy.

"Did you hear that?" Keiji asked his sister.

"Hear what?"

"Momo talked in my head!"

Sayuri stared at the cat, but Momo just waved his tail, then was still. Not fair, Sayuri thought. She ought to be the one who could hear the cat.

"It is a rare gift to hear so quickly," Yamanba praised. And Keiji beamed with pleasure.

The niggle of jealously turned into a small hard seed in Sayuri's chest. Momo turned to Sayuri and stared long with his strange green eye.

Keiji looked longingly at the mauve-striped cat but backed closer to the basin once more.

"The Water of Possibility makes things possible," Yamanba continued, "and it may make possible your passage home."

"Do we drink from it?" Sayuri asked, making a face. She was sure it would taste bitter.

Yamanba laughed, her shaking body making the lantern light dance across the walls.

"No, child. You must reach inside the waters and take out something that is good. Then you must reach again, and take out something that is bad."

Sayuri and Keiji looked at each other. In confusion and fear.

"What bad thing? What's in there?!" Keiji squeaked.

"Whatever you bring to the waters yourself. That is what you will find."

"Is this a trick?" Sayuri demanded. She looked suspiciously at the mountain woman, who smiled almost sadly.

"No, child. There is no trick. But I will not lie. There is always the possibility of danger. You must find strength in yourselves and in each other." Yamanba set the lantern on the floor next to the great basin and then gently touched the tops of the children's heads.

"I must leave you now." And the great woman quietly walked to the entrance, followed by Momo the cat.

"One last thing," Yamanba stood in the doorway. The light behind her was brighter than that of the room and her face was cast in shadows. As the dim lantern's flame flickered, expressions played across the mountain woman's face, wise, kind, sinister, and sad.

"Once you touch the Water, you must follow through and receive both the good and the bad. If you stop with just the good and leave the bad, the journey will not be complete. That which was possible would become impossible." Yamanba nodded her head.

"I am happy to know you." And she was gone.

"THIS IS JUST AWFUL! I DON'T LIKE IT ONE BIT!" Sayuri whispered. "Someone should save us. We're just kids. I don't even have hair under my armpits yet!"

"Yuuck!" Keiji pinched his nose and flapped his other hand in front of his face. "That's gross!"

They both giggled. The laughter helped. But the quiet pulled them into silence. Sayuri's fingers tingled, and the itch was so deep that she raised her fingers to her mouth and bit the flesh between her teeth. Keiji reached into his coveralls and took out his inhaler. Sucked in a comforting blast.

"Not too much," Sayuri murmured.

They faced the mysterious contents of the basin.

"Jun wouldn't like us sticking our hands into unknown liquids," Keiji whispered helpfully. "There might be germs...."

"Jun's not here! It doesn't matter! Weren't we saying we had to find some magic to get home?" Sayuri demanded, throwing her hands in the air. "There's a whole vat of it right in front of you! Ugh!" Sayuri exclaimed. She squeezed her hands into tight fists. Clenched her teeth. Then stopped. She consciously told herself to breathe deeper. Slower. Like swimming. Controlled breathing meant control over your body. Oxygen. Calm.

"Yamanba said one good and one bad. And they're only things we carry inside ourselves," Sayuri reminded herself.

"Like our guts?" Keiji clutched his middle, eyes wide open.

Sayuri giggled. "I think Yamanba meant things we think about, or our imagination. The hidden stuff. Those things inside us," Sayuri explained.

"B-b-but that's worst of all!" Keiji quavered.

Sayuri nodded solemnly. "It's like a test."

"This is worse than the root cellar!" her brother whispered. "I don't want to see my own bad thing."

"Good first," Sayuri reminded.

"Me not sticking my hand in there!" Keiji's bottom lip jutted out. And he spun away from the frightening basin.

"Listen!" Sayuri hissed. "Stop being such a baby! If you can't do this, how will you get home? We're lucky we met a friend here. What if the next thing you meet is a monster?!"

At this, Keiji dropped open his mouth and bawled.

"Baby," Sayuri muttered in frustration. Dragging her arm over the burning in her eyes. And when her brother kept on bawling, she clamped her hands over her ears.

They sat facing away from each other. And no one looked at the vat.

Well, Sayuri thought. She could do it. She could face her own hopes and her own monsters. She could pass the test and make her way home. Like swimming. She was good at tests. She never failed one lesson. She was strong. Not like scrawny, invalid Keiji.

Could she leave him? Could she?

13. CHOICES

OF COURSE SHE COULDN'T LEAVE HIM! WHAT, WOULD SHE come crawling out of the root cellar, wait for her parents to come home, then tell them she left her brother in a magical Dreamland, but with a very nice Yamanba, so they ought not to worry?! Aiii! Sayuri snorted. Rubbed her arm over her eyes.

"Come on, then," she said gruffly. "Let's think of something else...." She turned around.

Her brother was gone.

No!

"Keiji?!" Sayuri ran to the basin. The liquid was thicker than water, almost oily; the colour of nothing she could describe. Movement churned below the surface. Had he fallen inside? Jun had told her young children could drown in one inch of water. No, she would have heard something! Wouldn't she?

"Keiji!" she yelled into the vat. The liquid absorbed her cry and the surface rippled. A light grew from within. Sayuri stared, her mouth open, breathing in the pungent richness of forest growth and living magic.

The light inside the Water of Possibility grew orange, glowing like the embers of a fire. And inside the light, Sayuri saw. Movement. A small shape. A child running in the forest.

Sayuri's hand covered her mouth. Back in the forest! How? Who was chasing him? But as she watched, her brother's features became clearer. He wasn't gasping in terror. He was smiling, arms outstretched. Sayuri thought she saw a flicker of a tail...Momo! Her brother was chasing Momo!

"Stop!" Sayuri shouted. The light in the Water flickered, then vanished. Stupid! Sayuri berated herself. Keiji. Stupid child! Where was the cat taking him? Maybe the cat had bewitched him. Yes. In the Japanese legends, the cats were shape-shifters. And Sayuri couldn't remember one cat story that wasn't scary.

"Yamanba!" Sayuri ran out and burst into the room where they had sat by the fire.

There was no one there.

The plump moon shone through a small circular window and that was the only light, for the fire was completely out. The pot still hung above the pit, but it was empty. Sayuri crouched down, hand above the ashes. Cold. As if a fire had never burned there. Her fingertips clamoured in a sudden frenzy, the itching so deep she almost wished she could slice her fingers off. Sayuri scraped the skin against the edges of her teeth, hissing with the intense sensation. She bit her fingers hard, pain more tolerable than the itching.

Sayuri eyes watered. "Yamanba?" she whispered. Tears trickled down her cheeks. How could the mountain woman leave her like this? She had seemed like a friend. "Keiji!" she shouted. "Yamanba! Where are you?!"

Sayuri had never felt so alone in her life.

She sank on to the tatami and cried hot tears into the straw until she was exhausted.

KIMI PULLED SAYURI'S BLANKET OFF HER COSY SHOULDERS. Sayuri futilely grasped at the edges.

"Don't," she moaned. "I'm still sleepy. It's freezing!"

"Time to wake up," Kimi scolded. Folding the blanket, then shaking her daughter's shoulder. "Hurry! You'll be late!"

Sayuri sat up, heart thumping against her ribs. "Mom?"

She didn't know where she was.

It was completely dark. She could be anywhere. The thought was awful. Sayuri's lower lip trembled. She shook her head. Okay. Enough. She'd had a cry and that was fine. Now, she should Take Stock of her Situation. That's what Jun would do.

"Keiji?" Sayuri called out. There was no answer. Okay, Keiji was gone.

"Yamanba?" Sayuri tried. Nothing. Okay. She was on her own. The next step was to find her brother.

A challenge. A test. She liked them, Sayuri thought. She wasn't a quitter. "Don't worry," she whispered, "I'll find you."

Sayuri crawled on her hands and knees, for she couldn't see and she didn't want to fall into the firepit. Not that it was hot, but the last thing she needed was to be covered in ashes. She crawled in the direction she thought she'd seen the main sliding door.

"Oh!"

Her hand had touched something. Hard. Knocked it over and there was an oily warmth on her hand. "Yuck!" The liquid was thick, coating her skin. Sayuri tried rubbing her hand on the tatami to wipe the slickness off. She cautiously raised her fingers to sniff. Maybe the smell would give her clues.

Fatty. The oil lamp! Sayuri cautiously tapped around her. She'd knocked the lamp bowl over and the oil was all gone. Would nothing go right? Sayuri's thoughts brightened. She didn't have any matches to light the lamp with anyway, so she really hadn't lost anything! She tapped around and found the wick. Grabbed it, put it in her pocket. She'd take the lamp with her, matches or not. Something was better than nothing.

Sayuri wished she had her backpack. How did they carry things in the folk tales? Ah, she thought, with those bundles wrapped up with cloth. She couldn't remember seeing anything like that when the room had been brighter. And she didn't like the idea of crawling around all night, hoping to bump into Useful Items. Sayuri shrugged. She had to get out and start looking for her brother. Who knew how long she had slept? Sayuri shoved the oily curved bowl of the lamp into her front pocket. Good thing she wore her jeans baggy. She supposed the oil would leave a dark patch in the material, but there was nothing to be done about that. She'd rather look like she'd peed herself than regret leaving a light source later on.

Sayuri found the edge of the tatami and cautiously stepped on to the dirt floor. She turned toward the firepit and bowed formally, the way her grandmother had taught.

"Thank you for your generous hospitality," she said. "I hope you don't mind, but I have borrowed your lamp because I may need it. If I should return this way once more, I ask that I may again request your kind assistance."

Sayuri groped for the door. Slid it open and walked into the night.

14. JOURNEY

THE NIGHT WAS STILL COOL. WAS KEIJI WARM ENOUGH? Sayuri shook her head, turning in a slow circle. How would she decide which direction to go? She wasn't forest raised. She couldn't read a trail of broken twigs and pressed moss like words in a book that said, "He went that way!"

Think, she tapped her fingers against each other. Think.

Funny, she thought. When she tapped them together, the itch was gone. The skin felt silky cool. Almost pleasant. She frowned, squatting down and gazing at her hands. Was it her imagination or were they faintly glowing?

Crack!

Sayuri leapt to her feet. Her hands balled into fists, she crouched in the loose, knee-bent stance her mom had taught her.

A creature stood before her. Pale green, it glowed slightly in the dim. Slender and short, the creature was no bigger than her brother and a faint whiff of algae seemed to float in the air. She, Sayuri thought, though she didn't know why. The creature's head was strangely formed; the skull wasn't round but concave. A shallow depression like a bowl. And the face wasn't human. Like a frog, her face tapered to a triangular point, though her mouth was beaked like a turtle's. Shiny black eyes gleamed large and liquid. Nocturnal, Sayuri thought.

"What do you want?" she asked.

"What do you want?" the creature said.

Her voice was clear. Like water. Water, Sayuri thought. Water creature. Jun had told her tales of his childhood in Japan. When he spent one summer at his grandfather's rice farm. And the muddy rice fields had been filled with mysterious tiny footprints.

"Are you a kappa?" Sayuri grinned. Then her smile dropped. Kappa were mischievous and dangerous. In folk legends, they drowned children and pulled out the entrails of livestock!

"Are you a kappa?" the creature mimicked, a pained expression on her face.

"Will you stop that?" Sayuri said crossly.

"Will you stop that?" the creature sighed, her shoulders sinking with defeat.

Sayuri dropped her caution and pinched her upper lip thoughtfully. She asked questions and the creature repeated every word she said. And she didn't act like she was joking. Hmmmm.

"I am a kappa," Sayuri tried saying what the creature ought to say for herself.

"I am a kappa," the kappa smiled pointing vigorously to herself.

"You are a human," Sayuri grinned.

"You are a human," the kappa pointed at Sayuri.

"I get it!" Sayuri hopped up and down. "You can only speak in the manner you're spoken to!"

The kappa leapt joyfully, repeating Sayuri's words, nodding and nodding.

Sayuri stared at the little water imp. She didn't know if it was rude, but she couldn't help herself. She peered into the bowl-shaped head to see if it was true. If it really held supernatural water.

The bowl was empty. The kappa was shaking her head. Sayuri crouched down and stared into iridescent black eyes.

"What happened to your water?" Sayuri asked gently.

"What happened to your water?" the kappa sadly muttered.

Ugh! Sayuri frowned. Talking like this was so frustrating!

"There was trouble," Sayuri guessed.

"There was trouble," the creature nodded eagerly.

"I am cursed," Sayuri said.

"I am cursed," the kappa sighed, reaching to hold her head bowl tenderly.

"I must find a way to lift this curse."

"I must find a way to lift this curse," the water sprite said resolutely.

Sayuri sighed. The kappa had her own problems. And Sayuri still had hers. "Talking this way makes me tired. And I must find my brother. He is lost in the forest and I don't know where he has gone."

"Talking like this makes me tired," the kappa whispered.

She turned away, her slender shoulders drooping. Then she faced Sayuri with determination. "And I must find my brother." The creature pointed a webbed finger in the direction from which the moon had risen. "He is lost in the forest." The kappa jabbed east several times. "And I don't know where he has gone."

"What?!" Sayuri grasped the water imp's moist arms and stared into her midnight eyes.

"What?!" the kappa exclaimed.

"Can you help me?" Sayuri gasped.

"Can you help me?" the creature quavered.

"Yes!" Sayuri laughed.

"Yes!" The kappa leapt several metres into the air.

THE WATER IMP TOOK THE LEAD, her great eyes almost glowing. Sayuri held her cool webbed hand and was glad of the company. She had thought a forest would be still at night, but creatures were stirring and small chirps, the snap of twigs, sent tremors into her heart. The moss-covered trees were living beasts and the weight of branches creaked heavily above her head. But the night was ripening into morning, and though she was glad for the light, she yawned enormously. Unseen birds chirped with great cheer, calling for a day without rain and an abundance of insects to eat.

The kappa tugged her hand pointedly.

"What's your name?" Sayuri asked, forgetting the curse.

"What's your name?" the kappa asked woefully.

Sayuri sighed. It wasn't the kappa's fault. "I'm Sayuri," she said.

"I'm Sayuri," the kappa pinched her beaked mouth with frustration.

"I know," Sayuri said brightly, "I'll give you a nickname for now. How about, hmmm, Echo!"

The kappa repeated her words, a pleased smile coming to her mouth.

Sayuri smiled in return. "It's not for keeps. Only until you can tell me your real name," she explained. "I'm sleepy," Sayuri yawned.

"I'm sleepy," Echo yawned. She was squeezing her eyelids tight, so that only a thin slit of black showed.

"A kappa can't see very well during the day," Sayuri guessed.

"A kappa can't see very well during the day," Echo nodded.

Sayuri pointed in the direction they had been walking. North, she thought, in relation to where to sun was rising. "This is the right direction," she said.

Echo pointed her finger east. Directly towards the break of light. "This is the right direction."

"Oh," Sayuri frowned.

"Oh," Echo repeated.

Sayuri sighed. She knew the kappa was under a curse, but the repetition was so annoying! "I will lead until I find some shelter. Then, we will rest."

Echo repeated her eagerly and Sayuri took the lead. The kappa closed her eyes and held on tight to Sayuri's hand.

The mountain sloped downward and the trees grew fewer in number but were enormous in size. Sayuri gaped at the massive trunks, wondering how old they were. She touched the rough skin of a giant cedar and her fingers tingled electric. As if there were currents running beneath the flesh of the tree.

"Everything is so alive," she murmured.

"Everything is so alive," Echo whispered.

Sayuri glanced at her companion. The creature drooped with exhaustion and her skin was barely green. Sayuri didn't want to stop just yet. Who knew how far Keiji was? But Echo seemed to know. And if Echo got so weak she couldn't move, what then? Sayuri bit her lip. She looked down.

Noticed...a barely visible flaw in the body of the giant cedar. The tree wasn't whole. There was a crack in the skin of the tree, a fissure that led into the heart of the trunk. Sayuri sat on her haunches and peered inside. It was dark. Was the hole empty? It was big enough for a good-sized animal.... She grabbed a stick from the floor of the forest and gave the black hole a little poke.

Nothing screeched or ran out.

Sayuri crept closer and sniffed. There was a redolent animal sweetness. A burrow, then. But an empty burrow?

"I think it's empty," Sayuri decided.

Echo crept on all fours, too exhausted to walk. The kappa sniffed and wrinkled her nose. "I think it's empty," Echo agreed. Sayuri tapped the lamp from the outside of her jeans. There was an oily patch on the material. What she wouldn't do for matches or a lighter! Well, she'd have to find some fuel first, before she'd even need fire. Bear grease, maybe. She snorted. Yeah, she'd go hunting for bear. And the way everything spoke in this place, she could just ask the nice bear to please let her kill it so she could use its fat to light her lamp!

Sayuri laughed out loud, and Echo, surprised, laughed aloud too.

Sayuri gestured to the crevice in the tree and the kappa stuck her head inside, paused, then disappeared into the darkness. Sayuri crawled in after.

The hollow in the tree seemed bigger than it should be. Sayuri crawled quickly, afraid to be left behind, and she was glad that Echo's skin glowed. The twisting passage was smooth beneath the palms of her hands and she gulped. Wondered what had passed so many times to polish the wood so perfectly.

Finally, the tunnel spilled into a round hollow. Large enough for three Sayuris to lie down end to end. She could stand up without bending over, though something scratchy, like strands of dried branches, tickled the top of her head. How could this be? Sayuri thought. The tree certainly wasn't as big on the outside. But the heart of the cedar was warm. The animal reek was strong. As was a sweet green scent of grasses dried in the sun. Carnivore? Sayuri wondered. Omnivore? There was something soft on the floor, moss, and maybe feathers. Echo's faint glow was fading as the kappa sank into sleep and Sayuri, too exhausted to think any more, curled into a ball. "Be safe, Keiji," she murmured and fell asleep.

15. MISTAKE

"HAHAHHHH! WE HAVE VISITORS! WERE WE EXPECTING any? We don't think so. Are they friendly? Are they spirits? Are they well-mannered, hmmmmm?"

Sayuri jerked awake and blinked rapidly. A pointed muzzle of sharp white teeth almost pressed against her nose. The sweet smell of animal breath. An animal that ate flesh....

Sayuri slowly backed away. The den wasn't dark. A small lantern flickered light on bunches of herbs, flowers, and strangely-shaped roots hanging from the ceiling.

And sitting on his haunches was a small, scraggly fox.

"Please forgive us our intrusion," Sayuri bowed politely the way her grandmother had taught her. "We are travellers passing through the night and daylight found us tired. We have imposed upon your absence and humbly beg your pardon."

"Ho, ho, hohhhhh!" the fox raised his muzzle in amusement. There was a shiver of motion and the fox blurred, shimmering into a different shape. Fox no longer, a beautiful young girl in a patched kimono sat with her knees folded beneath her. A dirty slender hand raised to cover her mouth, she giggled. The pupils in her amber eyes black and sly.

"We are pleased to make the acquaintance of such a charming guest," the foxgirl giggled. "For we have heard tales told of human creatures, but have never met them."

Sayuri shivered. Foxes were shape-shifters and their nature was as changeable as their form. Had she ever heard a tale of a fox that didn't end with deceit or mayhem?

"I am pleased to make your acquaintance. I am not alone. My companion, the good kappa, Echo, has joined me in my travels." Sayuri looked around. But the creature was nowhere to be seen. Her heart plunged. Had the kappa left her already?

"You may come off the wall," the foxgirl commanded.

There was movement on the wall of the tree cave and Sayuri saw that Echo had been clinging to the cedar, skin adapted to the grain of the wood. As she watched, the kappa's skin slowly returned to its pale green.

"You may come off the wall," Echo said glumly, jumping to the soft floor.

"Is this kappa simple?" the foxgirl frowned, peering into Echo's face.

"Is this kappa simple?" Echo glared, jabbing the fox's sensitive nose with a green finger.

The foxgirl snarled.

"Please!" Sayuri raised her hand. "The poor kappa is afflicted with a curse that prevents her from speaking as she would like. Echo may only speak in the manner she is spoken to."

"Hohohohhhhh!" the foxgirl pealed gleefully behind her graceful hand. "What an imaginative curse, indeed! We wonder who might have thought of such a vexing punishment."

"I don't know," Sayuri answered. "I've only just come to this place and my brother is lost. I must find him so that we may return to our home. Echo has joined me and, together, we hope to find my brother and the cure to the curse."

A sudden squeeze of fear and pain gripped Sayuri's heart. What if the medicine in Keiji's inhaler ran out? She gasped, spun away, shoulders shuddering uncontrollably. Breathe in, she thought, breathe out. She dragged her forearm over her wet eyes and concentrated on air entering her body, releasing panic with every exhale. Controlled breathing meant control over her body. Sayuri breathed deep and smooth, the way she'd always trained to, and found a place of calm within herself. She turned around. The foxgirl was a fox once more. The animal was panting.

"Hah!" the fox barked. "We see you are in training too! We have recently graduated from the Academy of Fox Arts in the Burning Valley. We must train in our arts so that we may compete in the tournament held during the Festival of Fire. We might like to join you in your journey. For it sounds like there is room for great mischief."

"We are truly honoured," Sayuri bowed, thinking rapidly. "I would like to confer with my companion to see if Echo, too, would find this agreeable. For I am obligated to her needs before yours, you do understand?"

"But of course," the fox bowed. Swept his patchy tail and

retired to the entranceway. His large pointed ears flicked, one leaning slightly backward.

"What do you think?" Sayuri whispered to Echo.

"What do you think?" Echo clenched her webbed hands.

"You don't like foxes," Sayuri guessed.

"You don't like foxes!" Echo nodded vigorously. Her eyes squeezed into wedges of hate.

"A fox cast this curse upon you!" Sayuri realized.

"A fox cast this curse upon you!" The kappa grasped the girl's forearms.

"But not this one," Sayuri guessed.

Echo looked down. Shook her head. "But not this one."

Sayuri rubbed the kappa's back. It was obvious that she felt uncomfortable around the shape-shifter. Sayuri felt uncomfortable too. But a small tickling licked her thoughts, whispered down her arms to her fingers. Maybe the meeting was not mere chance. Sayuri anxiously rubbed her fingers against the outside of her jeans.

"I think he should come," Sayuri said slowly.

"I think he should come!" Echo jerked away from Sayuri's side.

"We could give it a try," Sayuri pleaded.

"We could give it a try," Echo muttered angrily. She wouldn't look Sayuri in the eyes.

What if she was making a mistake? Sayuri thought. Echo would know more about foxes and the ways of this world than she did. Sayuri stared at the fox's back. He gently swished his tail back and forth, ears twitching.

"Kind fox," Sayuri called, "we would be pleased and honoured to share your company on our journey. Your great skills and keen mind are sorely needed on this expedition."

The fox lightly leapt to his feet and minced closer on graceful paws. Laughing a mouthful of shiny teeth. "The honour is ours." He shimmered, the air warping around his body, his fur reshaped into the copper-coloured patched cloth of an old kimono.

"We have been a negligent hostess," the foxgirl whispered. "Please, my guests, seat yourselves and we shall prepare you some refreshments."

Sayuri tugged Echo's hand to pull her down. The kappa jerked out of her grip and sat a few feet away, refusing to look at Sayuri's face. The girl sighed. Could she afford to make Echo mad? How would she find her brother without the kappa's help?

The foxgirl rustled in a cleverly hidden cupboard. Sayuri hoped there was food. Her stomach squeezed painfully; the soup and fish she'd had at Yamanba's home seemed like years ago.

The foxgirl brought a small wooden tray to where they sat. On the tray was a small ceramic bowl, three cups filled with water. In the bowl were roasted chestnuts. Sayuri darted a glance at the foxgirl. Her beautiful features were blurring, shimmering, struggling to keep in form. The tray shivered in her hands. The cups started clattering and Sayuri reached to take the tray from her hands. The foxgirl collapsed into the form of the scraggly fox. He shuddered and gasped, shivering with exhaustion.

Echo peered at the fox with her large black eyes. Sayuri

rushed to the animal's side. She took a cup of water and held it before him, so he could lap up some of the liquid.

"Thank you," the fox said hoarsely. "I have been ill."

Sayuri stroked the fur on the fox's head. Wondered if it was rude. The fox didn't seem to mind, however, only closing his eyes and breathing a long sigh. "My name is Machigai," he offered.

"Really?" Sayuri asked. Echo edged closer.

"Hah!" the fox barked, "Funny, isn't it? I was named by my great uncle."

"Your uncle named you 'Mistake'? That's awful!" Sayuri said hotly. Funny, the constant itch in her fingertips was soothed by Machigai's oily fur. She ran her fingers over the patches that were thick, smoothed the skin where he was bald. The fox stretched with pleasure.

"Ahhh, the old Patriarch is a miserable beast. His idea of mischief borders on cruelty. The Fox Collective doesn't know what to do with him. He does not die. Only grows more powerful. When he found out I eat no meat, he cast me from my people. I am forbidden to return until I have eaten flesh."

"How awful!" Sayuri gasped. Echo inched closer still, and even patted the fox sympathetically on his haunch. Machigai twisted his head to glance back at the kappa. He winked.

"I wouldn't be surprised if the fox who cursed you was Great Uncle Mischief. The Old Fox Patriarch."

Echo hissed. Flapping her webbed feet in agitation.

Machigai's head dropped and he panted softly. "Please. Eat. Rest. We will have time for stories later."

Sayuri passed the cup of water to Echo who eagerly

poured some into the bowl of her head. But the water just disappeared. Her head wouldn't hold the liquid, so she was without supernatural powers. She was no better than an over-sized frog. Water ran from her enormous eyes instead and Sayuri put her arm around her slender shoulders.

"You mustn't cry. You're wasting water," she smiled.

"You mustn't cry. You're wasting water," Echo shook her head. She drank the rest of the water in great gulps. Picked up a chestnut and turned it around and around in her amphibious hands. She didn't have any fingernails.

A kappa who couldn't keep water. A fox who wouldn't eat meat, Sayuri thought. No wonder he was so weak. He needed more fatty foods like deep-fried tofu and sweet stewed beans. That's what the animal needed! Not boiled chestnuts! Foxes were active, athletic creatures. And who knew how much energy it took to shape-shift! He needed more calories!

Sayuri sighed. Bit into the skin of the dark brown nut and started peeling the shell. Chestnuts were a lot of work. She dug her nails into the crack, careful not to crumble the meat and so waste it. In the flickering light, she peeled all the nuts so they could share and eat together.

Instead of being closer to finding her brother, she thought, she seemed to have accumulated more problems that had to be solved. And where was Keiji now? Somewhere in the forest, cold and afraid of Clown-Face Man? That cat, Momo! Momo better be taking good care of her brother! Hot tears burned her eyes and she dragged her arm over the wet-ness. She stuffed a dry chestnut into her mouth and chewed angrily. The meat was sweet.

16. SOMETHING IN THE AIR

AFTER THEIR HUMBLE MEAL OF CHESTNUTS AND WATER, the three companions rested in quiet, each with their own burdens heavy upon their thoughts. They slept and woke; slept fitfully again. Machigai finally stirred, fanning his scraggly tail and stretching almost like a cat. His mouth dropped into a canine smile. The sweet smell of chestnuts on his breath.

"The night comes."

Sayuri rubbed her fingers on the outer seams of her jeans. She looked down. There were two bands of dirt along the outside of her thighs where she had been rubbing her soiled hands unconsciously to get rid of the itch. "Do humans live in this land?" she wondered out loud.

"Humans are creatures of myth and legend," Machigai explained. His eyes twinkled. "We think their lack of magic must, indeed, be a myth and their lack of wits is, of course, legendary!" He tipped back his sharp nose and barked at his joke.

"I guess you're feeling better," Sayuri snorted.

Echo tapped the girl's arm with a moist hand.

"There are no humans here," Sayuri guessed.

"There are no humans here," the kappa nodded.

Sayuri was relieved, though she didn't know why. Why would she fear humans more than animals? Murderers, kidnappers, she thought. Racism, sexism, war. She shuddered. Some humans, she thought, were more beastly than animals.

"Oh hohhh," Machigai leaned close. "Don't be mistaken in thinking there are no monsters in this place."

Sayuri jumped around. "How do you know what I was thinking?"

But the fox wouldn't answer. He rustled at the cupboard and took out a tan-coloured gourd. It was shaped like a figure eight, only the top circle was smaller than the bottom. The neck on the top was stopped with a plug of wood. A short cord was tied to the middle of the container. Sayuri could hear the slosh of liquid.

"We'll need to find more," Machigai muttered. He teethed the gourd to Sayuri and she picked it up. The container was smooth, hard, and light. She tapped her fingers against the cool surface. Hyotan, she thought. She'd seen illustrations of the old-fashioned gourds in her Japanese folk tale books, marvelled at how a fruit of a plant could be a natural bottle. Who was the clever person who thought it up?

Sayuri shook the hyotan and heard the contents slosh. She hoped it was water instead of sake! She looped the cord around her belt and tied it tightly so it wouldn't bang around.

Echo, eager to leave the den, nimbly slipped through the passageway. Machigai turned to the lantern and huffed. The darkness was heavier than a quilt.

"Aren't we taking the light with us?" Sayuri asked in a small voice.

"No," the fox murmured. "In the forest, a light will draw more toward it than we will be able to see. Come. The kappa and I see well enough. You may hold on to my tail. Don't pull out any hairs, mind!"

A scratchy tickle of fur swept across Sayuri's face and she giggled. She clasped the tail with a gentle grip. The fox led her outside.

NIGHT AGAIN. HOW MANY DAYS HAD PASSED? Sayuri wondered. Time seemed to stretch longer, though she couldn't say why. What if, she thought, what if time was passing more quickly in her own land? When she finally returned home, she might be like the fisherman, Urashimataro, who returned from his journey to the Kingdom Beneath the Sea, only to find that his parents were long dead, the village he knew a place in the past. And when time caught up with him, he withered under the sun – a passage of decades, centuries – until nothing was left but the husk of a man, hair, beard, white and brittle. Sayuri's heart thudded painfully. She couldn't move.

"Breathe," whispered the fox.

"Breathe," repeated the kappa.

Sayuri gasped and released her breath in long shudders. Echo patted her back with her webbed hand. Focus, Sayuri thought. Focus. I am looking for my brother.

The night air was sweet with pine and cedar. Stars glinted in the breaks between branches. Within the canopy of evergreens, Sayuri had no sense of season. For the night was chill, but there was no snow. Their breath didn't hang in the air, but there were no flowers. Nor was there the profusion of autumn mushrooms that come after the rains. Puzzled, she turned to Machigai who trod silently through the forest. Echo glowed faintly, a little ahead, sniffing the air now and then, though Sayuri could smell nothing except the rich perfume of pine.

"Is it summer or spring?" she asked. She watched the annoyed flick of Machigai's tail. If it weren't for the small patch of white, Sayuri doubted she'd see him at all.

"Shush!" the fox hissed. "There is mischief in the air." He pointed his nose to the skies, his dark eyes glittering starlight. "Be still!" he barked. And he bounded away.

Sayuri's heart thudded so loudly that she was sure everything could hear her. The hairs on her arms stood straight up and blood rushed to her extremities. Her fingertips tingled. The buzz skittered nerve endings and she furiously dug thumbnails into her flesh. There was so much mischief around, she could barely breathe.

Hide! her mind panicked.

Run! her mind screamed.

In the distance, there was a flash of pale light between massive trunks. A leaping glow of someone darting between the trees.

"Oh ho, ho, hohhhhh," laughter fading. The sound of the foxgirl's charming giggle. The glowing figure fluttered from tree to tree until it was swallowed up by the darkness.

"No!" Sayuri shouted. "Don't leave me!"

"HAH!" a gruff voice thundered.

A foul stench of stale sake and unwashed flesh surrounded Sayuri.

Fool, she thought. Blood pounding in her ears. You fool.

A thick coarse hand grabbed the back of her neck and she was lifted high into the air. She kicked her feet, but her struggle was as futile as an insect's. She was raised up, up, almost level with the giant cedars. Level with the horrifying face of an oni.

His bright blue skin was pitted with lumps and pale scars and his teeth were sharp and black. The ogre's eyes were red with blood and two golden horns spiralled from the top of his head. Dirty knotted hair tumbled down his back like the mane of a horse and the reek of spilled and rotten food emanated from the fur hides that clothed his filthy body.

Sayuri turned her head as far as she could, away from the nauseating smell.

"WELL, WELL!" boomed the oni. "WHAT HAVE WE HERE? A MOUSE? AN INSECT? A NICE LITTLE MORSEL TO EAT?"

Think, she demanded of herself. Though she wished she could just faint and hope that someone would save her. Oni. What had Kimi told her about oni? Can't overpower them. No. Then –

"I am, indeed, most privileged to make your acquaintance," Sayuri said brightly, though her heart quaked inside her chest. "The wondrous tales of The Great Blue Oni have travelled far and wide and your fame precedes your awesome presence."

"HA! HA! HA!" Blue Oni bellowed with pleasure. The reek of rice wine almost knocked the girl senseless. "SO YOU HAVE HEARD OF ME?" He pulled Sayuri closer to one red eye and he gave the girl a little shake.

Sayuri's neck ached. Tears dripped from her eyes, but she laughed and raised her voice.

The adventures of the Great Blue Oni
have been sung from land to land.
How mighty are his feats of strength.
His foes dissolve like sand!

Sayuri sang as loudly as she could. Desperately making up the words as she went along. Were Echo and Machigai captured too? How long could she think up rhymes?

His legs are pillars of the skies,
his arms are limbs of lead,
his hands crush all his enemies,
crush them good and dead!

"HA!HA!HA!HA!HAAAAAAAA!" the giant ogre bellowed. "CLEVER BIRDIE," he cooed.

Sayuri thought the rhymes were pretty simple, but they were the best she could manage, being dangled by the neck in the hands of a stinking ogre.

Blue Oni chuckled and reached down to open the flap of a pouch draped over his massive shoulder. He dropped Sayuri inside.

"Umph!" She landed on a jumble of lumps, fur, and sticks. The stench was overwhelming. The pouch was made from the uncured hide of a deer and the reek of rancid grease, dried flesh, and spilled sake overwhelmed the girl. Weak with hunger and terror, she fainted for the first time in her life.

17. BLUE ONI'S CAVE

WOOD SMOKE BIT THE BACK OF SAYURI'S THROAT, CREPT into her lungs. She coughed hoarsely, pushing herself off the rough floor she lay upon. She blinked in the dim light. The sun cast diagonal lines of dust into the mouth of an enormous cave. A rumbling roar waxed and waned. Sayuri frowned, until she saw the source. The Blue Oni was sprawled on a pile of furs near a smouldering fire, snoring so loudly that tiny stones tumbled down from the ceiling.

Sayuri was in a wooden cage, hanging from the ceiling of the cave. The slats of her prison were far apart; there was plenty of room to slip through, but the distance from the cage to the floor of the cave was instant death. Sayuri peered over. Her weight tipped the cage slightly, the floor of her cage tilting, sliding her toward the edge – she scrambled back to the centre, shivering. The cage swung slowly back and forth. Sayuri sat with her legs drawn up, her arms clasped tightly around her knees. She remained motionless until the cage stopped swaying.

Sayuri's eyes darted about. A rope was looped through the

middle slat on the top of her cage and strung through a hook in the ceiling. The line ran from the hook to a narrow piece of rock that jutted halfway down the side of the wall. The rope circled the jutting rock, knotted once, with the end of the line trailing the ground. Could she somehow climb to the top of her cage, then slither down the rope to escape? She didn't know. She felt so weak. And thirsty. Sayuri's mouth was grainy and her tongue tasted sour.

The water gourd! It still hung from her belt! Thanking Machigai, she brought the bottle to her lips. The liquid tasted so sweet she almost wept. She gulped once, twice, then blinked. Stopped. Ration the water, she thought. Her throat ached for more, but she put the stopper back into the neck of the gourd. Retied the cord around her belt with shaking hands. Sayuri stared at them for a moment, then drew her knees to her chest, wrapped her arms around her body. She dropped her head and closed her eyes. How could she save her brother? She couldn't even save herself. Hot tears stung her cheeks. Stop crying, she told herself. You're wasting water....

"Sayuri!" A whispered hiss.

Sayuri looked up. Darted a glance at the sleeping ogre, then crawled slowly to the edge of her cage. Her prison swung gently. She lay on her stomach and peered over.

Machigai waved his tail. Echo held a webbed hand over her mouth, pointing to the oni with the other hand.

Sayuri smiled, a hiccup of pleasure almost spilling from her lips.

Echo motioned to herself, then to the cord that held the girl's cage. The kappa mimicked the letting down of rope as

Machigai shimmered into the form of the foxgirl. Echo leapt to the walls and almost seemed to disappear into the stone. Sayuri could only locate her when the kappa blinked her large black eyes.

The foxgirl ran to the mouth of the cave and stood in the sunlight. "Ooh hoo, hoo, hoo!" she giggled. Then began to sing:

> *Big Blue Oni is a smelly clod,*
> *reeks of dung, and brains of sod.*
> *Stupid lout without a hope,*
> *have you ever heard of soap?*

The blue ogre woke slowly as the words sank into his brain. Then he roared a great roar that shuddered the walls of the cave. He pounded to where Sayuri cowered inside the cage. His fist raised to crush her like a bug.

"My sister," Sayuri cried, pointing to where the foxgirl was standing. "My naughty sister makes fun of you, oh lord! You must catch her so that she may be punished."

The oni roared once more, then thundered to where the foxgirl stood. Sayuri stared with horror. He was big, but he moved so quickly. Foxgirl leapt from the mouth of the cave and bounded quickly across the field. Flitting in and out of the grass, her giggles trickled back to sting the horrible ogre.

"I WILL TEAR YOU TO PIECES!" he roared. "I WILL MASH YOU AND CRUSH YOU AND SQUISH YOU TO NOTHING!"

The floor lurched beneath Sayuri and she gasped as the

cage fell several metres. She swung her head around. Echo was being dragged by the weight of the cage, though she strained at the rope with all her might. The cage started to swing and the walls and floor of the cave lurched like a carnival ride. The rope slid a few more metres. And Sayuri saw. The roughly-made cord was being sliced by the rock. Strand by strand, the rope was fraying, as the cage lurched downward, then stopped. She was still twenty metres above the ground. If the cage dropped, she'd be smashed.

Sayuri scurried to the side closest to the cave wall. She slipped through the slats so that she was on the outside of the cage. She spun around, pressed her back against the bars with her hands gripping behind her. Sayuri bent her knees and pressed down with her weight, making the cage swing even harder. The wall of the cave swung closer, then farther away, back and forth. Using momentum, she pushed harder and harder, even as the cage lurched, dropping several more metres. Now or never, Sayuri thought. Now or never!

She leapt.

The rope shredded, the cage fell to the floor and splintered into tiny pieces.

Sayuri clung to a small outcropping of stone. Stunned. "Move," she hissed. "Move now!"

"Move now," Echo moaned.

Sayuri took a quick glance down. The kappa was lying on the ground. Sayuri scrabbled for footing. The rough walls of the cave had many pockets for her feet and hands. Sayuri bit her bottom lip to stop herself from crying out as she clambered down with hands skinned raw and bleeding.

The ground came sudden and solid and Sayuri fell to her bottom. She shuffled on her knees to where the kappa lay. Echo was so pale, she was almost white. Curled up in a ball, she held her hands awkwardly outstretched.

The kappa's beautiful webbing was ripped clean away.

"Oh," Sayuri cried. "Your beautiful hands."

"WHERE IS YOUR NAUGHTY SISTER?!" a voice bellowed from outside. Coming closer.

"Oh," Sayuri gasped, "you must get up. Quickly. Echo, stand up!"

The kappa only smiled sadly. Then her eyes closed.

"No!" Sayuri gasped. Tears spilling. "No!" She lifted Echo by the armpits and draped her over her shoulder. Echo was lighter than Keiji! She would save Echo, then she would save her brother. She would not be a caged singing pet of a stupid ogre!

Sayuri lurched to her feet and stumbled to the mouth of the cave.

"LITTLE BIRDIE!" Blue Oni panted, his hard feet crunching the stones outside the cave, "HAS YOUR SISTER COME BACK TO SEE YOU?"

Sayuri ran back inside, Echo sliding awkwardly over her shoulder. She ran further into the cave. Back into the deeps where there was no light. Only the faintest glow from the kappa's faded skin. Sayuri lowered Echo to the ground, so she was sitting up, back against the wall. The girl squatted in front of the kappa, and reached behind to drape Echo's arms over her shoulder.

"I have to piggyback you, okay?" Sayuri whispered. "It'll be easier to carry you."

Echo didn't answer.

Sayuri leaned forward, cupping the kappa's weight with her hands. The girl hissed with pain but she stood up, hunched over so her back was almost horizontal. She shuffled beneath Echo's limp weight.

"BIRDIE!" Blue Oni roared. "WHERE ARE YOU!"

Sayuri scurried along the back wall of the cave, heart thumping so hard and fast she was afraid it might explode.

"Huh! Huh! Huh!" she panted, the sweat of fear wet on her forehead. She felt a small rush of cold air.

Cold air!

There was a triangle of greater darkness in the face of the rock. So small the giant oni would never have known. A triangle of darkness that tunneled deeper into a universe of utter black.

But what made the tunnel? Sayuri tiredly thought. Her mind refusing to rest. What's on the other side?

"IS BIRDIE HIDING IN THE DARK?" the hoarse voice was very close. A wave of ogre sweat and filth swept into the enclosed space.

Sayuri, with Echo clasped to her back, disappeared into the soul of stone.

18. THE SOUL OF STONE

THE CRACK IN THE ROCK WALL WAS NARROW AND TWISTY. The small trace of light from the cave quickly disappeared. And though the kappa's skin gave off a tiny glow, this too became dimmer and dimmer. Please, Sayuri thought, please don't let it mean that Echo is dying.

Sayuri could see nothing at all.

Absolute darkness pressed oxygen out of the air, the crushing weight of a million tons of rock bearing down upon Sayuri. A scream spiralled from her belly, rising, growing, trying to burst from her throat like a hidden monster....

And she had been afraid of a little root cellar!

She giggled. Gasped. Eyes squeezed shut. Coughed up her fear in chunks of laughter. How ridiculous! Root cellar! She chuckled weakly, one hand cupping Echo on her hunched-over back, one hand leaning against the rough stone.

When she opened her eyes, the darkness seemed less complete. Was it her imagination? She blinked and blinked and lights seemed to dot her vision. Sayuri didn't know if it was real. She awkwardly shifted Echo's weight. The kappa was lighter than her brother, but her limp body was hard to hold. Sayuri couldn't feel the pain in the palms of her hands. She bit her lip, hoped it only meant that they were numb. Gangrene, her mind shouted. Dead nerve endings!

"Shut up!" Sayuri hissed. "Just move!" She shuffled forward, bent over, sweeping her lead foot on the sandy ground to toe out rocks she might stumble over, or sudden holes in the ground that would swallow them up. Her right foot scouted the dark terrain and the left foot dragged to catch up.

She walked like this for minutes, hours, she had no way of knowing.

She might have walked for days.

IT WAS COLD BENEATH THE BONES OF THE EARTH. The dragging walk into the eternity of darkness wasn't enough to keep her warm, but the kappa's weight pressed heavier and heavier upon her back, cold sweat dripping off her icy brow.

"Echo," the girl gasped, "I don't know how much longer I can do this."

Echo didn't answer.

Was she – dead? Was Sayuri just carrying around a corpse? She shuddered. No!

Sayuri sank to her knees and gently propped Echo against the wall. Free from the weight, Sayuri stretched. Her back was drenched with sweat and the wetness quickly turned cold. She started shaking, her arms twitching with exhaustion.

Sayuri turned to Echo, reaching to tap out the lines of her face. Sayuri traced down the angles of cheek and gently pressed her fingers into Echo's neck.

No pulse. Nothing.

No!

No, the kappa mightn't be dead! How could Sayuri know? Maybe kappa didn't have pulses in the first place! Okay, Echo's skin felt dry and icy cold. If she was human, she'd be dead for sure, but maybe kappa were more like frogs? Maybe she was cold-blooded and was sort of hibernating? The temperature surely wasn't a problem. But the dryness was. The only dry frogs Sayuri had seen were dead ones.

Water! Water would help. Sayuri fumbled with the knot around her belt, her cold fingers clumsy. When it finally came undone, she gave the container a little shake. The slosh was light, barely enough for one. So.

Sayuri gently followed Echo's curve of skull to the bowl-shaped indentation on the top of her head. Keeping her hand against the side, she pulled the stopper out of the gourd with her teeth, then poured a little into Echo's head. The smell of the water was dizzying and Sayuri clamped her teeth together. Her hand shook with want.

The girl gently cupped the back of Echo's head and tilted it slightly back.

"Sorry," she murmured, using her dirty fingers to open the kappa's beaked mouth. She trickled the tiny amount of water into the back of Echo's throat, hoping none of it was wasted. When she could hear no more, Sayuri lay the kappa on her lap, then she tipped the empty bottle to her own lips.

Her dry tongue soaked up the last few drops like a sponge. She desperately sucked for more, but the gourd was empty.

Rage burned hot in her chest. She threw the bottle away from her and it clattered against something. Sayuri sobbed. Gasped. Breathe in, she shuddered. Breathe out. Control over your breathing means control over your body. The heat of anger quickly burned out. She was too weak for it.

That was stupid, she thought dully. If they made it through the cave or found a source of water, they'd need the container.

Sayuri gently moved Echo off her lap. She groaned. Her muscles ached worse than after the hardest swim training she'd ever had. She crawled along the sand, one hand held before her. Tapping all around. Sand, sand, everywhere. Where did all the sand come from? This way, she thought she threw it this way.

"Just wait, Echo," she murmured. "I'm just getting the bottle. I'll be right back." Sayuri tap tapped at the loose sand, forcing herself to go forward. Alone.

"Where are you, bottle?" she called softly. Just to hear her own voice. For the silence was heavier than stone.

"Oh!"

Something hard. Rock. Not sand. She giggled. Of course there was rock! Wasn't she lost in a cave?! She tapped out the shape in the sand. One, two. Two rocks, smooth and the same shape. Smooth? Or smoothed by someone. Something.

She reached with both hands and ran her fingers along the two flat and long shapes, shapes that were connected to two stone columns that went upward like legs....

Sayuri jerked back.

How had a statue come to be in this place?

Was it a tomb?

Sayuri made a small noise, her hands pressed to her chest. Her fingers suddenly flared with a feeling so intense she almost screamed.

Kimi, she thought, holding her hands to her chest, Kimi! I can't bear it any more. Sayuri shook, desperately holding the sobs inside her body, because if she started, Sayuri knew she wouldn't be able to stop. Mom. Mommy, I want to go home. Sayuri squeezed her eyes shut. Please come get me.

And then a swirl of bright clouds rushed inside her mind, the mist rising, lifting, and her mother! She could see her mother! So real Sayuri almost called out. Kimi! Silly Kimi. Staring blankly in the car, stuck in rush hour traffic. Kimi's faraway eyes and her hands holding a shape, fingertips to fingertips, thumb to thumb. The shape of a triangle.

The vision disappeared.

Sayuri shook her head. Blinked and blinked to call it back, but the comforting image of her mother was gone. Ugh! Stupid Kimi! She would have broken her ankles a long time ago if she were stuck in this place! Why did she do that stupid thing with her hands! Orienteering! That's what Sayuri would learn as soon as she got back. As soon as she –

She gulped. Shook her head. No more crying. She needed to find the gourd. Return to Echo. Find water. Find a way out. Those were the things she needed to do.

But all she had been doing since leaving Yamanba's home was running and hiding and surviving. She felt all scattered.

The image of Kimi came back to her thoughts. Why did her mom do that thing all of the time? There must be a reason.

Sayuri sat down in the sand. Pressed fingertips to fingertips, thumb to thumb and shaped a triangle with her hands. "Focus my thoughts," Sayuri murmured, breathing deeply. "Open my heart."

19. AN OPEN HEART

A BURST OF HEAT AND GLOWING SWELLED FROM THE TRIANGLE of her hands. The sensation crept up her arms like warmed blood, soft and comforting, it encompassed her entire body, and the chill that had plagued her since leaving Yamanba's hearth finally disappeared.

"Oh," Sayuri mouthed with wonder. Afraid to open her eyes. For what if it all vanished? The warmth grew cooler with her doubts and the girl calmed her thoughts once more. My heart is open. My mind is still. The heat licked her body and the tickling sensation made her almost giddy.

She opened her eyes.

Inside the triangular space that her fingers and thumbs shaped, a glowing orange light floated. A flame that didn't burn, only warmed everything that it shone upon.

Sayuri laughed out loud.

She could see! She was in a long, curving tunnel, not much wider than the hallways of her house. The walls sparkled with a crystalline glint, throwing shards of pink, coral, amber, and azure. A marvel of light and movement.

The glow she framed in her hands shone upon what she had felt in the sand.

It was, indeed, feet and legs. Only not a statue. A head taller than Sayuri, the stone-like figure looked like the calcified remains of an upright tanuki. The animal was frozen, turned to stone, by what force, Sayuri could only guess. The raccoon-like creature stood on its hind legs, arms extended, the paws reaching. Or warding off. The tanuki's face was twisted in the opposite direction. Whatever had happened to the poor creature, it couldn't have been pleasant.

Sayuri reached to touch an extended paw, but she pulled back her hand. What if it broke off? The poor thing. She offered a prayer as her grandmother had taught her.

"Tanuki-san, I hope you are in a better place and that your suffering was brief in this world. Living is hard but there are joys also. And our journey, both in life and in death, may take us to wondrous places."

Sayuri wished she had some incense to offer. But she had nothing.

Wait! The lamp she'd picked up in Yamanba's home!

But what would happen to the light if she pulled her hands apart? If the light went out, could she call it back? Her heart skipped. Now that she'd had the brightness, she couldn't bear the thought of the dark again. But then, she'd have to sleep. She couldn't hold the shape forever. Sayuri took a deep breath. Dropped her hands.

The light went out.

Okay. Don't panic. Sayuri tapped out the shape of the lamp. It wasn't broken! She set it on the sand, reached into her pocket for the wick. She propped the wick into the lamp, then shaped her hands into a triangle again. Opened her heart: peace.

The small light came back. Sayuri smiled so sincerely that brightness glowed from her face. She held her hands over the small wick. Though she knew it made no logical sense, she knew that she could light the lamp. The rules that governed the reality of this world were not the same as the ones she'd learned in the place she called home. She knew she could light the lamp.

And so she did.

Without a source of fuel, the wick burned brightly with a merry flame. Sayuri laughed joyfully, clapping her hands with glee. The little lamp flickered warmly upon the cold shape of the tanuki and the glint of azure and coral from the crystalline walls of the cave was a colourful magic.

"Please accept this gift," Sayuri smiled, leaving the burning lamp close to the tanuki's form. She was happy to be able to do something. Shuddered to think about how long the creature had been trapped in the darkness.

Sayuri glanced about in the sparkling light for the gourd. The hyotan lay behind the calcified tanuki and she picked it up, retied the empty container to her belt. She triangulated her fingers once again, centering her thoughts and opening her heart to all possibilities.

Without crawling or groping, she returned to where Echo was slouched against the cold wall of the tunnel. The orange glow lit up the poor creature. Warmth seeped outward and the blanket covered them both. Sayuri crouched next to her companion and watched, mesmerized, as the glittering fragments of colours, pink, coral, amber and azure, played on Echo's skin.

The kappa's eyelids flicked.

No. She must have imagined it. But they flicked again and Echo opened her large black eyes. Smiling.

"You're all right!" Sayuri gasped, hugging the small creature. The light slowly faded, so the girl quickly released her friend to call it back.

"You're all right," Echo smiled weakly.

"Look at what I can do!" Sayuri boasted, holding the warm flame aloft.

The kappa repeated her words wonderingly, for the magic filled the room with a glow that warmed but didn't burn or glare.

Sayuri's arms suddenly felt weaker. Heavier. The struggle from the oni's cage and the long trek through the stone's soul had pushed her muscles to their limits and beyond. Her shoulders sagged, the triangle of light dimming.

"We must still find water," Sayuri said. Her tongue was brittle inside her mouth.

"We must still find water!" Echo said brightly, holding her arms out so that Sayuri could help her up.

Sayuri frowned. "You're still weak," she protested.

"*You're* still weak!" Echo exclaimed. Sayuri helped her friend up, then called her light once more. It was even dimmer than before.

"Water," Sayuri muttered.

"Water!" Echo exclaimed, sniffing the air. The kappa retraced their dragging footprints in the sand. Sayuri hobbled after her, desperately keeping a sliver of light aflame. Echo stopped suddenly and Sayuri almost ran into her back. There was a split in the passageway, one that she had completely missed in the dark. Echo pointed to the tunnel not taken and gestured with her ruined hand, bringing the cup of her palm to her mouth.

"You smell water!" Sayuri gasped.

"You smell water!" Echo beamed. Her beaked mouth grinning as wide as it could.

"Whoooop! Woohooo!" Sayuri leapt with joy and Echo laughed with her, filling the cavern with childish glee.

FOR A MOMENT, they thought they heard the sounds of stone beginning to crumble behind them. Then they skipped down the sandy path, giddy in their pleasure.

20. WATER

THE PASSAGE OPENED INTO A GREAT CAVERN. LIMESTONE pillared the great cathedral and crystalline icicles hung from the roof of the ceiling in a profusion of green, pink, and yellow. The icicles dripped into nests of rock where stone eggs lay waiting to hatch. The ripple of calcium was liquid in slow motion, waiting through the ages to slide across the floor of the cave. The organs of the mountain were heaving with life.

"Ooooh," Sayuri sighed. What wonders lay beneath the earth's surface!

"Ooooh," Echo agreed, then slipped to where a stream trickled a path. She sniffed. Bent low and licked a taste. The kappa turned to Sayuri and smiled. Nodding.

Sayuri stumbled, slid, dropped to her knees, and broke the formation of her hands. The glow faded from between her fingers, but some of the light was held in the phosphorescent walls, in the stalactites, and the room didn't return to complete darkness.

Sayuri plunged her hands into the warm water and sucked the liquid in great gasps. Once, twice. Echo grabbed the girl's arm and shook it. Sayuri glared at her friend, almost wrenching out of her grasp.

Echo shook her head, then turned to the stream. Showed Sayuri how to cup water with one hand only, and to drink very slowly.

"Oh," Sayuri nodded. Of course. Like when she trained at Compet. You didn't gulp water at the end of the day. You took it slowly. Carefully. Already, she could feel the unaccustomed weight in her shrunken belly. Sayuri sat back and controlled her thirst. There was a whole stream. It wasn't going anywhere.

Sayuri clucked her tongue against the roof of her mouth. She'd been so desperate to drink she hadn't even noticed, but now a faint aftertaste lingered in her mouth. She dabbled her fingers in the stream. Yes, the water was warm. She hadn't imagined it. A hot spring, then, and she brought her fingers to her mouth. She sucked the moisture. And realized there was a slight tinge of sulfur, a small taste of blood.

Echo sprang into the water with a small splash. She leapt back out, something white flipping in her hand. Sayuri hurried over and her friend, grinning, showed off her catch.

A white, eyeless crawfish flipped weakly in her palm. Echo quickly twisted off its head and sucked the juice. Sayuri thought of the special tiger prawns her family ate for Christmas and her mouth watered. Echo passed the tail to Sayuri, who ran her fingernail down the belly side of the crawfish. She flipped off the skin and brought the white flesh to her mouth. The meat was slightly soft, almost mushy, but the flavour was sweet and the juices filled her mouth. While Sayuri chewed, Echo waded back into the water again, her keen eyes catching the flicker of white tails scurrying under limestone ledges. Echo's hands darted faster than Sayuri could follow. Her companion flipped crawfish to the shore where she stood, chewing and laughing.

Sayuri joined her. She chased darting white movement, always one scoop behind. Her foot slicked off a wet mound of limestone and the ground shot out from under her. Sayuri landed with a giant splash. Echo ran over on her webbed feet, but the polished limestone proved to be too much for her as well. She flipped neatly into the stream, dousing Sayuri in a spray of warm water.

They laughed and laughed, clutching their weakened stomach muscles, and the sound was a music that filled the cavern that had been silent for thousands of years.

SAYURI LAY BACK IN THE WARM, HEALING WATER. They had eaten the crawfish slowly and sipped small mouthfuls of water. Sayuri kept her clothes on, so that they would be washed along with her body. Echo lay beside her. The kappa raised her hands and spread her fingers. Stared. Sayuri called the glow back to her hands. Raised the light so that they could see more clearly.

New webbing was starting to grow between the kappa's fingers! A whispering of cells, skin stretching, growing tight and elastic between the slender bones. The new webbing wasn't green. The skin was dappled with the play of coloured lights that glittered inside the great cave. The kappa's hands glowed like jewels.

"Oh, Echo!" Sayuri sighed happily. Blinked. Turned her own palms upward and stroked skin newly healed smooth and soft.

If only her brother was here.

Stupid. She only thought of him when she was safe herself. And what about Machigai? Where was the fox now? At least, Sayuri consoled herself, the stupid Blue Oni hadn't caught him. And the cat, Momo. He was so fat he must keep himself fed somehow. If Keiji could understand what the stupid cat said, maybe he could talk to him too. Sayuri sighed.

Okay, she thought. We've found the water. Next, find an exit.

"Oh!" She hadn't filled the gourd! How could she forget? Sayuri unstopped the mouth of the bottle and listened to the cave water trickle inside. "Thank you, cave, for sharing your wealth with us," Sayuri whispered. Echo repeated the words reverently, staring at her healing hands. Then Echo glanced up, a mischievous grin squinting her large liquid eyes.

Echo pushed against the wetly slick limestone and shot down the stream like she was greased.

"Wait!" Sayuri giggled, pushing off after her.

The slick channel of the stream was a slide that plunged them faster and faster. They giggled as they whipped past colourful pillars of stone. Only, the slope of stream was becoming steeper. We should stop, Sayuri thought, as she tried clutching at anything to slow herself down. The water had polished all the rocks to a smooth surface. Her hands slipped on everything she grasped. Gasping. Not fun anymore. Sayuri vainly raised her head, but she could see nothing but the spray of water. Picking up speed, they shot out of the cavern of coloured icicles, the stream turning into a narrow, twisting tunnel, plunging them into a thick velvety dark.

The stream was a tube that twisted wherever the water had worn through. The water temperature changed from warm to hot, hot to cold, as they slipped, shot along, helpless in their momentum.

"Echoooo!" Sayuri called, but she was sliding so fast, she left her voice far behind. Tossed from side to side, she couldn't call her light. She could only sense, with the changing pressure of air, passage through vast caverns that, in turn, squeezed narrower again into tubes.

And suddenly, the bottom dropped out from beneath her. For a brief moment, Sayuri felt as if she floated in midair, a microsecond of weightlessness.

Then she fell.

Brightness so sharp she was blinded. Eyes squeezed shut, she plummeted. Down, down.

Please, she thought. Please, let there not be any rocks.

21. OUT OF THE MOUNTAIN

THEY PLUNGED DEEP INTO A POOL OF GREENBLUE WATER. Ahhhh, Sayuri thought, in the buoyant liquid embrace, this is where I belong. Eyes open, she slowly released a steady stream of bubbles. She could feel the pressure of the depth inside her ears, so she pinched her nostrils with her fingers and gently, ever so gently, pushed air through her nose. When the air stopped at her plugged nostrils, the pressure equalized inside her ears. Sayuri resumed blowing air bubbles as she turned a slow, graceful somersault in the depth. A small green creature darted past her and Sayuri languidly turned to watch.

It was Echo, joyfully zipping about in her element. The water imp swam with grace and ease, an undulating green ribbon.

Sayuri, feeling the burn for oxygen far more quickly than Echo, kicked her legs and stroked upward, still exhaling a small thread of bubbles. Daylight jewelled the surface of the water and Sayuri broke through with a gasp.

The bright sun felt glorious on her face. When was

the last time she'd seen the sun? Years ago, she was certain. Sayuri trod water for a moment, looking up, up to where the cave water spilled from a hole in the mountain cliff. Sayuri gulped. She breaststroked her way to the shore.

The pool they'd plunged into was incredibly deep, but small. The water quickly narrowed into a small river flowing into a light forest. The plants, Sayuri saw, had changed. They weren't the evergreen giants she'd passed through, but leafier trees with thinner skins. Groves of whispering bamboo. It must be warmer here, Sayuri thought cheerfully.

Don't be so comfortable that you're not ready for the unexpected, Sayuri thought sternly. She sighed. It was rather tiresome work, surviving. Then she laughed. How ridiculously human, she thought. Did she imagine she could survive and be entertained at the same time?

Still, she looked around carefully at her surroundings. She saw no marks of camps or activity, though she might be in the middle of an animal freeway and never know it! There were two large flat rocks next to the pool. Sayuri pinched her lip. Were they "naturally" there or had something placed them? Echo, though, still swam. If her friend was so comfortable, Sayuri decided she could afford to relax a little. Besides, she had to dry her clothes.

Sayuri carefully hung the water gourd from a branch in a tree. She kicked off her soppy runners, peeled off her socks, tugged her T-shirt over her head, and jerked the wet jeans off her legs with difficulty. She wrung her clothes and lay them out on the larger flat rock that held the heat of summer inside it. Sayuri giggled at the human shape outlined in cloth. It would be so much easier to walk around naked like Echo did. Though, Sayuri reasoned, she'd probably freeze to death at night. She glanced down at her chest. Her nipples hadn't hurt the whole time she'd been here. She had that to be grateful for. Had they stopped growing in this place?

Sayuri stretched and yawned. She was still hungry, but the sun heated her skin. The water was drying rapidly, and she blinked slowly, like an owl. Birds chirped merrily in the trees and Sayuri thought she could hear the mesmerizing hum of bees. She sank on to the smaller rock, the heat from the stone sinking into her tight stringy muscles. Do sunburns exist in this place? Sayuri wondered sleepily. I don't have any sunscreen anyway....

She fell deep into sleep.

"Do you think it's a baby oni? It's skin is all red."

"But it has no horns!"

"Maybe they grow in when they're older."

"Do you think it's good to eat? It's hairless like a pig."

Sayuri's heart plunged, though she kept her eyes closed. The sun felt further away, not directly above. And her skin prickled painfully. And Echo? Where was she?

"It no longer sleeps," the first voice declared. "Open your eyes. We can smell your wakefulness."

"Perhaps it doesn't talk," another voice tittered. Several voices joined her in laughter.

"I beg your pardon," Sayuri said indignantly and sat up. "Ouch!" Her skin was as roasted as the delicious crackling pig she'd seen hanging in the restaurants in Chinatown. No wonder they thought she might be food.

They. They were four fat tanuki women. Their small black eyes glittered curiously in their furry faces, faces that looked like a cross between a badger and a raccoon.

Tanuki, Sayuri thought rapidly. Jun loved tanuki stories, although, he always qualified, they ought not to drink so much sake. They loved to hold feasts and they played tricks for fun. They shape-shifted too, but usually harmlessly.

Sayuri held caution in her spine and shoulders, but the tanuki's glittering black eyes held only curiosity. And they had nothing that looked like weapons. The tanuki held vegetable-filled woven baskets with their nimble paws.

"I am a visitor to your lands, journeying from one place to another. Please forgive me if I have intruded in your forest." Sayuri tried to look casually around for her kappa friend. But Echo could be camouflaged anywhere. Maybe she was hiding in the water.

"Well! You should be sorry," the largest tanuki sniffed. Her fur was patchy and a few bald spots were shiny with dark skin. "You have been bathing your foul body where we wash our vegetables!"

"Oh!" Sayuri blushed. "I'm terribly sorry."

"Hmph!" a second tanuki sniffed.

"Humph!"

"Ke!"

Sayuri stared glumly at the animals. Now what?

"Well!" said the large, scraggly-furred tanuki. "You'd better come along with us. Dusk comes and the oni have been making trouble."

"Oni!" Sayuri hissed.

"You have seen them?" the patchy tanuki tilted her head.

"I just escaped from the Blue Oni's cave, through the heart of this mountain." Sayuri pointed to where the mineral-rich water tumbled from the side of the cliff.

"Hohhhhhh!" the tanuki women hissed. "Hehhhhhhh! This is a tale you must share tonight at the village hearth!"

"Go!" the patchy tanuki gestured to the smallest of her companions. "Tell the villagers we bring a stranger with strange tales!"

The two others clapped their hands with glee. "A feast. A party. Call for the musicians!"

Sayuri let out a small sigh. The tanuki would treat her as a guest. "I have a travelling companion, though she is shy and hiding," Sayuri said.

"Is she one like you?" the tanuki peered around, her sensitive nose twitching. "Ahhhh. I smell a kappa! Kappa!" she cried out. "We bear you no ill if you do not drown our children."

Echo rose from the water without leaving a ripple and placed her wet hand in Sayuri's. The girl gave it a little squeeze. "This is my friend, Echo. A curse has been cast upon her so that she may not voice any words of her own. She can only repeat what someone has already uttered."

"Hssss," the tanuki hissed sympathetically. "Truly you have a strange tale to share. Save the telling until all may hear. Come, help us wash the vegetables."

When they were finished, Sayuri grabbed her clothes.

They had stiffened in the sun so she beat them against the rocks to soften the material. Still, the cloth felt rough against her stupid sunburn. The tanuki watched her dress with a great deal of amusement, chuckling behind their paws. Sayuri's pride stung as much as her sunburn. Grimacing, she tied the precious gourd to her belt and marched after the giggling tanuki women.

22. THE TANUKI VILLAGE

Sayuri didn't know they were in a village until the tanuki stopped. In a clearing was a great hill. A piece of the hill lifted up and a tanuki head popped out. The villagers lived underground!

Dusk purpled the sky and Sayuri noticed a thread of woodsmoke rising from the top of the mound. The smell of smoked fish and roasting tubers wafted in the air. Sayuri's stomach growled.

The tanuki led Sayuri and Echo to the rounded earth. The "roof" of the hill was completely covered by sod. A flap made of reeds acted as a door to the hatchway and Sayuri could see a ladder made of branches leading into the darkness below. The smell of food made the girl's stomach clench. They crawled down the ladder.

"Welcome to the Earth Lodge of the Mountain's Blood Clan," an old voice croaked near the firepit. Thirty, forty adult tanuki sat round the fire, preparing food, whispering and giggling. Kits tumbled about, hiding behind the pillars that supported the roof. The tanuki children stared with glinting eyes from the dark edges of the great circular abode. Sayuri looked upward. The sod "ceiling" was supported by a hexagon of timbers. The firepit snapped with a clean and bright orange flame. Beams, four metres above their heads, circled around like the spokes of a bicycle wheel and a wisp of smoke snaked up, up, to escape out the small hole in the ceiling.

"Come," the old voice croaked. An ancient female tanuki sat on a chair woven of rushes. A blanket of orange and brown covered her fat stomach and her great breasts sagged down her chest. The fur on her face was frosted with age, but her small black eyes glittered with life and wisdom. "Ahhhh! A human child. What great mischief wanders the earth? For I have oft heard tales of mythical humans, but have never cast my eyes upon such a creature."

"A human! Human child! Not a pig!" Sayuri heard whispered round the room. Echo squeezed her hand with her moist grip and Sayuri felt better.

"Shush!" the Old One admonished. "Let the guest introduce herself."

The entire clan sat around the central timbers. Smoked fish, roasted tubers, and berries were heaped on large leaf platters that circled the fire. Sayuri, her heart thumping, faced the masked tanuki who stared at her with great curiosity. The girl's eyes darted, looking for a friendly face, and she caught the glance of the first tanuki who had spoken to her, the one with the patchy fur. The tanuki winked!

Well, Sayuri thought, gulping. At least one of them liked her....

"Greetings, people of the Mountain's Blood Clan," Sayuri raised her voice, deepening the pitch. Just like her mother did when she had to read in public. "I, and my good companion, Echo, thank you for your kind hospitality. My name is Sayuri Kato and I come from a place called Earth As I Know It." Sayuri twisted her fingers. Was she supposed to keep on talking or was that enough?

"Welcome!" the old woman tanuki called from her chair.

"Welcome!" roared the tanuki clan, and the children shrieked with excitement.

"Let the feasting begin!" the Old One shouted.

Friendly paws drew Sayuri and Echo closer to the fire, and fish and mountain yams were passed around with great generosity. The fish was pungent with smoke and crisp with salt. Sayuri couldn't get enough of it. The tanuki had thoughtfully left a platter of fresh greens for Echo, who crunched through the stems with great enjoyment. Child tanuki edged closer to Sayuri to watch her chew her food. When their parents scolded them for their ill manners, the children giggled and scurried away. Great jugs of sake were passed around and around the fire. Sayuri could barely hold the clay container, and when she took one little sip, she made a face and passed the jug to the patchy-furred tanuki beside her.

"Arara. So the human child does not drink rice wine," she winked. And tipped the jug to her own lips. Gulped and gulped. She wiped her mouth with the back of her paw and cried out, "Bring the human child water!"

Sayuri stared into the clay bowl that was thrust into her

hands. The water caught the glint of flames. Warm, her stomach full with good food, Sayuri turned her thoughts guiltily toward her brother. Where was Keiji now? How long since they'd been apart? Did he have enough to eat? Did he still have his inhaler?

The patchy tanuki thrust her scruffy nose against Sayuri's cheek and peered into the cup. "What do you see in the water?" she whispered hoarsely.

Sayuri stared and stared, the water pulling, hypnotic. A flicker of movement, a glimpse of a child's face. Dark shadows beneath sad eyes.

"Me miss Sayuri."

Sayuri gasped. Looked wildly about. So dark. Smokey. Not enough air. She was surrounded by animals. Animals! Sharp teeth and glittering eyes. Claws and stink of animal fur. What was she doing here? She half rose, her fingertips clambering, all her senses telling her to flee. Sayuri sought wildly for the ladder.

Then she caught the Old One's eyes. She had been watching the whole time and the aged animal's gaze was soft with compassion. Sayuri gulped hard.

Breathe, child, she thought she heard. Sayuri gasped, for she had been holding her breath without knowing. She inhaled deeply and exhaled, shuddering.

Look again, the voice murmured.

Sayuri nervously glanced into the cup. The water was water. The tanuki were tanuki.

Drink, the voice said.

So she did.

THE FEASTING AND DRINKING CONTINUED LONG and the tanuki who had eaten their fill went to retrieve assorted instruments – small leather drums, long-handled shamisen, tiny bronze cymbals, and bamboo flutes. The musicians filled the lodge with great cheer. Zun chaka! Zun chaka! Zun chaka! The rest of the tanuki clapped their paws in a light-hearted one-two beat until the plaintive voice of a singer rose in a haunting song. The drums stilled their festive beat and only one shamisen accompanied the mournful discordant melody.

When the myth of life began
our people shared life with humans,
stone to earth, fire to water, trees to sky.
But the spiral turning
saw humans break
the pattern
as if they were their own masters.
Instead of magic they wrought death.
They broke the living law.

So Great Mother Tanuki,
Old Baba of Tanuki Mountain,
enchanted humans into story
and they were never seen again.
So many ages of peace
and life
flowed like the mountain stream.

Until a troublesome fox was born —
out of whose imaginings was he wrought?
A fox who seeks to be a master
outside of living law.

Old Baba Tanuki
had retreated from mortal things.
But the people begged:
The spiral has come undone,
the fox has broken the pattern,
and the very stones scream.
Great Mother went to her mountain lair
to hone her lore and magic.
Alas, since then, we've heard no more.

Where has Old Baba gone?
Has she left us all alone?
We sing to our missing Mother:
Come back. Come back.
Your children weep.

Great tears rolled down the singer's furry cheeks and small children wailed in their mothers' arms. Sayuri blinked away tears at their sorrow. How long ago, it seemed, since Kimi had told her the story of the yamanba. Kimi would love this place, Sayuri thought fiercely. She dragged her forearm over her burning eyes.

"This is a song we have been singing for one hundred tanuki ages," the old tanuki called out from her chair. She raised her paw in the air and traced the shape of the spiral. Then she clapped her hands sharply and the mood shifted. "Sayuri Kato, of Earth As I Know It, please tell us your tale."

Sayuri slowly rose to her feet and faced the circle. In the tanuki's song, humans had been banished into story for breaking the law of life! What if they thought she was evil? But the faces that stared back at her weren't angry. They were curious.

Sayuri breathed deeply. The tanuki people had welcomed her into their home. She was being treated as a guest. Sayuri deepened her voice so her words would ring true across the great circle.

She told them them how she and her little brother had made the passage from their world to this one. Told them about meeting the Yamanba and about the Water of Possibility.

"Ohhhhh," the people sighed, when they heard of the Water.

Sayuri told how her brother had chased the cat and how she had set out to search for him. When she explained how she met Echo and found out the nature of her curse, her friend stood up and bowed to the clan. Everyone clapped their paws. Sayuri spoke on, of meeting the fox, Machigai, and of how she had been captured by the Blue Oni.

"Hsssssss," the tanuki hissed, "The Blue Oni!" And they spit over their left shoulders.

Sayuri described her great escape and the children squealed with terror. They clung to their mothers and covered their furry ears. Sayuri spoke of the passage into the mountain and her discovery of her own light and the stone tanuki –

"What! Made of stone?"

"Turned to stone, she said!"

"Who do you –"

"It must be –"

"The Great Mother!"

"Silence!" the Old One bellowed from her chair. When they were quiet, she turned her sharp eyes to the girl. Sayuri shook. Had she done wrong?

"Continue with your tale, child. Questions may be asked when you are finished. No need to be frightened, for we will not harm you. Just tell your story as you remember."

Sayuri swallowed. The patchy tanuki handed her a small jug of water. Her eyes were kind and the girl drank gratefully.

So Sayuri continued with her telling. The cave of many-coloured icicles and the blind crawfish. Their plunge through the veins of the mountain and the escape into the tanuki clan's water hole. When she was done, the tanuki were silent in appreciation. The youngest kits had fallen asleep in their fathers' arms. The older children's eyes were round with wonder.

"A tale well told," the Old One's voice rang. "Now people may ask questions, but only one by one."

A thin tanuki with a long scar across her cheek stood up quickly. "Was the tanuki-of-stone you found inside the mountain a statue or a creature that had been turned to stone?"

Sayuri bit her lip. "I don't know. If it was a statue, it was very realistic. But why would it be placed there? If such things are possible here, I would guess it was a real creature turned to stone."

The clan muttered, whispered furiously. A short plump tanuki child stood up.

"Could you lead us to this place?" There was a murmur of approval.

"It would be impossible to enter the mountains from where we spilled out," Sayuri explained. "The only way to enter is through the Blue Oni's den."

The people whispered fearfully. Some voices rose and fell as they argued over the risks of attempting entry.

"Why couldn't you have brought her with you?" a small child asked tearfully.

Her father shushed her and cast an apologetic look at Sayuri, but everyone stared. The child had only asked what everyone was feeling.

"The tanuki-turned-to-stone was much too big for me to carry. And I had no way of knowing her importance. I'm sorry." Sayuri looked down. She knew it wasn't her fault, but she wished she could have done something for the clan. Then she remembered!

"I did leave a lamp, burning, so that the tanuki wasn't left in darkness."

"Ahhhhh," the clan sighed with one voice.

"That is, indeed, a great gift," the old tanuki woman sighed. She wiped her eyes with a trembling paw.

"What," a small voiced piped, "what about the fox, Machigai?"

The tatty tanuki who had first spoken to Sayuri at the water hole stood up and faced the circle.

"What, indeed?!" the patchy-furred tanuki leapt up and flipped into a back somersault. Landing lightly, the tanuki shimmered, rippled into the form of a scruffy fox.

"Fox! Fox! Fox in the lodge!" The tanuki cannoned about, rolling into each other, running into the timbers and scrambling up the ladder. Those who had powers shape-shifted into rabbits, voles, boulders, and kettles. But the excitement was too much and they burst into their natural forms. Sayuri and Echo watched with rounded eyes, open mouths.

Machigai was laughing so hard he lay on the ground, front paws pressing his stomach.

"Be still!" the Old One bellowed. And the force of her words caused everyone to freeze, even the ones in the midst of falling off the ladder.

"If you are not our sister, Burdock," the old tanuki said sternly, "where is she?"

"Old One," Machigai bowed extravagantly, "your most loyal Burdock is sent on a fishing trip to the pools farther down the stream. I told her to fish all she could for two days, dry the fish she'd caught, then to return."

The old tanuki stared fiercely at the fox. He sat formally on his haunches and inclined his head. The Old One's eyes softened.

"A trick well wrought." She shook her head and began to chuckle.

The frightened tanuki looked sheepishly at each other and began to giggle. Jabbed each other in their round stomachs and nodded their appreciation to the fox.

"Good one," they chuckled. "You fooled us."

Machigai's shoulders began to convulse with laughter again.

Sayuri ran to the gasping fox and threw her arms around his neck. "You naughty, terrible thing!" she laughed.

Echo shook her head at the big upset he had caused.

Machigai barked with glee, great teardrops dropping from his eyes. "Oh," he crowed, "oh, this was my best trick yet! Oh, I hope the tale is told at many hearths. Oh, my stomach," he moaned. Laughing and laughing.

"That was, indeed, a trick worthy of being retold," the old tanuki shook her head at the disarray of her people. She chuckled.

"More sake!" she bellowed. "More song!"

The tanuki reorganized themselves, good-humoredly laughing at their silliness. The jugs of rice wine were passed anew and the zun chaka! zun chaka! music rose up with the woodsmoke, lifted into the night air.

23. TANUKI NIGHT

W AKE UP, DUCKY." KIMI SHOOK SAYURI'S SHOULDER GENTLY.
"Nnnnnmph," Sayuri groaned. "You're always waking me up."

"The cat's coming back," Kimi said softly.

"I don't like that cat," Sayuri moaned, pulling the blankets over her head.

"Doesn't matter, duck. There's work to be done." Kimi pulled off the covers.

Ugh! Sayuri hated it when her mom took away the blankets. It was a miserable way to be woken.

Sayuri sat up. She was on a sleeping platform that edged the sides of the earth lodge. The fire in the centre of the great room had dimmed to red-orange embers and the air was filled with the whistling snores of tanuki who had drunk too much sake. Young kits, impressed with her story, had slept all around her, their limbs sprawled in their childish dreams.

Sayuri shivered. Her fingers tingled, the feeling zipping up her arms to tickle the back of her neck. Something was wrong.

"Echo!" Sayuri hissed. "Echo!"

No answer.

"Machigai!" Sayuri whispered. "Where are you?"

She saw a copper snout poke up from a mound of fur, but Machigai's nose sank back down with a groan.

Ugh! They'd drunk themselves stupid. And Sayuri could smell trouble in the air.

Claws clamped on Sayuri's shoulder and she almost shrieked, but a second paw covered her mouth to stop her voice.

"Yes," an old voice croaked, "there is mischief about. I smell it too. Be still. We will wait to see what form it takes." It was the old tanuki woman. Sayuri sagged in relief. The old tanuki's white whiskers quivered, her eyes black and shiny.

They waited.

An edge of the great ceiling was peeled open by huge fingers. The Old One and Sayuri saw a brief field of stars before the sky was blotted out by a great red eye. The eye rolled about, taking in the sleeping forms. A hungry glint burned in its depth. Sayuri gasped, but the old tanuki's paw held the sound inside.

It was the Blue Oni!

No! Sayuri thought. How will we fight him? We are so small. Her eyes cast about. And all the little children!

"Yes," the Old One whispered, "stay with the children. I will lead the other tanuki to dissuade our uninvited visitor."

The ogre ripped off the roof of the lodge with a horrible bellow.

"Yattsukero!" the aged tanuki cried and her people awoke with a roar.

"Children!" Sayuri screamed. "Come to me! The Old One said to come to me!" The kits, bawling, ran to the girl's arms.

Blue Oni dipped his hand into the open hole of the lodge. Warrior tanuki leapt for their short spears and stabbed at the swinging arm. The others ran to the wall to make a ladder with their bodies, clasping wrist to wrist, standing on bent knees, constructing a tanuki pyramid. Warriors clambered up their comrades' backs with spears clenched in their teeth.

The oni grabbed three fat tanuki who had been too frightened to move. He started lifting their bodies up to his maw when the Old One raised her paw and drew the shape of a circle. The circle lingered, hung in the air with the brightness of stars.

"The cave closes," the old tanuki said calmly. Her eyes shut.

Sayuri, the children pressed behind her back, watched in wonder as Blue Oni's mouth slowly closed against his own will. The ogre rolled his bloody eyes, and swung his fist in fury, but he couldn't keep his mouth open. He dropped the tanuki he held in his hand so that he could wrench his lips open with all of his fingers. The tanuki, fat as they were, tucked into round balls. They bounced and rolled out of harm's way.

Sayuri whipped her gaze to the old tanuki. Her face was still calm, but the whiskers on her nose shook with effort.

Meanwhile, the warrior tanuki had all climbed out of the hollow of the lodge. The ogre, roaring, moved away from the open roof. Sayuri could hear their fighting cries from the surface. But how could they fight the ogre with force? He was much too big.

"You're right, of course," Machigai grinned his canine smile. He shook himself vigorously then lightly swung his tail. "Why use force if you can use guile?" Machigai's tatty fur looked worse than ever, but his leap over the lip of the earthen wall was quick and light.

"Oooh, hoo, hoo, hoo." Sayuri could hear the familiar giggle of the foxgirl.

"NAUGHTY SISTER!" Blue Oni bellowed! "HO! YOU LED ME ON A MERRY CHASE. MAYBE YOUR BIRDIE SISTER IS INSIDE THIS NEST!"

Oh, no! Sayuri darted a panicked glance at the old tanuki, but her power was spent. Her whiskers drooped and she was kneeling.

Blue Oni peered over the hole of the roof.

The children screamed and the remaining adult tanuki ran to surround them. But there was no point, Sayuri thought. He could just reach from above and take what he wanted.

Oh! It wasn't fair! Fear and rage choked Sayuri's throat. The heat burned her tongue. She would kill him if she could!

Could she?

Would she?

No, thought Sayuri. That's not the way.

Think, then.

Think.

Sayuri closed her eyes and breathed deeply. Sank to the dirt floor and crossed her legs, resting her arms on her thighs.

She pressed fingertips to fingertips, thumb to thumb, while taking long and slow breaths. Sayuri formed a triangle with her hands and opened her mind, her heart.

Why does the oni attack us?
Because he is hungry.
Why is his hunger so great?
Because he is so big.

Sayuri saw Kimi lying in bed. Lying in bed with Sayuri when she was a little girl. Before Keiji was born. Sayuri watched herself as if she was hovering high above her own bed. Her hair floating in the air as if she was under water. She could hear voices, but the sound was muffled through the cushion of time. Kimi was reading a story. And little Sayuri giggled as Kimi acted out the tale, ichi, ni, san! They both chanted, striking the magical mallet. One, two, three.

"Ichi, ni, san," Sayuri mouthed. How did that story go? Little Issun-boshi! The little manling who grew bigger with the magical double-headed mallet! Pounding on one side of the mallet made things bigger, but pounding on the other side of the mallet made things smaller!

Sayuri opened her eyes. Inside the triangle of her hands floated a mallet made of golden light! The tanuki children stared with round black eyes and Sayuri laughed out loud.

"WHO LAUGHS AT THE GREAT BLUE ONI?!" roared the ogre. "I WILL CRUSH YOU AND MASH YOU AND SQUISH YOU TO NOTHING!"

Sayuri grasped the mallet with a light heart. "Ichi, ni,

san!" she laughed. Swinging the little hammer to pound the dirt floor. The children giggled with joy. "Ichi, ni, san!" they shouted all together.

"WHO LAUGHS?!" the oni bellowed. "I WILL CRUSH YOU AND MASH YOU AND SQUISH YOU TO NOTHING!

Ah! Sayuri almost dropped the mallet in dismay. The tanuki children shrieking. Because the Oni was getting bigger, enormous, blotting out the entire sky.

"Wrong side!" Sayuri gasped, quickly flipping the mallet over. She pounded like mad, "Ichinisan! Ichinisan! Ichinisan! ICHINISAN!" The monstrous oni shrank and shrank, his great mouth gaping open in surprise. He dwindled, smaller, tinier, until Blue Oni had disappeared from the gaping hole of the roof. They heard the barking laugh of the fox, then a great roar from the tanuki warriors.

"Heads up!" Machigai shouted. Something small and blue fell through the air.

"Umph!" Blue Oni fell onto a pile of bedding. The kits gathered round in a circle, giggling, and poked the small blue mousling with their fingers, flipping it on its back to watch its swinging arms and legs.

Sayuri looked at her hands. The golden mallet was gone.

"Children," the Old One said sternly. The kits stopped teasing the tiny oni and clasped their paws behind their backs.

"What was the lesson we learned three days ago?"

One young kit with a dirty tail stepped forward and chanted loudly. "Cruelty calls cruelty and kindness calls kindness!"

"Sayuri, could you please tell the children the nature of Blue Oni's actions?" The Old One's eyes glowed.

Sayuri crouched with the kits and looked at the cowering ogre. His arms covered his head and his knees were drawn to his chest. "The oni attacked not because he is cruel, but because he is always hungry."

"Ohhhhh," the children sighed. They whispered amongst themselves, about how they fought when they were hungry too.

"Should we feed him?" they asked.

The old tanuki woman laughed. "Yes. Yes, feed our little guest." The Old One cast her eyes upon the remains of their home. "Lower the ladder!" she shouted. "I must see to the wounded."

There was movement behind the old tanuki and Sayuri leapt to her feet.

A pale green arm lifted, then, a pale green face rose slowly from a pile of bedding. Round black eyes blinked slowly. Gazed blearily at the drama around her. Echo squeezed her eyes shut, clasping both hands to her head. She burped stale sake, groaned, then slumped back to sleep.

Everyone roared with laughter.

24. REPAIRING THE LODGE

Daylight brought much work to the Mountain's Blood Clan. Many were wounded, though none had died. Sayuri, remembering how the water in the cave had healed their hands, ran about with her gourd, pouring just a little on the warriors' injuries. They rested easier.

The roof of the great lodge had to be rebuilt, so work, first, went to making temporary shelters. The small domed wigwams were made out of springy saplings. They covered the curved frames with birchbark so the wounded had a place to heal. Sayuri marveled at how hard the children worked too. They ran about, fetching water from the pool, retrieving bundles of dry rushes to twist the strands into rope. Echo went to catch fresh fish, though Sayuri suspected the kappa just wanted to get away from the boisterous voices of the tanuki.

The Blue Oni was fed until he could eat no more. Then he slept. When he woke up, he started scurrying about the village, but he wouldn't leave.

The tanuki laughed, rubbing their stomachs with pleasure.

"Go on!" they chortled. "You can go home now."

But the ogre was intent on staying. He collected small green twigs the adult tanuki discarded in stripping the saplings. Blue Oni watched how they made the wigwams and he started work on his own. The littlest kits, who couldn't do much work, offered advice and helped lash the twigs together with their nimble paws.

The work went on for several days. Those who were well enough made journeys to farther woods for the long straight timbers needed to fix the ceiling. And the gathering and preparing of food was constant. Every night, all slept exhausted.

THE TANUKI WERE TAKING THEIR MIDDAY REST. They had lunched on a heavy meal of water lily seed cake, crushed berries, and the fresh fish that Echo had caught. Sayuri saw the wisdom of the nap, but couldn't sleep. She sat, a little apart from the others, on a small rise at the edge of the meadow. Machigai had slipped into the nearby meadow, murmuring something about herbs, and Echo had returned to the water hole for more fish. Sayuri stared at her hands.

How many days had passed? Her fingernails were jagged and hard calluses had formed on her palms. How long ago had she lost her brother? She looked at the tanuki folk and all the work that was left to do. She could stay forever and there'd always be something that needed to be finished.

Did Keiji have enough to eat? How could she know? How could she know if he was still alive?

Sayuri clenched her hands into fists.

"I can hear your journey calling you," a voice croaked.

Sayuri jumped. The Old One was sitting next to her. How did she do that?

The aged tanuki's eyes twinkled. "Oh, I still have a few tricks," she chuckled.

Sayuri sighed. "Sometimes I forget what I'm supposed to do. I forget I'm even here. I mean – everything happens all around me. I'm just being pushed along!" Salty tears rose inside her mouth, burned her eyelids. Sayuri hid her face against her knees.

The old tanuki shifted beside her. And Sayuri felt a hum.

"Look," the Old One said gently.

Sayuri slowly raised her wet eyes.

A window had opened in the air before her. Like a small hole into someone else's dream, the image was fluid, without hard edges.

It was Keiji. He played in a square where a fountain sprayed water and pigeons fluttered, looking for bread. Keiji was chasing a ball, his cheeks flushed with health, lips red, hair shiny. He was plumper, his face full and not hollow with weakness. He yelled jubilantly, though Sayuri could hear nothing. Three children his own age played with him, two girls and a boy. But something was odd about their eyes. They were round and tawny amber; without any whites. In one motion, the three children turned toward the window and stared directly at Sayuri.

Sayuri shivered and dragged her burning fingertips down the outer legs of her jeans.

What? her brother mouthed at his companions, though there was no sound.

"Keiji!" Sayuri shouted aloud.

Her brother turned to the window with a confused look. Something passed over his face, like a thought half-remembered, then he shrugged. Kicked the ball and ran down the cobblestone street. The children turned and loped after him.

"No!" Sayuri raised her hand. As if to reach inside the window and pull him back.

The vision faded into a shimmer of air, then disappeared.

Sayuri whipped around. To beg the tanuki to show her more. The old creature was hunched over, her saggy breasts resting on her great belly. She was panting softly.

The girl stroked the Old One's soft shoulder. "Thank you," she whispered. When the aged tanuki regained her breath, Sayuri helped her to stand and they walked back to the village.

THE OLD ONE SENT SEVERAL TANUKI TO GATHER TRAVEL SUPPLIES. Green tubes of bamboo filled with spring water. Tiny salt-dried fish, the length of Sayuri's forefinger, crushed with sweet berries, then spread out in the sun to dry. The children chased Blue Oni away from the travel fare, though he kept sneaking back to where the fish and berries dried. The kits squealed and giggled as they ran after the small ogre, their little legs swift despite all the baby fat.

The Old One thrust a sack of small nuts into Sayuri's hands. The old tanuki untied the cord with her black claws and Sayuri peered into the bag. She had never seen the like; the nut meat was spiral, like a snail, and dark green. Sayuri popped one into her mouth. It was hard as dried peas, oily as avocados. She chewed hard and a sweet, rich flavour filled her mouth. Good, Sayuri smiled. Machigai could really use it.

Echo brought out the water gourd and gave it to the girl. Sayuri smiled at her friend. The kappa had not spoken since coming to the village. For the tanuki chattered so, and repeating all their words would have been too much.

Sayuri shook the gourd with the healing waters. A faint slosh. She sighed. She was saving it for Keiji.

Machigai loped into the clearing, a sprig of tiny yellow flowers in his mouth.

"What?" Sayuri teased. "Picking flowers when there's so much work to be done!"

Machigai swished his scruffy tail in Sayuri's face and she sneezed. Laughing.

"Old One," the fox bowed, "we are in your debt. You and your kind will always be welcome at my hearth."

The old tanuki bowed solemnly in return.

Sayuri blushed. She had forgotten her manners! Her grandmother would be so angry with her!

Machigai laid the yellow flowers in the Old One's paw. "This is HealAll. A tea, made from the flowers, cures the coughing fever, and the roots of this plant, pounded into a paste, will stop the rotting waste of wounded flesh."

"Ahhh," the Old One squinted and brought the spicy

blooms closer to her face. Sniffed. "This one we did not know. Thank you, brother fox." The old tanuki's eyes twinkled. "And if you should ever decide to live a better life as a tanuki, your family, here, is always waiting. For truly, your nature seems more tanuki than fox."

Machigai barked once, then impudently licked the Old One's whiskered snout.

Sayuri threw her arms around the old tanuki's plump neck.

"Oh!" the Old One said, startled. Then she chuckled, gently stroking the dirty knots out of Sayuri's hair.

"Thank you so much, Grandmother," Sayuri whispered salty tears into the tanuki's neck. "Thank you," she said fiercely.

"Ahhh, child," the Old One crooned. "Your life spiral will take you to many wondrous places."

25. JOURNEY RESUMED

"Sayuri's steps were swift. She was glad to be moving again. The travel bundle pressed awkwardly on her shoulders, but she carried the burden gladly.

Echo walked slightly ahead, eyes half-closed against the light. The kappa had seemed adamant about walking in daylight. Gesturing that the trees provided enough shelter. Sayuri had been grateful. She was tired of a nocturnal lifestyle and she could travel much more quickly during the day than at night. Echo had seemed to approve of the fast pace. As if she felt closer to lifting the curse which plagued her.

Sayuri wished she could offer the kappa sunglasses, although, she suddenly realized, the kappa didn't have any external ears to speak of. The companions travelled on a small path pressed into the meadows, wended through copses of trees. There were many ponds but few streams.

"Must you clatter so?" Machigai called to Echo. The green bamboo water containers slung over her shoulder clicked, clacked, against each other.

The kappa turned around and blinked. "Must you clatter so?" she snorted and continued clattering though her steps were silent.

"Who do you suppose made this path?" Sayuri asked, looking back from where they had come and looking forward to where they were going.

Machigai shrugged. Sniffed the trail. "Rabbits, tanuki." He sniffed some more. "Snakes, and foxes." The fox's eyes narrowed. "And something else – it smells strange...."

"Do you know anything about cats?" Sayuri asked.

Machigai shrugged again. "They shape-shift, of course. The powerful ones. But most are content with immediate pleasures. I have heard that there is a land of cats far to the north, where the sun only rises one day of the year. They dive for fish as large as trees and they sing strange songs that sound like the howling of snow. I, however," the fox yawned, "have never seen a cat."

"Oh," Sayuri sighed. "Then I guess you've never seen the great purple cat called Momo?"

Echo stopped suddenly and placed her cool hands over Sayuri's mouth. Startled, the girl flinched. The kappa frowned, pointed to the fox's ears, then covered Sayuri's mouth again.

"I don't have any secrets to keep from Machigai!" Sayuri jerked away from Echo's grip.

Echo shook her head in frustration. She pointed to the girl's mouth, then the kappa placed her green hands on top of her head like two great ears. She pointed to the forest, east, south, west, north. And looked expectantly at Sayuri.

"Yes," Machigai murmured, sweeping his tatty tail. "There are ears everywhere. The kappa's counsel is wise. We travel a trail well trod."

Sayuri gazed at the way the dappled light broke through the glittering leaves of aspen. It looked so cheerful and the path was so easy to walk on. So unlike the great forest of giant cedars. Sayuri sniffed the air. Listened. Heard nothing.

Of course.

The trees and meadows should have been a chorus of birdsong and insect chitters. But Sayuri could hear nothing. Only the sound of her heart growing louder and louder. She gulped. Nodded her understanding to the silent kappa.

Echo smiled almost sadly. Stroked her cool hand against Sayuri's burning cheek.

A strange hot wind swirled leaves and grass into the air, brushed past the three travellers and clambered skyward with a howl. Sayuri grabbed hold of Echo. Machigai bared his teeth, snarled. The ill wind twisted into the distance, leaving behind a strange and thick odour.

DUSK CREPT PALE AND LAVENDER ACROSS THE SKIES. Somehow it felt of autumn. Sayuri shivered. Machigai had forbidden a fire, so the tinder and flint the tanuki had provided went unused.

"Where," Sayuri mumbled through a mouthful of fish and berry meal, "do the kappa live? Why haven't we seen any of them?"

Echo pointed in all directions, her dark eyes unreadable.

"Mountain kappa are shy," the fox chuckled, "though there are kappa villages in the south." He tapped out a few oily nuts from the pouch with his dainty paw. He crunched on the spiral meat and tossed back his head to swallow. Licked his muzzle. "Unlike our friend, most only come out when they feel an urge to wrestle."

"Oh! That's right. They like to sumo tori. I bet you know some great moves," Sayuri smiled at Echo.

"I bet you know some great moves," the kappa shook her head and turned away from her companions.

Sayuri glanced at Machigai. He shrugged and started grooming his patchy fur. Sayuri sat next to Echo and draped her arm over slender moist shoulders. "We'll find the cure to your curse. Don't worry. And then you'll be able to wrestle again."

Echo was still. Then she stiffly shrugged Sayuri's arm off her shoulders. She stood up and disappeared into the growing night.

"W-Wait!" Sayuri started to call out, fumbling to her feet.

The fox batted the girl's shin with his paw.

"What?!" Sayuri glared at Machigai.

"I think," he stretched dramatically, "the kappa fights some demons of her own."

"What do you mean?"

The fox shrugged. Sniffed the air, the ground, then circled two times. Curled into a ball and closed his eyes.

Sayuri glared at her friend. What kind of answer was that? Sayuri snatched up the bag of nuts and retied the string. Stuffed it angrily into her pocket. Maybe the light would help her! She sat back on her haunches and triangulated her fingers and thumbs. Called peace to her heart and opened her mind. But her emotions were jumping like grasshoppers and her thoughts flew with no direction. The light wouldn't come to her hands. Her fingers wouldn't even glow!

"Ke! Ke!" Sayuri stomped around in a snit. She unpacked the small coarse travel blanket that the tanuki had given to her. Curled up next to the fox. She breathed heavily through her nostrils, eyebrows frowning and teeth clenched.

After a while, the fox raised his snout and prodded the girl's side with his cold nose.

"Eeep!" Sayuri shrieked.

"Would you mind breathing a little more quietly?" Machigai said icily.

"Hmph!" Sayuri sniffed. She noisily turned over, rustled around to find a comfortable hollow. Forced herself to breathe slow and long. She sighed. They'd walked for many, many hours and her legs were sore, her shoulders tight from the supplies she carried. Sayuri yawned. And stared out at the forest.

She didn't notice when the kappa came back to join them. For she was sound asleep.

26. BETRAYED

SOMETHING SHARP JABBED SAYURI'S SIDE. SHE JERKED away, rolled onto her hands and feet like a forest animal. A brilliant blue light glared and she hissed, raising her arm to shield her eyes.

A croaking laughter rose, a sound that circled around the girl like a cage. Blindly, Sayuri cast about, looking for her comrades.

"Your friends are here, you needn't worry," a voice sneered. "Your friends...."

The glaring light was turned away from Sayuri's face. She was surrounded by a small platoon of kappa. Kappa who wore dark clothing and hard boots. Kappa with artificial flashlights. Kappa with red eyes instead of black.

Echo! Machigai! Where were they? Maybe they got away! Maybe –

Then she saw. Machigai's long snout was muzzled in a cage of metal. A chain bit into his neck. He jerked backward, his tawny eyes snapping, but the chain choked

harder the more he struggled and the fox's eyes rolled. He lay
on his belly. Panting desperately inside the muzzle.

And Echo.

No.

Not Echo.

She stood with the platoon. The soldiers smacked her on
her back and she smacked them back, laughing.

"This is the one, eh?" the kappa with spear nodded. A
piece of his bowl-shaped head had completely broken off, so
he could never hold water.

"This is the one, eh," Echo nodded, pointing at Sayuri,
but refusing to meet her eyes.

"Not much to look at," Broken Bowl laughed. Prodding
the girl with the butt of his spear.

A hollow roaring filled Sayuri's head. The taste of blood
in her mouth. She wanted to vomit.

"Echo," she choked back the acid in her mouth. "Echo.
Don't do this." This was why the kappa had been so eager to
walk during the day. So that the rendezvous with the kappa
soldiers would come as they slept.

"She already has," a kappa jeered. He poked Sayuri with
his flashlight. "Get up."

Sayuri rose to her feet. A cluster of soldiers picked
through the stores the tanuki had provided, but when they
saw the contents, they disgustedly kicked the supplies about.

Oh! Sayuri brought her hands to her mouth. The tanuki
had worked so hard for the things they made, the gifts they'd
given. Old One! she thought. Help me....

The kappa soldier who held the chain around Machigai's

neck kicked him hard in the rump. The fox screamed and Sayuri tried to run to her companion. Broken Bowl tripped the girl with his spear and she thudded to the ground, face first. The soldiers roared with laughter, and Echo...Echo laughed with them.

Sayuri spat the grass from her mouth. Raised her head to stare at her betrayer.

You will pay, she thought. A bitter taste filled her mouth. You will be sorry.

THEY WERE MARCHED ALONG THE PATH, the kappa soldiers encircling Sayuri and Machigai. The soldiers didn't walk like forest creatures – they swatted limbs of trees, cracked dry branches beneath their hard boots weighed down by heavy packs. They shone their bright torches and the beams of light glared unnaturally bright. Even Sayuri had to blink and blink, she had grown so used to the soft glow of stars. They marched for hours and hours until Sayuri stumbled with fear and exhaustion. Finally, they came to a small clearing. Trees had been cut into low stumps and some were uprooted, the roots writhing upward like screams. The girl stared blankly around her. A sound escaped her lips. The destruction to the land was the most horrible thing she had seen since coming to this place.

Sayuri shook her head. What did she care? This wasn't her home. And at home, they did this kind of thing every day! She'd lived in a city her whole life!

But the wrongness filled the air with a thick weight of

mourning. The tree spirits were wailing and Sayuri could barely keep her hands from covering her ears. She had no tears. Her heart felt dead and her head felt stupid. She looked down at her hands, the palms grubby and rough with calluses.

They hadn't bothered to tie her up. She was no forest creature.

A soldier tied the fox's chain around a thick root of an overturned stump. Then the strange kappa all dropped their heavy packs and started to set up camp. Sayuri, exhausted, dropped to her knees. She awkwardly straightened her legs. The damp of the dirt started seeping into her jeans, but she was too tired to care. Machigai scrabbled to where she sat, resting his nose on her lap. Listlessly, Sayuri looked down. Maybe she could remove the muzzle, if only for a little while. She traced over the metal bands, looking for a buckle. It was shut with a lock.

"I'm sorry," Sayuri whispered. "I can't get it off."

Machigai sighed. And kept his nose on her legs for comfort.

Sayuri absent-mindedly stroked the fur on his head.

Machigai growled.

Sayuri jerked her hand back. Afraid. Maybe the fox had turned too? Maybe his eyes would turn red.

But the fox was growling at a mark etched into the back of someone's backpack. The brand was a shape of an eye. Inside the circle of the pupil was a spiral.

"What does it mean?" Sayuri cried. For she had never heard the fox growl before.

"Patriarch!" the fox managed to spit out.

27. CAPTURED

Sayuri huddled close to Machigai. She couldn't think. Panic crumbled her reason and strength. As if the very earth was falling out from beneath her, she would plunge, plummet eternally into a never-ending chasm of fear. She couldn't breathe. She was so scared. She wanted to go home. Please, Kimi, Mom. I want to go home. Her lower lip wobbled and her chin quivered. Salty tears pooled inside her eyes, inside her mouth. A wail almost seeped from her lips. Broken Bowl smacked the butt of his spear right next to Sayuri's body and she jumped. The kappa snickered. Sayuri gulped and gulped. What was wrong with her? She mustn't show any weakness now. That was what they wanted. That was what they fed from. Cruelty and pain. Machigai softly nudged her with his head and the girl blinked and blinked. The warmth of his head was a small comfort.

They silently watched as the soldiers set up a rough camp under a small stand of leafless trees. They threw a large plastic tarp over a metal frame and huddled beneath.

"Those are human things," Sayuri whispered. "Where did they get them? They're not using them right."

"Shhh," the fox managed.

The soldiers started a smouldering fire and a large pot of water was set to boil. When it was hot enough, the kappa broke up plastic wrappings and deposited dry discs into tin mugs. Water was poured into the cups and a kappa screeched when he was splashed. The soldiers roared with laughter. They sat on the ground and ate their soup.

Echo sauntered to where Sayuri and Machigai sat huddled. Hot anger seared the girl's veins and her hands clenched so tight her knuckles bulged white in the growing dirty light of morning.

Echo threw a package at them. A round disc of dehydrated soup. It bounced off Sayuri's shoulder and fell to the dirt. Sayuri picked it up and threw it, hard, back at the betrayer.

Echo gazed at the human. Sayuri couldn't read her eyes at all.

"Leave the prisoners!" Broken Bowl yelled from the makeshift tent. Echo shrugged and joined her companions.

Sayuri let out a shuddering breath. Machigai set his paw on her leg. It pressed uncomfortably on something hard and lumpy in her pocket.

The spiral nuts!

The girl flicked a glance at the kappa soldiers, but they were busy eating their rations. Sayuri reached furtively for the rich food. She carefully drew the small sack from her jeans and hefted the weight. If they were careful, they could get by for a few days.

Slim green legs silently stopped in front of Sayuri. Echo had returned and Sayuri quickly twisted her body to hide the precious food. Something nudged her shoulder. The girl hissed; her back still toward the enemy, she twisted her head around to glare with hate and fury.

The kappa had brought her the long tubes of bamboo. The water tubes. Sayuri wanted to throw those at her too, but she wasn't that foolish. She snatched the bamboo from the betrayer and turned her back again. Waited until she heard Echo walk away.

Sayuri shook the bamboo tubes and listened to the reassuring slosh. Enough for four or five days. Funny. Echo knew about the gourd with the healing water. But she hadn't taken it away from her. Sayuri stroked the smooth curves of the hyotan.

She shook her head. The kappa had forgotten was all. She shouldn't waste time thinking about the traitor. Sayuri passed a nut to Machigai, who whined softly. He held the spiral meat in his long snout. He couldn't chew. The fox tossed back his head and let the nut drop into his gullet. He swallowed with a choking cough.

"Sorry," Sayuri whispered. She quickly popped a nut into her own mouth and she chewed until the flesh was mealy between her teeth. She fed the muzzled fox from her fingertips and Machigai gratefully licked. They ate four nuts each, then Sayuri hid the pouch deep in her pocket. She unstopped a water tube and took a small mouthful, holding the liquid without swallowing. She turned to Machigai and, pursing her lips, passed water directly into his jaws. Machigai gulped awkwardly, but none was wasted. He managed to give Sayuri's cheek a tiny lick. She smiled, then took her own small sips of water. They rested against each other. Comfort in the warmth. The sun was rising, but the sky was grey with something other than rain.

The kappa had finished their meal and two of them stayed awake, on guard duty while the rest slept. Just two! Sayuri thought. "Can you shape-shift?" she asked Machigai.

The fox scratched the muzzle with his paw in frustration, his golden eyes glinting. Couldn't he just shape-shift out of the muzzle? Sayuri thought. Then, she pictured the foxgirl with a muzzle too narrow for her face. Shuddered.

"What about a snake? Snakes are long and skinny. You could just slither out, couldn't you?" Sayuri whispered desperately.

Machigai shook his head. Tapped the muzzle and sank into a heap. He turned his nose away from the girl's confusion.

"No talking!" One of the guards prodded Sayuri's back. She spun around, snarling. The kappa jerked back, alarmed. Then laughed nervously. "Funny hairless ape," the guard jeered. "Maybe the Patriarch will keep you alive as a pet." She returned to her post.

Sayuri threw her arms around Machigai's neck and pressed her hot tears into his sweet-smelling fur. The girl's shoulders shook and shuddered. What did the kappa want with them? Why would the Patriarch imprison them? They hadn't done anything. Unless he hated humans. What would they do to a human who didn't belong in this place?

Machigai whimpered softly. After a time, exhausted, they both fell asleep.

SO THEY MARCHED FOR SEVERAL NIGHTS.

The kappa slept during the day and travelled under the cover of darkness, but Sayuri could see how the landscape had changed. The stretches of forest and meadow became fewer and fewer. The land, razed of living things, was dry with death. Trees that had been hacked were now overturned stumps. Bleached roots were piled into heaps like bones. Meadows had turned into deserts. Dry ponds were hollow cups of empty shells and bones. Sayuri saw that the awful destruction stretched farther and wider whenever they stopped at the rising of the sun each morning. She tried to imagine what could have done such work, since she hadn't seen any machines in this world, but she had no answers. Most of her thoughts stayed on putting one foot in front of the other, conserving strength to stay alive.

THE NIGHT WAS INKY DARK and Sayuri couldn't see the stars. The last two bamboo tubes clattered awkwardly against her hip and Machigai padded wearily next to her knee. The weight of the muzzle pressed his head low. Sayuri didn't know when she'd last seen the moon. She stared glumly at her fingertips. When was the last time they'd lit up with magic? Maybe she'd made it all up.

The glare from the flashlights caught the writhing roots of

overturned stumps. Then the columns of soldiers stopped. A jubilant roar rose from the kappa troop.

They had come to the edge of a paved road.

Paved road! Sayuri blinked and sniffed. It didn't smell like tarmac. But a paved road! Had they somehow walked back to her own world? She gazed along the side of the pavement, but there were no power lines.

The road was an unnatural thing in the forest world, but it was easier to walk on. Sayuri didn't have to stumble over branches and roots. And the remaining tubes of bamboo didn't swing so wildy against her body. It was easier to think.

Her clothes felt rough and stiff. Sweat had wet then dried, wet and dried so many times that her armpits and jeans smelled tangy and animal-thick, like the inside of a winter den. When was the last time she'd bathed? Jun, Sayuri smiled weakly, would be appalled by the potential for disease.

Sayuri had tried to call back the magic to her hands. But she couldn't. She'd sat huddled on the ground after the end of the long marches, begging calmness and silence to come to her soul, but all she could hear was the pounding rhythm of panic in her ears. Maybe, she thought, maybe it was the nearness of too many evil kappa? Maybe the destruction of nature? Oh, what did she know? What was the use of the power if it didn't come when she called it?

Sayuri turned to her friend. The fox's sharp nails clicked on the surface of the road. Sometimes, the sound of the marching boots swelled like ocean waves pounding on stones, but then Sayuri shook her head and the noise returned to normal. She dragged her dirty palms over her sweating face. She was too tired to make any sense. Sayuri dropped one hand to gently stroke Machigai's back. The fox moved his tail a few centimetres but didn't bother looking at her.

Sayuri bit her lip. *Old One*, she called desperately inside her mind. *If you can hear me, we really need your help.*

Sayuri pulled her feelings deep inside herself.

There was a small shout from the soldiers at the front of the formation and Sayuri looked up, saw a kappa pointing into the distance. Dawn creeping another day into the ugly world. The troop came to a halt. Sayuri rose on her toes, though she was taller than all of the creatures, and stared.

Far away, bluish lights glittered, spread out. A glow reflected off low dark clouds. Not the lavender of dawn, as she had thought.

"Oh!" Sayuri clapped, excited. "A city!" There would be food! Coffee ice cream and tonkatsu and curry rice and hot water and showers and, and – Sayuri dropped her hands. She was a prisoner. And this wasn't her world. She had no idea what a city meant here.

There was a small sound. Sayuri looked down. Machigai's teeth were bared as much as the muzzle would allow and the girl took one step back from her only friend.

"Poison," he hissed.

Ice slipped inside Sayuri's veins. Fool to think a city would somehow bring comfort. There was no comfort or safety for her. She sank to her knees and clung to the fox's coarse fur. How would she ever save her brother? And home. Home was a make-believe story. A dream she might never wake up to.

Her brother!

When the Old One of the tanuki clan had opened the window, her brother had been playing in a village square. On cobblestones. Maybe he was in the city!

"Machigai!" Sayuri hissed. "We need a plan!"

The fox slowly turned his head and stared into Sayuri's eyes with his amber gaze. He winked!

Sayuri's heart lightened and, for the first time since their capture, she felt a small seed of hope.

28. TOWARD THE CITY

THE KAPPA TROOP DIDN'T STOP AT THE COMING OF DAWN. The sight of their home seemed to fill them with a grim determination and they forced an even faster march, well past the hour they would normally have rested. Sayuri took quick drinks from the last bamboo tube and nobody stopped her. There was no way she could give a drink to the fox with the almost jogging pace they were forced to keep. She cast helpless looks but Machigai made no sound, just jogged steadily, his nails click-clacking against the surface of the road.

The sun rose. Sayuri stared at the dead landscape all around them, razed into an unnatural flatland. The temperature rose without the canopy of branches, the deep roots of trees. The heat started to melt the surface of the road and it stuck to the bottom of her runners. A smell in the air so familiar but out of place; Sayuri couldn't remember. The countryside dotted with piles of drying stumps and branches. No birds. No chattering insects. Nothing but the sound of pounding feet.

It didn't make any sense. The land wasn't being used for

crops or even construction. What was the purpose of razing the land and leaving nothing in its place? What kind of lunatic destroyed his own home? Sayuri stared in bewilderment. Sadly compared it to the beauty of the forests she'd seen, the home of the tanuki clan. A dry wind swirled dirt against their faces and stung their cheeks. Sayuri blinked the dust from her eyes. How could the kappa keep on walking in the sun, the heat? They were creatures of moisture. Not that she should care. They were her enemies.... Sayuri's eyes darted to catch sight of a kappa without clothing and boots. But she couldn't see one.

They marched until a soldier toppled. Then, like a chain reaction, three, four more crumpled to the burning pavement. The heat of the sun melted the surface and the stink that wafted was like pine sap. Pine sap! Sayuri thought. They must have bled the trees for the road. What a stupid idea.

"Halt!" croaked a kappa. Broken Bowl, Sayuri thought, barely recognizing his voice. "Set up temporary shelter. We will rest, then march again after the sun has set."

A murmur of relief rippled through the columns of the soldiers. Wearily, they lowered their packs and the stronger ones set up awkward tents. Machigai was jerked to a tree stump and Sayuri followed. They hunkered in a tiny curve of shade and Sayuri unstopped the last bamboo container. She sucked some water in, passing the liquid directly into the fox's mouth. Machigai whined his thanks. He sank his nose heavily onto his paws. They were too tired to eat the last of their spiral nuts.

Sayuri turned wearily toward the city. They were much

closer. The sun reflected off bulbous metal, turrets of glass and razor edges. The buildings twisted and Sayuri wondered what kind of person designed it and how they had managed to keep everything from toppling. Metal spiralled from the peaks of fluted towers, and there was no sense in the profusion of glittering walls and roofs tiled with glass. The city trembled between grotesque and weirdly beautiful in a way that twisted the girl's stomach. The city glimmered, shimmered, and she could almost hear a metallic hum.

This city didn't belong here, Sayuri thought. Her fingers spasmed with pain.

She jerked her head away from the hypnotic pull and gazed at her captors. The exhausted kappa slumped beneath the shade of their tents. The two soldiers on watch had crept beneath a shelter and slept too, skin brittle and cracked.

She could escape! Her heart pounded inside her throat and she could barely breathe. The exhausted kappa would never be able to catch up to her. She could run, run back to the forest and find the tanuki. They would help her. She had cast off the bamboo tubes once they'd emptied, but the last one held quite a bit of water. Enough to see her back to the forest. And Machigai. Machigai was smart. Of course he'd think of something once they arrived at the city, he'd be all right....

Machigai raised his head from his paws and his amber eyes were bright. Unblinking.

Sayuri held his gaze, then she swallowed. Turned away.

Run! Her mind shouted. Now's your chance!

Sayuri slowly rose into a crouch. Cast her eyes once more

over her sleeping enemy. She didn't look at the fox. Hunched over, she scurried away from the road and darted south. The heaps of tree remains would provide some cover. And by the time the kappa made it to the city to call for fresh soldiers, she'd be long gone. Unless they had soldiers that flew. She ran, scurried, panting too loudly, looking back and upward at the sky.

No one followed.

SHE RAN TOO FAST IN THE MIDDAY SUN. The heat, caught in the dark dry earth, sucked the energy from the fleeing girl and she gasped too hard, her head growing dizzy.

"Pace yourself!" she heard her swim coach yell over the splash of water being churned by her arms. "Control your breathing! Control your body!" Sayuri shuffled to a stop. She was breathing so hard she started to retch. Sank to her knees and vomited a small trickle of water. She watched it disappear into the dry soil.

She took a shuddering breath through her nostrils. Looked wearily around her, saw a clump of tree trunks and branches, a wedge of shade. She crawled to the welcome shelter. It was a few degrees cooler than the direct sunlight and for that she was grateful. Sayuri breathed long and slow. Until her heart no longer pounded inside her eardrums. She took a small sip of water. The wetness seeped into the parched lining of her cheeks, disappearing before reaching her throat.

Who would give Machigai water?

"Damn!" Sayuri hissed. Her hands clenched into fists. She pounded the dirt with the heels of her palms. "Damn you! Damn you!" She rocked on her hands and knees, clasped her hands to her head and pulled her hair. Her nose running, she rubbed the mucous with the back of her hand. Stared at her palms. Her face must be a mess. Sayuri breathed in, held, then breathed out. She did this until she could breathe again without pain ripping at her heart.

She rose from the dirt and looked at the darkly forested horizon in the west. Looked at the destroyed landscape in the north. She ran again. A controlled pace. She ran with purpose.

29. ENTERING THE CITY

"I'M SORRY," SHE BABBLED, WHISPERED, THROWING HERSELF at the tatty bundle of fur. "I'm not like that. I'll never betray you."

Machigai slowly raised his pointed snout. The weight of the muzzle had started to cut into his flesh, and raw bands along his nose and head were caked with dried blood.

"Oh," Sayuri cried. "Oh." She unstopped the plug on the bamboo, ready to pour some water to clean his wounds, but the fox shook his head.

"Drink," he managed.

Sayuri tipped the water into her mouth so she could pass the liquid to the fox. He drank slowly and with great concentration. Then rested his head on his paws once more.

Sayuri squeezed her hands together, afraid to touch her friend.

Machigai's eyes glinted. Then he winked.

Sayuri pressed her face into his matted side and she sobbed silently, his fur absorbing her tears. He patted her back with his tatty tail. So the fox comforted the girl until they both fell asleep.

THEY MARCHED IN THE NIGHT and Sayuri stumbled with exhaustion. Each step pounded in her head and the thudding remained inside her skull, pulsing with her heart. Yellow lights flared and scattered before her eyes and she swung her hands through them. Fireflies, she thought dimly. But the flickering lights would disappear. Her eyes burned dry. The heat of the day was trapped beneath her skin.

Machigai whined. Sayuri felt a wet nose in the palm of her burning hand. The coolness crept up her arm and she shook her head.

"Sunstroke," she muttered. She groped for the last bamboo tube and let water trickle down her throat. Gone. She wearily dropped the empty container. She could still hear a slight slosh of water. The gourd. She stroked the smooth roundness with her filthy hand. She smiled weakly. She still had it. There was water inside. Why wasn't she supposed to drink it? Saving it for someone.

"Halt!"

They had come to the city. Sayuri, so intent on staying on her feet, hadn't noticed. Blue lights shone pallid from windows. They didn't flicker like flames. The lights were like things dead.

Why, the girl wondered sluggishly, why were they stopping?

Broken Bowl was croaking to several other kappa. The

troops shuffled. Throats were cleared and fingers tapped on spears, beams from their flashlights shining restlessly. Night pressed heavily upon them and the march had wearied all, but no one made a move to step inside the city.

A barely visible wall stood in their way. Barely visible because Sayuri could see through it.

No, thought Sayuri, her senses waking. Not a wall. Something else. A shimmering buzz...was it electricity? The surface of the "wall" shimmered slightly. Like liquid. And the girl realized that the "wall" was a rippling dome that surrounded the whole city. The city wasn't made of fantastic shapes that skewed beyond reason, the see-through dome just made them look that way.

But why were the kappa so troubled? It was their city, wasn't it? Why didn't they march right in?

"He asks too much!" a soldier gasped.

"Silence!" Broken Bowl hissed. "He sees and hears everything!"

"She's right," another soldier muttered. "Every time we pass through this wall, we lose more of ourselves. Are we so weakened that we don't recognize that the final outcome is total nonexistence?"

A few more kappa muttered in agreement. The others were silent, only darting quick glances over their shoulders. Above their heads.

Sayuri stared at her feet. The kappa weren't loyal subjects. At least not all of them. The Patriarch ruled with fear.

"Ahhh!" A gasp broke out from several of the soldiers and Sayuri looked up.

The surface of the dome shivered, undulated like fluid. The wall rippled, a slow-motion liquid, and lines formed in the transparent surface. In the shape of a great eye.

"Ohhh," the kappa moaned, falling a few steps back. Then they stamped upright, chests out and chins held high.

The great colourless eye slowly closed and Sayuri's skin pebbled all down her back, the hairs on her neck standing frozen with fear. Her fingers burned as if they were plunged in acid.

The eye opened. A brilliant amber. Alive.

Machigai whined deep in his throat. Run! Sayuri's mind screamed, but her legs were made of stone.

The great amber eye rolled about, staring at the dusty troops, passing over Machigai and Sayuri. The eye narrowed. Glared something so intense, that Sayuri turned away.

"Noooo!" a kappa shrieked. It was the one who had complained; the kappa who had dared voice her knowledge of the dome. She was rising in the air. Not floating, it was as if some invisible thing held her by the neck.

"Ahhh!" another screamed. The kappa who had agreed with her. She was lifted too, and two, three more who had muttered their agreement. Legs thrashing, they desperately tried to kick themselves free, but they rose in the air like puppets. Sayuri spun around to the hated eye. Its corner was crinkled, laughing, and the pupil followed the kappa rising higher in the air.

"Remember who and what we were!" shouted the brave kappa. "We are not soldiers! We are not slaves –" The kappa was tossed into the side of the dome. She was sucked in, absorbed so quickly it was as if she had never existed. Her boots fell heavily to the ground and her clothing fluttered after. One by one, the kappa were pulled in, their forms dissolving like water. Not one of them screamed.

Sayuri staggered, sank to her knees. Retched and retched. Nothing came up. She slowly raised her head. Her fingers were on fire. She pulled her hands to her stomach, cradling them, palms upward. And she understood. The dome. Wasn't electric at all. Wasn't a mechanical force field. It was magic. Magic harnessed into a terrible form.

The giant eye stared into her face.

Welcome, child, a melodious voice rang inside her head. And as Sayuri watched, the amber faded from the great eye, shrinking from the outside in, the colour disappearing into shades of liquid sheen. The shape of the eye bled smooth, melting outward, peeling back from itself into an opening which grew in the wall of the dome. The hole grew larger, large enough for three kappa to walk side by side, then stopped. A doorway into the city. The dome had fed on the disloyal. The toll had been met.

Enter.

"Forward!" Broken Bowl's voice quavered.

Sayuri lurched to her feet. They entered the city.

30. END OF THE ROAD

THE STRANGE PINE SAP ROAD GAVE WAY TO CITY STREETS OF pale cobblestone. Yellow, Sayuri thought dimly, though it was hard to tell with the lighting. An unwavering bluish glow shone from lampposts, neither flame nor electric. The kappa boots marching in unison sounded like dull glass being crunched.

Pretty, Sayuri thought. The cobblestones must be pretty in the day. Day. Cobblestones. Her brother. What was his name? She started giggling. How could anyone forget their brother's name? Her runners, she decided, were a mess. Tatters. Jun would be mad when he saw them. Why were her fingers so sore?

A small furry form rubbed her calf. Shocked, Sayuri shook her head. An animal! What – her head plunged, or was it her heart? Vertigo, the ground skewed almost ninety degrees and she scrabbled with her hands to keep from sliding off. Scrabbled, clung to the cobblestone, ground no longer, but an upright wall. She tried to dig her runners into the rock face for a toehold, but her feet slipped over the smooth stones.

"Ah! Ah! Ah!" Sayuri panted. Sobbed. She was slipping. She would plunge to her death. She huddled to the ground as if she were clinging to a cliff.

"Get up!" Someone shouted from far away. Across a huge chasm. "Up! The Patriarch awaits!"

Sayuri whimpered. She couldn't go up. It was all she could do not to fall off. She could feel someone tugging her wrists. She was saved! Her eyes burned beneath her closed lids. Her fingers must be scraped down to the bones. But she would live. She had been saved!

The hands which clasped her wrists let go.

Sayuri, wailing, plunged into complete darkness.

31. MEETING THE PATRIARCH

"OH, SWEETHEART. LOOK AT YOU." JUN'S ALWAYS WARM hand felt cool on Sayuri's hot forehead.

She sighed peacefully. Her dad would take care of her. He knew exactly what to do when she was sick. Sayuri tried to open her eyes, but they were caked shut. She wanted to lick her roughly cracked lips, but her tongue was swollen inside her mouth.

"It'll be all right now."

Sayuri felt a moist cloth pressed to her lips and a small trickle of water seeped into her mouth. The sweet coolness tasted better than anything she'd ever known.

"More," she croaked. Her lips tore apart and the taste of blood was metallic.

"Shhhhh."

Sayuri could hear the towel being dipped into a basin, the lap of water, droplets falling back into the bowl. The towel was gently placed to her lips again and she sucked the moisture.

"Not too fast. It'll make you ill."

Sayuri tried to raise her hand, to pick at the caked hardness sealing her eyes shut, but couldn't. Her arm, her whole body was stiff with pain. With great difficulty, she turned her head toward a glow of light.

"Dad," she managed. She swallowed slowly. Every movement a small miracle. "Have I been sick?"

"Here," he murmured.

Funny, Sayuri thought. He sounded different. Maybe she had an ear infection too.

"Let me wipe this from your eyes."

The light slap of water, the towel being wrung. Sayuri held herself still, expecting damp cold, but it was warm and she relaxed. She felt the seal over her eyes start to melt. Her lashes fluttered. Sticky. Everything blurry. She blinked and blinked, turned her gaze toward the hands that had comforted her.

The hands were long, slender. The fingers tapered. The skin, white and uncanny, seemed to glow from the inside. They were not her father's hands.

Her eyes followed the length of hand to a fine wrist covered in fur. A soft sleeve fitted loosely over the rest of the arm. Was the person wearing a furred undergarment? Who would wear fur inside a house? The coppery red hairs were sleek and shiny. Not a bad idea for winter, Sayuri mused. The loose sleeve was made of a rich blue fabric. Glossy and stiff. What was the word? Brocade? Maybe that was why a softly lined undergarment was used...what a beautiful jacket! White hair in the neck of the coat. A beard? Strange beard....

She gazed into the face of an enormous fox.

He wasn't heavy or fat. He was a slender fox but he stood

on his hind legs, like a human. If Sayuri stood beside him, they would see eye to eye. His fur was glossy and sleek with good food. Not like Machigai's tattered coat. His long whiskers quivered and his shiny black eyes glittered. They looked neither cruel nor kind but extremely intelligent. Sayuri's heart beat slightly faster. She supposed he could hear her fear with his great ears atop his head.

"The Patriarch," Sayuri said evenly.

The fox dropped the damp towel back into the basin with the warm water. The human hands on the ends of his animal limbs made Sayuri's skin crawl.

"Please," he smiled a row of shiny teeth. "No need for formality. Call me Great Uncle. I've been waiting for you, human child." His voice was melodious. Kindly.

"Where is Machigai?!"

"Shhhh," the Patriarch soothed. "He is being cared for as you are."

Sayuri pushed herself upright. Her head pounded with blood and stars burst inside her eyelids. Bile rose in her throat, but she swallowed hard. Panting. "I must see him!"

The whole room swung into focus. She was lying on a low bed. A table with two basins of water had been drawn near. Darkness spilled through a curtainless window. Small nubs of light spaced along the walls lit the large room. A hinged screen kept the draft from her bed. It was painted in bright colours, but her eyes couldn't make out the pattern. She cast about the room. Stiffly. Was this her prison?

Next to the door, a little boy in overalls sat on a cushioned chair. His feet didn't reach the ground and he stared at his sneakers, swinging them back and forth.

"Keiji?" Sayuri whispered. "Keiji!"

The boy looked up. "Hello," he said politely. Then he dropped his eyes to stare at his feet again.

Sayuri gaped at her brother. She tried to push herself upright, to swing her legs around, but her limbs felt like dead things and would not move. Sayuri glared at the fox. "What have you done to him?!"

The Patriarch sighed and dipped his uncanny hands into the basin with the cold water. Wrung it softly, then turned to press the moist towel to the girl's dehydrated lips.

Sayuri smacked the towel from his hand. It fell with a wet plop.

"That," the fox said coolly, "was silly."

Sayuri gulped. Her heart thudded painfully in her chest.

"The boy is fine." The Patriarch bent to retrieve the towel. "He enjoyed his stay here. But then he began to pine for his kind. He became inconsolable and refused to eat, so I took away his painful memories. He's been much happier since. Hasn't he grown under my care?" the fox said proudly. Like he was a new father.

It was true. Keiji's cheeks had filled, as she had seen in the window the Old One had opened so very long ago. Her brother's skin looked healthy and the dark bags under his eyes were gone. But his eyes, though not unhappy, stared blankly back at her. As if Sayuri was of no more importance than anything else.

She dug her teeth into her wobbling lip. All this way she had come. And the boy in front of her – he didn't know who she was.

"Give his memories back!" Sayuri cried. "He is an empty shell without them! Why have you brought us here?! Why do you keep us as prisoners?"

"Shhhh," the Patriarch soothed. "You're still sun-drunk. You must rest and regain your strength. And then everything will make sense." The fox drew his unnatural hand over Sayuri's eyes, and though she tried to pull back, she found she was incapable of movement. The fluttering bird-like panic in her head and heart slowed, leaving her sleepy and heavy. She sank back onto the softness of the bed. For it was true. She was still tired. And sleep would be very sweet....

THE NEXT TIME SHE AWOKE, IT WAS SWIFT. Without the eternity of wondering if she was awake in some strange dream. Sayuri opened her eyes, completely conscious. The ceiling was arched high above her head. Her room must be on top of the building. Bright colours caught the corner of her eye and she turned to the painted screen. On an inlay of gold, brilliant foxes with human faces, foxes with human legs and animal torsos, were depicted in a city setting. The paintings weren't realistic, but they glowed with a brightness that bordered on movement. All of the creatures wore clothing. A fox with human limbs but animal body was wearing knee-length leggings. It was buying fish in a market. A fox walking on furred hind legs had a woman's body with an animal's face. It was scolding a fox child that had a human face but walked on all fours. There was no sound, but they all seemed alive. Somewhere far away in slow-motion time. The child was jerked to its hind legs and made to mince unsteadily across the cobblestones. As Sayuri stared, the figures seemed to move slowly from one panel to another.

Sayuri squeezed her eyes shut, then stared again. The painting was a painting. Had it ever been anything else? Not even done well. Some of it was chipped. The girl shook her head and sat up. Swung her legs over the edge of the bed.

She was alone in her room. Bright sunlight spilled through the open window. The low table was still beside her bed. On it were a small silver pitcher of water and a silver cup. Both were engraved with foxes. Sayuri poured herself a cup and sipped slowly from the delicious water. The cool wetness trickled down her throat, down, down, the liquid absorbed by her dehydrated body like desert ground.

Water! The gourd!

Sayuri, looking down, desperately smacked at where the hyotan had been tied to her belt. It was gone. No! Her chin sank to her chest. What was the use any more? Could she just give up? Because that would be so much easier.

And saw. The hyotan and been left on the floor near the foot of the bed. Sayuri snatched it up and clasped the gourd in her arms. She shook gently and the splash of water seemed to be the same as before. "Thank you," Sayuri whispered fiercely. To all the forces that helped her. She retied the hyotan to her belt and sat on the edge of the bed. She poured herself another cup of water and sipped it slowly.

Think.

WAS SHE IN DANGER?

Probably. She'd been forced here by soldiers, after all.

Was she a prisoner?

Only if she was prevented from leaving whenever she wished.

What if the Patriarch had taken away her will to wish?

Then she was a slave.

What should she do?

Don't act on guesses unless it's a matter of life and death. Observe. Listen. Wait. The kappa soldiers were soldiers now, but they might have been forced against their will. She had been looking for her brother. And now she had found him. At least he was alive....

The door swung open. A fox awkwardly minced into the room on hind legs. She was dressed in a shapeless tunic. Sleeveless, it hung to where her "knees" ought to be. She bore towels. Because of the shape of her limbs, she couldn't hold anything, for despite being upright, her forelimbs were limited to a fox's movement. She couldn't turn her "palms" upward, so the towels were draped over her long slender forelegs, her paws facing down.

"The baths are ready."

A bath! A hot bath!

"Come, then." The fox's voice was not unkind.

She would act with dignity, Sayuri thought. She would act like a guest.

The girl stared at her grubby toes. Her runners were tattered. They probably smelled so bad they'd start running away from themselves! Sayuri followed the fox with the towels. Maybe they'd have slippers she could borrow.

The floor was tiled with squares of yellow stone. They pressed cool against her filthy feet. *Did the Patriarch take off my disgusting socks?* Sayuri wondered. Giggled at the image.

The Towel Fox darted a look with her glinting eye. The human didn't look mad.

Sayuri glanced up and thought of Machigai. Winked.

The Towel Fox gasped. Almost dropping the perfectly white and fluffy towels.

Sayuri giggled again. She felt a little giddy. Probably still dehydrated. But she hadn't lost her wits at all. She was capable of laughter.

They walked down twisting stairs, around and around; they must be in a turret, Sayuri thought, as triangular windows blazed patterns on the steps. The stairs opened to a long passageway with golden doors at regular intervals, but they didn't go through them. The fox turned a small corner and more stone steps plunged downward. The air felt cooler. Moist. And there were no more windows. Small lights glowed from tiny nooks in the stone walls.

They must be beneath ground level, Sayuri thought, thinking of the basement of their new house. When had they moved? It felt like centuries ago.

Sayuri could smell moisture in the air.

The baths were in a cavern beneath the great building. The ceilings were wet with the humid heat and hot condensation dripped on their heads. Somewhere, there was a soft roar of water falling in a steady torrent. The noise filled the room.

The baths weren't in tubs. They were like natural pools of

water. Three large irregular-shaped ponds, lined with rocks and more yellow stones. Steam rose, twining in the low lighting. The water looked almost black. And at the far end of the central bath, a lone fox rested its pointed snout on a smooth rock, its body otherwise completely immersed.

"Machigai?!" Sayuri yelled. Her voice echoed overloud in the enclosed space.

"Ahhh!" he leapt with a splash. Crossly glared at her. "Have a care! My hearing is slightly more sensitive than yours."

"Sorry," Sayuri mumbled. Her ears burning. She stomped toward the central pool. "Sorry! I was only worried you were being tortured! Maybe even dead!"

Machigai paddled to the edge of the pool. His pink tongue starting to slip out from between his long jaw. He frowned. The smallest curl of his snout. Then he sighed. And licked the girl's cheek in a fox kiss.

"Your loyalty is touching," he said almost sadly. Then he laughed, the laugh of the foxgirl. "Oh, ho, ho, hohhhhh!" He didn't shape-shift, but for a moment, his eyes became human. "You must join me in the baths," he said in the foxgirl voice. "A banquet awaits."

Sayuri's heart clenched small and hard. Why had Machigai said that about loyalty? Was he a servant of the Patriarch, after all?

She turned away. Clasped her arms around her middle. She could trust no one.

She breathed deeply and slowly, with great concentration, so she wouldn't fall back to the panting breath of fear. She breathed calm back into her body and felt slightly better. She added another idea to her list.

Assume nothing.

The Towel Fox stood behind the girl, waiting silently. When Sayuri finally turned to her, the fox gently said, "If you remove your clothing, it will be washed for you."

Sayuri wondered if she ought to ignore her. Remembering something Kimi had told her. How to fight without fighting. What was it called? Passive resistance! She could do nothing at all. She could be silent and do nothing.

But her mind talked back. What use would that be right now? The Patriarch didn't care if she bathed or not. He would just think her uncouth and filthy. He lost nothing. But she would feel better about herself if she bathed. So. Bathe first. Do nothing, be passive when it counts. Sayuri nodded to herself. It felt good to have a plan.

She carefully removed the water gourd and tied a knot in the cord so she could loop it over her wrist. She eagerly unbuttoned her jeans and kicked them off her feet. Pulled the crusty T-shirt off her head. She looked down at her body. The sunburn she'd developed at the tanuki's water hole had peeled off in unsightly patches. Dark bruises covered her legs. And sweat and dirt were etched into every crease of her body. She tried running fingers through her hair but the strands were knotted clumps of dust, sweat, and twigs.

"You must wash off the dirt before entering the baths," the Towel Fox murmured. She followed the fox to where the roar of falling water grew louder. A stream of hot water plunged from a large spout in the stone wall. It didn't spray, like a shower, but poured, like something tipped from a giant pitcher. Sayuri looked dubiously at the hyotan on her wrist. It would be awkward washing her hair.

"Why don't you leave it here on the floor?" Towel Fox said gently. "No one will take it."

Sayuri stared intently at the animal. Sighed. If someone really wanted to take it away from her, she couldn't stop them. She set the precious gourd on the ground and stepped beneath the downpour of hot water. The wet heat pounded on her like a hard massage. Pounded the travel and dirt and sweat away. She stepped out to gasp for air.

"Here," the fox nudged. She passed Sayuri a jar and a scratchy sponge. The girl stared dubiously at the sticky brown contents. It looked like axle grease.

"Thank you," she said doubtfully, lifting the jar for a whiff. Honey! And something herbal. Sayuri dipped fingers into the container and scooped out a handful. When she rubbed the sticky soap into her hair and over her body, a fragrant perfume filled the air.

She shampooed her hair three times. Then, she scrubbed and scrubbed her body until she glowed pink and shiny. The tanuki, she decided, would definitely think she was a piglet! When she was finished, she felt she'd washed away several pounds of dirt and dead skin. She felt brand new.

Sayuri returned to the three pools, the hyotan swinging from her wrist. Machigai sat on a low bench, his nose on his paws. Next to him were a bowl, a pitcher, and a glass. Condensation beaded the glass pitcher. Sayuri poured water for herself and the fox and they drank. Sayuri could feel the passage of the cold water from her mouth, all the way down her throat and into her stomach. She dabbled her toe in the third pool.

"Ow!" she yelped, jerking her foot back.

Machigai barked a small laugh. Sayuri glared.

"I'm sorry," he apologized. "The pools are all different temperatures. You need to go into them in order or they're too hot. I couldn't manage this last one at all," he admitted.

Sayuri went to the first pool and cautiously dipped her fingers. Bearable. Barely. Even hotter than the baths her grandmother had poured in Japan. She eased her body slowly, slowly, into the pool and a great sigh hissed from between her lips. The hyotan bobbed on the surface next to her wrist. She rested her head back on the smooth stones that lined the edge of the bath pool. Her body quickly went from pink to red.

The steam rose from the water in twining strands and she dreamily followed the movement. The pounding massage of the shower and the hot water of the bath was sapping her wits. Sayuri let her eyes slip out of focus, a trick she'd developed when she first started memorizing the times tables. Expanding her pupils, she saw everything but focussed on nothing. Eyes open, she stared at a point just beyond the blurred nothing in front of her. The steam curled into shapes, faces, far away.

Old One. Old One was on a litter, carried on the shoulders of strong young tanuki. Rows of tanuki. There weren't that many at the Mountain's Blood Clan...and was that an oni, bringing up the rear? The steam faded and a new figure coalesced, a tanuki older and larger than the others. But walking at the front of the procession. Something familiar about the figure, but Sayuri couldn't remember a creature of that size when she'd stayed with the clan. She frowned, blinked, the movement making her blurred vision begin to focus and the steam became nothing more than steam.

"Ho hohhh," Machigai whispered.

Sayuri jumped. For she hadn't noticed the fox had crept closer. His snout peered over her shoulder from the edge of the pool.

"What have you seen in your far sight?"

"Didn't you see anything?" Sayuri asked. Still uncertain how to treat the fox.

"Just whispers," Machigai nodded. "Hints."

"That's all I saw too," Sayuri said. Not entirely untrue, because she didn't know what the vision in the steam meant.

"The key," Machigai sighed, as he leapt back on his bench, "is knowing what is the past, the present, or the future."

Sayuri sighed too. "There's always some sort of catch." She held her breath and sank under the water. The gourd floated on the surface like a small buoy. Releasing a slender stream of bubbles, Sayuri opened her eyes, everything blurry but with no visions. Crying under water wasn't exactly crying.

32. OUT OF THE BATHS AND INTO THE FIRE

JUST AS SAYURI TIRED OF THE BATHS, THE TOWEL FOX returned with Sayuri's clothes washed and carefully pressed. Holes in the knees of her jeans had been patched with squares of dark red material and she ran her fingers over the cloth. As she dressed, Sayuri glanced at her chest. The material of the T-shirt didn't sting her nipples the way it had back at home. Maybe they'd stopped growing. She didn't know how she felt about that. Then a thought came to her. She crouched down and stared at her clean toes. Her toenails. They were even and clipped short, like always. Like always! Sayuri knew she couldn't measure with her fingernails, because she'd climbed cliffs and fallen through tunnels and rebuilt a roof. Her fingernails were ripped and tattered with survival. But her toenails had been protected inside her runners. And the toenails hadn't grown! She'd been here for more than two weeks, she was certain. Back at home, she clipped them once a week! If her toenails hadn't grown, that might mean time had slowed to a rate immeasurable to her body!

Or, toenails didn't grow here.

She giggled. Okay. Okay. Assume nothing. But she breathed easier. Her parents might not be worried out of their heads. Or dead and turned to dust like Urashimataro's parents because time had passed too fast. Her parents might not even be home yet. Sayuri smiled hopefully.

Machigai watched her with unreadable eyes. Didn't say anything. Just nosed the water gourd with his snout. "There is plenty of water here now. No reason to burden yourself needlessly."

Sayuri clutched the container. Then forced herself to let go. "It gives me comfort," she said. And that was true enough.

The fox shrugged. Sayuri could see that the cuts in his snout were clean and starting to heal. Machigai took a few steps away and shook vigorously, droplets of water scattering in a fine spray.

"Hey!" Sayuri gasped.

"Oops," Machigai smiled. "Sorry." He turned to the quiet Towel Fox, still standing on her hind legs. "Don't fall over," he whispered out of the side of his mouth.

The fox twitched her ears but said nothing. Sayuri wondered if foxes blushed. Maybe, she thought, they gave off a blushing smell.

Machigai seemed pleased with himself, trotted out of the room, swishing his tail.

The Towel Fox sniffed. Sayuri giggled silently as she followed Machigai from the room.

MACHIGAI SEEMED TO KNOW WHERE TO GO. His nose in the air, he turned from one hallway to another with an assurance that made Sayuri's heart squeeze with fear. Was Machigai an agent of the Patriarch too? Had she made a terrible mistake in turning back to save him from dehydration? But then the fox paused at a doorway, sniffed deeply, then turned away farther down the corridor.

Oh, the girl thought. He's just following his nose. Then she, too, smelled an orchestra of flavours. Her stomach twisted and groaned and she trotted even faster after Machigai.

Was that tonkatsu? Her mouth pooled with want. Curry? Steamed dumplings? Stewed daikon? Udon soup? Ohhh, was that toasted rice cakes?

Machigai nosed a great golden door. It swung open into a vast room with a glass ceiling. Daylight was turning to a lavender mist. Not a cloud. The sky curved a half circle above their heads. Sayuri couldn't tell where the ceiling ended and the dome that enclosed the city began.

"Come, join us," a rich, melodious voice rang out.

One wall was made of glass as well. And a dining table, about six metres long, was centred next to the great window. Too large for the small group that sat at the banquet – the Patriarch at the head of the table, Keiji to his right, Broken Bowl next to Keiji, and then Echo. The seats to the Patriarch's left were empty and he inclined his head toward Sayuri and Machigai. Sayuri made a small bow. Not so low as to be humble, but just enough to be courteous.

"Thank you for your hospitality," she murmured, thinking furiously. Being polite had helped her in awkward situations before. She had nothing to lose by being polite. A lot to lose if he was angered. "I have been remarkably refreshed by your amazing baths. They are certainly a great wonder."

The Patriarch raised his eyebrows slightly. "Indeed. I am pleased they pleased you."

Sayuri stared at her brother. She longed to run to him, check his arms and legs and neck and spine for injuries just as Jun would do. Keiji, who talked baby when he was scared. She tried to catch his eyes, for some sign of recognition, but her brother was gazing at the lavender mist turning purple in the evening air.

Sayuri swallowed. Then calmly sat in her seat. Were his memories erased? Or were they saved somewhere?

"Great Uncle." Machigai made an elaborate bow, with an arm flourish that looked like something from a pirate movie.

"Hah!" the Patriarch barked. "The Great Mistake. Behold, everyone. The Fox Who Eats No Meat!" The great fox pointed a tapered finger at Machigai, who swung his tail around to half cover his face. He peeked from between the long strands of fur and he fluttered his short eyelashes. Everyone chuckled politely. Except for Sayuri.

"No more strange," she said coolly, "than a fox with human hands."

The silence was heavy enough to shatter the glass ceiling. Then the Patriarch barked and howled with laughter. He wiped the tears from his eyes with his human hands and everyone else laughed with relief. He thought it was funny. No one would be punished.

"Indeed, child," he gasped, "you speak a truth. You will do well in my court."

Sayuri bowed her head. As if she was bowing with gratitude. But her thoughts ran wild in her head. He intended them to stay?

"Eat! Enjoy!" The Patriarch swung wide his hands, then lifted his golden chopsticks.

Sayuri looked down at her bowl and plate. Gold. She lifted the bowl and the weight was astonishing. Golden dishes, how silly, she thought. Heavy, easy to scratch and dent. But the food. The food was all she'd imagined and more. There were heaps of fried greens with ginger and soya sauce, fish steamed with forest mushrooms and savoury noodles mixed with sesame seeds. Sayuri reached out with her chopsticks to snatch a golden fried pork cutlet while she looked around for the sauce.

Machigai touched her forearm with his paw. "Your stomach is still shrunken. Eat small and slow at first or you will make yourself sick. And don't eat meat for now."

"You see!" the Patriarch snorted. He stretched across the table and snatched two fried cutlets at once.

"Did you ask this pig if he consented to becoming a meal, Grandfather?" Machigai flicked his tail.

The pork fell from Sayuri's chopsticks, her free hand covering her mouth. "You mean," she whispered, eyes round, "that the pigs you eat can talk?"

"Everyone talks," Machigai frowned. "Don't the creatures on your Earth As I Know It speak as well?"

"Bah!" the Patriarch scoffed. "Does speech mean special

treatment? Foxes eat meat. That is our nature."

Where did you draw the line? Sayuri wondered. She didn't know. But the idea of eating a pig that talked seemed, well, inhuman. She replaced the meat on the platter and picked small portions of greens and udon soup.

"You see!" The Patriarch tossed his head. "You've ruined her appetite, and after such a fast. Eat!" he smiled with all of his sharp teeth. "Eat as your brother has!"

Keiji looked up from his full plate and smiled dutifully. Then he dug in again, scooping rice and noodles into his mouth. Chewing big chunks of tonkatsu.

He ate with no pleasure at all.

Sayuri felt ill. What if she couldn't find his memories? Would he still be able to go back home? Would his memory return when they left this place? Sayuri didn't know. She felt sick, but she had to rebuild her strength. She bit into the greens and the bitterness mixed with sweet soya sauce was a delicious combination. Sayuri darted a glance at the betrayer. Echo was crunching into long stems much like celery but a darker green. Her eyes were still black. Not red, like Broken Bowl's. The kappa looked up and caught Sayuri's eyes. The creature looked sad.

Sayuri scowled. The creature looked evil, not sad!

The girl returned to her bowl of noodles. Ate and drank the salty soup. Her mouth was happy for the salt. She hadn't realized she wasn't getting enough. She drank a little more soup, then pushed her bowl away. The fox was right. Her stomach had shrunk, for she was full already.

"May I ask a question of your greatness?" Sayuri asked,

turning to the Patriarch. She smiled like she meant it.

"Hoh! Hoh!" he chuckled. "Ask me anything."

"Why is it that your soldiers bear human things? Why do you wear clothes and use artificial lights?"

"That is more than one question," the Patriarch smiled, "but I will tell you. When I magicked my new hands, they began longing for things human."

Sayuri stared at her empty plate. Was that why she and her brother were brought here? She gulped. Stared at the abundance of food on the banquet table and frowned.

"Where does all the food come from?"

"Why, the kitchens," the fox smiled indulgently. As if he thought her a slightly stupid child.

"Yes, but where do you grow the vegetables? Where do the foodstuffs come from?"

The great fox frowned slightly. The tiniest curl along his snout. His human hands tapped the tabletop, then he reached for his cup of rice wine.

"From afar!" he pointed vaguely at the window. "The kappa farm fields to the south. They are good at that. They enjoy the outdoors."

"Oh," Sayuri said softly. "The way they enjoy being soldiers too, I suppose."

"You know nothing," the Patriarch murmured. "Watch you don't push my patience too far."

"I know what I saw," the girl persisted. Fear squeezing her gut. Hadn't she decided she'd be polite? What was wrong with her?

She couldn't help herself.

"I saw you kill those kappa soldiers who spoke against you."

"And are you so eager to follow?" the Patriarch whispered, not looking at her. He stared at Keiji instead.

The girl shook. Her legs trembled beneath the table. Machigai pressed a paw on her knee and she clasped it desperately.

"You are tired," the Patriarch decided and he smiled. Clapped his hands lightly. "Come. It is time to reward the loyal!" He gestured to Echo and she rose quickly to her feet. Keiji looked up briefly, but his eyes uncaringly drifted to his plate.

Sayuri's heart pounded. Would the fox tear out the kappa's eyes and replace them with the monstrous red ones?

Echo knelt before the Patriarch and Sayuri's hand covered her mouth. No! she wanted to scream.

The great fox stood above the kappa and raised his human hands. He pressed his fingers along fingers, thumb to thumb, in the shape of a triangle.

"Oh!" Sayuri gasped. That's how she'd called the magic! Machigai kicked her leg with his paw.

The Patriarch closed his eyes and a red light grew inside the triangle of his hands. The light shone like glowing liquid. It spilled fat and thin, molding like hot plastic into the form of a gleaming pitcher. It hung in midair. The fox snatched the handle just as the pitcher began to fall and he grinned his sharp teeth. The Patriarch poured a small amount of water back into the bowl of Echo's head. Not full to the rim, not even half full. But Sayuri could see that the water didn't fade away. Echo stood and bobbed her gratitude, not bowing, for she had to make sure the precious liquid wouldn't be spilled.

"I will give you eyes tomorrow," the Patriarch promised.

Sayuri shuddered. Echo turned to stare at the girl. Sayuri stared back, her feelings snakes that writhed in her belly.

"Forgive me," the kappa spoke.

The girl started. For the kappa spoke with her true voice and the sound was like water rushing over pebbles.

Sayuri's cheeks burned. She didn't know what to say. She looked away.

"Come, come," the Patriarch encouraged. "Show some compassion. The kappa had little choice. She intended you no harm."

Sayuri's ears burned hot. Her heart pounded in her throat. Her brother was staring at the sky and his mouth hung open. "What kind of monster are you?" she hissed. "You curse the kappa and force her to befriend then betray me. Then you turn to me to forgive her? You're crazy! You care for me in sickness and bathe me when I'm dirty, but you take away my brother's memories. You've destroyed the land around you and you kill creatures at will! And you sit there, pretending we're all dinner guests?!" Sayuri shouted, somehow standing, her hands flat on the table.

The Patriarch dabbed his napkin down the length of his jaw, first one side then the other. "Well," he said mildly, "if it's so unpleasant being a guest, then by all means, be a prisoner." He clapped his hands smartly, four times, and four kappa soldiers marched quickly into the great dining hall.

"Take the prisoner to the dungeons," he sniffed, pointing

his snout toward the girl. "Now, we must call for the entertainment!"

The anger that had filled Sayuri's body with heat froze into icy shards.

Fool, she thought as she was led away. Fool.

33. TO THE DUNGEONS

THE SOLDIERS TOOK HER TO A NARROW PASSAGE THAT twined down, deeper than the baths. The air wasn't damp. It was icy with the terror of thousands of prisoners before her. Sayuri's teeth chattered and she could do nothing to stop herself.

The kappa soldiers said nothing.

They marched deeper and deeper into the darkness. The passage was not lit and the kappas' eyes gleamed like red pearls. The guards had to use their flashlights to see the steps going ever downward. The stairs finally ended and small doors lined a long, narrow hallway. It smelled of sweat, urine, filth.

And I just took a bath, Sayuri's mind giggled senselessly.

A small triangular window was cut into the thick wood of each door. The glow from the flashlights must have bounced into the cells, for small cries could be heard. Whispers for water and pity. None of the prisoners stuck out their hands. The doors were barred with big pieces of timber that fitted into brackets, the wood at least ten centimetres thick.

Sayuri had no thoughts left.

They came to a stop. The last cell at the end of the hall. Two kappa grunted, heaved to raise the timber, then shoved the door open. A soldier placed a hand over Sayuri's head and made her duck to fit through the frame. The ceiling of the cell wasn't much higher than the door, and when Sayuri straightened her knees, she bumped her head on the stone ceiling.

"Oh!"

The door was shut and the heavy timber dropped into place. Her heart fluttered in her rib cage. The bobbing glow of the flashlights grew dimmer. Then silence. Just her blood, pounding in her ears.

The darkness was as complete as in the tunnels behind the Blue Oni's cave.

Sayuri held out her hand. The dark was heavy against her skin. And cold. Her bare feet were icy on the stone floor and she tried to curl her toes closer to her feet. She started groping toward a wall, anything. Stopped. Her teeth chattered, clattered. She clapped her hands over her mouth.

What if there were skeletons chained to the walls?

She moaned and sank on her haunches. Wrapped her arms around her knees. She stared at the darkness until false flashes of light burst in her vision.

Something *moved* behind her.

Sayuri spun around. Panting. "Hello?" she quavered. "Who's there?"

Movement behind her again. No noise. Just the movement of air.

"I am a prisoner just as you are," Sayuri said wearily. She was tired of being terrified. The adrenaline and the relief were exhausting. She plunked to the ground and sat with her legs straight in front of her. "I mean you no harm."

A thrumming vibration. The wings of a giant insect? Sayuri thought dully. Who could guess what kind of creature would pop up next, talking?

No, the girl realized. Not insect.

Purring!

"Momo," she said hopefully. "Momo, is that you?"

"Mreow."

A huge furry weight knocked the girl over as the enormous cat pressed two massive paws on her chest. The purring vibrated into Sayuri's body. The great cat started licking around the girl's mouth for traces of her dinner.

"Ow!" Sayuri screeched, giggling. "Ouch! Cut it out!"

The giant cat stopped and contented himself with heaping his heavy body over the girl's lap. Sayuri pressed her nose in the cat's fur. A faint scent of shiso.

"Oh, Momo," Sayuri sniffed. "I guess Yamanba doesn't know what's happened to you. I almost forgot all about her. So much has happened. I've been looking for my brother. I thought you led him away, but you're just a prisoner too." Sayuri sniffed again. She ran her fingers through the cat's thick coat and, though the creature was too heavy on her legs, the warmth was a great comfort.

"The Patriarch took away Keiji's memories and now we're trapped. I don't know who my friends are. I – I –" Sayuri swallowed back her tears. "I want to go home." Breathed deeply. "We *will* go home."

You've grown, child.

"Momo?"

Yes?

"I can hear you!" Sayuri cried gleefully.

Of course. The cat swung his long tail and gently batted her face. Sayuri giggled, then sighed.

"What part does Yamanba play in all of this?" Sayuri asked.

She is a keeper of gates. She looks through doorways and watches. She is One Who Watches. How could something happen if no one witnessed?

"Why must things happen?"

Why indeed?

"That's not an answer!"

Nor was it meant to be.

"Do you talk like that because you're a cat?"

Am I a cat because I talk this way?

"Ugh!" Sayuri snorted. Pushed the feline off her legs. "How annoying!"

Momo thrummed with pleasure. *Oh, I have been terribly bored!* The cat heaved a great sigh. *And hungry.*

"Oh! I'm sorry. I wish I'd had the sense to grab something. They don't bring food often?"

Once a day.

Sayuri sighed too. "Have you tried digging out? And why can't you just jump through the wall anyway? Like you did at my house!"

The Patriarch has twisted the lines of magic. I cannot read them in this place.

"Is that why Yamanba doesn't come to save you?"

The cat sat up and licked his paw and began washing his ear. Sayuri could only hear fur being wetted, the swipe of motion. The inky blackness made every movement sound louder.

Have you not listened? Yamanba is One Who Observes. We are the ones who act. Or not.

"Does that mean she's watching us now?" Sayuri said hopefully.

She has many gates to ward, many acts she must observe. We are one of many, but she may be watching us now.

"But she can't actively help." Sayuri sighed gently. "Well, what are you, Momo? What were you doing in my bedroom?"

I felt a call.

"From whom?"

I know not.

"Can you help us get home again?" Sayuri whispered. She dragged her finger over the cold stones of the floor. Dirty! Jun would wince if he saw her. Sayuri smiled sadly in the dark. She couldn't see the dirt.

As Yamanba said, You must seek the passage yourselves through the Water of Possibility.

"I don't know if I could find Yamanba's hut again." Sayuri raised her knees and rested her head, encircling her legs with her arms.

That. That I may aid you with.

"Thank you!" Sayuri threw her arms around the giant cat's neck, then let him go.

Well! she thought, she shouldn't assume that the Patriarch would let her out any time soon. She would look for an escape. Sayuri started to crawl, sweeping her hand around to tap out the walls.

Child, there is no escape from this cell. I have tried.

"We can't just give up!" Sayuri said loudly.

I have not suggested such a thing.

"What do we do then?"

We wait.

"Wait? Wait?! What has waiting done for you?"

Are you not here?

"You had no control over that!" Sayuri shook her head, though the cat wouldn't be able to see. Could he? "Can you see in this dark?" the girl asked.

The cat said nothing.

"Momo?"

No, child. I can see nothing.

Sayuri yawned hugely, dragged the back of her hand over her eyes. Straining her eyes in the dark made them tired. She might as well close them, it didn't make a difference anyway.

Lie next to me. You should rest now, for you smell weary.

"I just took a bath!" Sayuri protested, though she curled close to press her back against the cat's soft and warm belly. Her feet were cold, but there was nothing to be done about that. She tried to wiggle her toes into the cat's fur.

Momo purred and laughed at the same time. A bumpy thrumming sound.

"A friend – someone – told me there's a land of cats far to the north," Sayuri murmured sleepily. "Where cats dive for fish as big as trees and sing songs that sound like the howling snow. Is that true?" She yawned again. For the cat's fragrant fur was warm and sweet. She snuggled the comforting roundness of the hyotan against her belly.

Yes, child. There is such a land. Even now, the cats gather for the one day of sun, to tell tales and sing the snow back to the world....

So Momo softly shared his stories. Even after the girl had fallen asleep.

34. NIGHT VISION

A HUGE FURRY PAW CLAMPED OVER SAYURI'S MOUTH AND she jolted awake, her eyes bulging wide. It was so dark she wondered if she was dead.

A dream! She shouted to herself. It's just a dream.

Sorry, child. I hear something. We must be prepared.

Only Momo. Sayuri sagged with relief, then turned her senses toward the door.

For there were faint noises, wood dragged across wood, a panting breath. Whoever had come, it was without a light.

Did ghoulish demons wander in the dank hallways?

Momo dropped his paw and crept to the door.

A muffled grunting sound. A loud THUD echoed on the stones, then the flap, flap of wide feet running, fading into nothing.

I think we have an ally.

Sayuri scurried to where the sounds had come from. She reached, placed careful fingers on the rough boards, and curled her fingers around the uneven surface of wood. She gently pulled.

The door swung open.

The hallway was as dark as the cell, but the air shifted to spill outward.

"We're free!" Sayuri squeaked.

Wait.

Momo went first. Keeping his body inside the cell, he cautiously stuck his head out the door and sniffed the air. Sayuri could almost picture his ears turning like radar dishes.

The hallway is empty. Come.

Sayuri tapped with her hand and turned right of the door. Theirs had been the last room in the long hall. Her feet were so icy they felt numb. She had to find something to wrap them. Or how could she reach the forests?

All those cells....

They were not the only prisoners.

She couldn't leave them behind, could she?

But it would take so long. What if they were caught setting others free? Then her only chance would be wasted.

Should she overlook the suffering of others?

Ahhh! Sayuri clamped her hands over her head. She couldn't stop her racing mind. And Momo said nothing! Sayuri bit her lip. And tried to think of nothing. But her conscience refused.

They could come back later, she rationalized. After she'd got her brother.

What if this chance was lost? And prisoners died?

She hadn't placed them in their cells!

But she had the power, now, to free them....

"WE MUST FREE THE OTHERS!" Sayuri hissed.

Momo thrummed, soft and steady. Rubbed against the girl's back in the absolute darkness.

Yes, we must. Mustn't we?

Sayuri ran her hands along one wall and Momo took the other side. The girl came to the first door and she yanked, upward, the timber barring the door. Pain wrenched her shoulders.

"Ow –!"

Hush. Take care.

Sayuri clamped her lips shut and hopped up and down silently in pain. Returned to the door. She crouched down and placed her right shoulder beneath the middle of the beam and straightened her legs. The timber rose and she tottered beneath the weight, awkwardly shuffled to the side. She wanted to drop the heavy wood, but the noise! They couldn't drop those timbers left and right. Might as well bellow, "Escaping! We're escaping now!" She tipped the weight to one side and let the rough length slide down her back.

It felt like her skin was being shredded.

How many cells were there?

She pushed the door open. Paused. Just because the Patriarch was evil didn't mean all of his prisoners were good. What if he'd jailed horrible monsters?

A little late to think of that, her mind chided. Sayuri gulped. "You can go free," she whispered to the prisoner. "We're escaping. We've opened your door."

What if there were gentle giants who would help open the rest of the cells? Sayuri thought brightly.

"Is it t-t-true?" a voice quavered near her ankles. Sayuri crouched down.

"Yes. Who are you?"

"I-I-I'm a t-t-toad."

Sayuri sighed. Toad would be no help. "Fear not," Sayuri said gently. "Could you go to the end of the hall and be our sentry? If you hear someone coming, moan as if you're in pain."

"A-A-All right," Toad answered. "My thanks."

"You're welcome," Sayuri grunted, shouldering the next beam. It felt heavier than the first.

Sayuri could hear a raspy voice behind her. Momo must have opened his door as well.

A rank odour of dirty fur and urine spilled around Sayrui's head. She choked and coughed as a thick paw thumped her back.

"Momo said to help Sayuri," a rough voice rasped.

"Thank you," the girl coughed. The beast-like thing lifted one end of the beam and Sayuri lifted the other. Piece of cake, the girl grinned in the dark.

"We're escaping. You're free," she whispered and went to the next door.

As each cell was opened, the freed help unlock the other doors, and soon the hallway was filled with warm bodies, whispers, grunts, groans, squeaks, and the pungent odour of fur and flesh long unwashed.

"We're free!" they murmured. Some fearfully, for they knew not what to do.

Sayuri panted after the hard work. Her forehead was

damp. She darted her head about, though she couldn't see in the darkness. Where was Momo? Maybe, she thought, maybe it was a mistake to free the prisoners. There were so many of them and the noise was growing like a tide moving to shore.

Why didn't Momo make them stop?

"Quiet!" Sayuri ordered in a loud whisper.

The rising mutterings trickled to a low murmur.

"We must remain silent until we've escaped from this dungeon." Sayuri's heart pounded in her chest. Who was she to tell them what to do? But no time! Someone had to do something. Or all would be lost. "We must work together to overthrow the Patriarch. If we scatter, we will all perish trying to pass through the outer dome. Alone, we are weak. Together, we are strong."

"The Patriarch," someone moaned. Another started to cry.

"What about the soldiers?" a beautiful voice rang like small perfect bells.

"Yes, soldiers!"

"Not all serve the Patriarch through choice. This I have seen." Sayuri wiped the sweat off her forehead with the palm of her hand. It was hard speaking to convince people and she wished desperately for a glass of water. "If we fight the Patriarch, some of the soldiers will turn and fight for their own freedom as well."

"Hah!" a gruff voice scoffed. "You don't know that! I say everyone run and hide. The odds are better that way."

Sayuri gritted her teeth. How could she convince them? This was a chance to break the Patriarch's stronghold. Quick escape didn't mean they wouldn't be his prisoners again!

"I-I-I think that Sayuri's p-p-plan makes sense!"

Toad! the girl thought. Thank you!

"Bear's with Sayuri!" the rough voice rasped. "Bear helps Sayuri!"

"If only we had some light in this terrible darkness!" Sayuri said softly. "Then we could see each other and measure our strengths. Can anyone call a light?"

Complete silence. Shocked, everyone had stopped breathing.

"Hah!" the first gruff voice coughed, part laughter, part choking. "Fool child! You want to follow after a Fool child?" he called out to all. None answered. "Hah!" The gruff voice was right next to Sayuri's ear and she cringed from the panting heat, the rage.

"We are all BLIND!"

Oh! Sayuri clamped a hand over her mouth. No! It was all so terrible. They would only be rounded up and pushed back into their pens. Punished. Kinder to have done nothing. Kinder to have not brought hope. She was a fool. A fool. And the fool would be caught with the blind. Tears stung her eyes and she gulped. What could she do now? What?

Child?

"Oh, Momo! Are you blind too? I'm so sorry!"

Indeed? It was not you who blinded us.

"What can I do?" her voice was heavy. Her head dropped with despair.

Look inside yourself. Maybe you carry answers you have not yet seen.

Sayuri sank to the cold floor and sat with her legs crossed.

Not that it was any use. She had nothing left. She would stay a hairless ape in the Patriarch's court. She would speak her mind and the great fox would be either amused or angered. She'd move back and forth from the banquet room to the prison at his whim. With or without her eyes.

"What does the creature do?" a voice whispered.

"Who does she speak to?" the bell-like voice rang.

"She's lost her sense!" the gruff voice scorned, moving away from the crowd.

"Be quiet! Sayuri thinks!" Bear whispered a shout.

Sayuri's lips curved slightly upward. But she stopped listening. Or the words turned to murmurs, wisps of sound, not meaning. Sayuri pulled her thoughts deep inside and rested her arms on her thighs. Gently aligned her fingers against fingers, thumb on thumb.

Peace, she called. Calm. And opened the door between heart and mind.

Light swirled behind her closed eyes, twining colours of opal, amber, teal. Sayuri stretched her thoughts and followed the twisting strands, flowing weightlessly in air that smelled like honey and ginger. Where, she wondered, bemused, are we going?

She hovered, floated high above a yard, where little children played together. One child stood in the middle, arms outstretched, and the other children circled her, darting in to touch her back, then darting away before she could clasp them.

How cruel, Sayuri thought, what cruel games they play. Then she realized, the girl in the middle was blindfolded.

The girl in the middle was her! Little Sayuri untied the scarf and shouted at her companions. Sayuri Who Watched could hear nothing. The girl marched into the house and the friends looked at each other and shrugged. Little Sayuri marched back out, her arms filled. She handed scarves out to everyone and had the children blindfold themselves. And the game started again. Now all the children stumbled about with arms extended and Sayuri Who Watched could see the children shrieking with laughter as they fell against each other, unsure who was "it" or not....

Sayuri's bottom was icy. Her fingertips tingled and when she opened her eyes a faint glow remained in the triangle of her hands. She smiled.

She could see the creatures closest to her and the sight pained her. Tanuki with concave bellies, a medium-sized bear, a rabbit with one ear, an enormous spider larger, still, than the bear, and a dried husk of a toad, and so many more; they turned their eyeless faces toward Sayuri's light. For though their empty sockets couldn't see, their animal senses felt the small warmth.

"Sayuri have powers! Bear knew it!" the black bear nodded his blunt head.

"Hah!" the gruff voice broke through the circle. A short and stumpy tengu pushed his way angrily toward the girl. Of all the folk creatures, the tengu looked the most human. His matted filthy hair was black and his tengu nose was long and red in a surprisingly human face. "Not power enough to beat the Patriarch!" the tengu scoffed, snapping his small wings angrily.

Anger burned in Sayuri's chest. But the heat dampened

the small glow in her fingers. Sayuri breathed in deep, slow, to calm her feelings and her thoughts. Fury wouldn't serve her here. Did fury ever serve anyone well?

"Force against force causes much destruction," Sayuri mused.

"Well, you don't seem especially clever!" the tengu insulted.

"And you," Sayuri countered, "don't look especially brave, but it would appear you refused the Patriarch's gift of eyes."

"Ha! Ha! Ha!" Bear laughed.

"Shhhh!" several creatures hissed, though some also tittered.

"Humph!" the tengu sniffed. But Sayuri saw that his hands were no longer in fists.

Sayuri rose to her feet, her fingers still cradling the small glow of light. She lifted her hands high, so the soft warmth would fall upon all. "My name is Sayuri. I am not a creature of this world. I came to find my brother whom the Patriarch has kept prisoner. I only wished to return to my own world, but the Patriarch has done a great wrong to many people. We can right this wrong if we unite. Who is with me?"

"I!" a small roar filled the hall.

"And I," the tengu muttered. Kicking something with his toes.

Sayuri smiled wide and her face seemed to glow with a golden light. "Come. Let us learn each other's names. Then I want to share my plan."

The creatures all came close and they sat together.

"Boulder," the bear proudly slapped his chest.

"D-D-Dew," Toad croaked.

"Autumn," the spider's voice chimed.

"Blossom," the gruff tengu grinned.

"Lake," the one-eared rabbit whispered.

And as they called their names one by one, Sayuri heard Momo begin to purr.

35. FLIGHT

"Now," Sayuri said eagerly, "you may be blind, but we might be able to use that to our advantage."

"How?" Blossom, the tengu snorted. "Do you imagine that our remaining senses are extra special now that we no longer have sight?"

"Bear doesn't like Blossom's tone!" Boulder warned.

"Hush," Sayuri placed her hand gently on Boulder's huge paw. "It is useful to know the weaker links." The girl turned to the tengu. "I was thinking that you have grown used to being blind. Blindness isn't surprising. But what if all of the soldiers and the Patriarch were to become suddenly blind?"

The creatures gasped. Then were silent. "Y-y-you would d-d-do as the Patriarch has d-d-done to us?" Dew, the toad asked sadly.

"No, no!" Sayuri shook her head. "The city is brightened with some kind of artificial light. I haven't seen a single fire or lamp since I've been here. That means that somewhere there is an energy source. If we turned off the switch, the whole city would be in darkness. The creatures have become used to living at night with lights on. If we suddenly took it away, they would be blind."

"Ahhhh," said Autumn, the giant spider, with her lovely bell-like voice. "There is much sense in the girl's plan."

"Can you still cast thread, Autumn?" Sayuri asked, stroking the spider's hairy face.

"Yes. But I cannot see to throw."

"I will be your eyes," Sayuri said. "I need someone with great strength and someone with a loud voice to accompany me, Autumn, and Momo."

"Bear!" said Boulder. "Bear is strong!"

"M-m-my v-v-voice is loud," Dew croaked.

Sayuri looked down at the little dry toad. Her eyebrows raised. "Thank you," she said.

"What will the rest of us do?" the tengu asked gruffly.

Sayuri smiled. She had won him over. "Blossom, while we search for the power source, you and the others must make your way to the upper floor. I think the power for the light must be within the deeps of this building. Find the upper floor, then hide in nooks, cupboards, closets. When we've cut the light source, you will know that it is so, for the guards who keep watch will call out an alarm. Everyone will be confused in the darkness. When you hear the signal that Dew makes, everyone with Blossom make loud noises and frighten the kappa soldiers, because they're not very brave. Mill about so they do not know who is friend and who is foe."

"What about the Patriarch?" Blossom asked drily. The

tengu crossed his arms. "A little darkness will mean nothing to that fox!"

Sayuri gulped. "Boulder, Autumn, Dew, Momo, and I will seek him out. We will confront him." Her courage failed her and the light in her fingers went out. "Will you come with me?"

"Bear always goes with Sayuri!" Boulder thumped the girl on her back. She staggered, took a few tottering steps forward.

Gently, Momo murmured. *Know your own strength, bear.*

"Sorry, Sayuri! Bear's so sorry!"

"Hush," Sayuri murmured. "I'm fine. Autumn, are you with us too?"

"Of course," Autumn's voice rang sweetly. "But who's Momo?"

Sayuri giggled. "Momo the great purple cat. He only speaks with his mind. Have you not heard his voice?"

"Bear hears Momo's talk," Boulder proudly thumped his chest.

"I have not," Autumn chimed.

Momo, purring, curled around the huge spider's back and nudged her face with his wet nose.

"Oh!" Autumn exclaimed. Then giggled. "I know his scent now."

"Good. All right. When the signal is made, we want to cause great confusion so that we can confront the Patriarch without his guards. The important thing is to overcome the Patriarch. He is the key." Sayuri raised the light of her hands. She stared at the maimed all around her. They stared back with their eyeless sockets, but she could read hope and courage in the way they held their faces. "Peace, clarity, and wisdom be with you."

Well said. Momo purred louder.

Sayuri bent down to lift the toad into her hands. She snuggled into the girl's fingers for the last trace of warmth.

"Are you sure you want to come with us? It might get rough."

"Y-y-yes," Dew croaked. "I'm certain."

"It'll be dangerous for you on the ground," Sayuri said. "Could you stay on if I put you on my shoulder?"

"Y-y-yes," Dew nodded. "M-m-my toes and legs are strong."

Sayuri gently lifted the toad to her right shoulder.

Dew curled her sensitive toes over the neck of Sayuri's T-shirt. "I will be f-f-fine."

"Boulder, please open the door," Sayuri called out. She triangulated her hands to call the light.

The bear opened the door and stuck his head through. Snuffled the air as if he was eating it.

"Bear smells no one!" he grunted.

Sayuri turned to Blossom and kissed his coarse cheek. "Lead them well," she whispered.

The tengu grinned fiercely and patted the girl on the head.

The next room was empty. A narrow stairway spiralled upward and two doors stood on either side. Sayuri placed Blossom in the lead, then guided the one-eared rabbit's paw to the tengu's shoulder. On Lake's shoulder, she placed the first tanuki's paw. And on and on so that all filed, a long train, holding paw to shoulder as they twined up the spiralling stairway.

"If we are forcefully separated, then sit on the floor and howl," Blossom advised. "Hah! No point in being quiet after we're caught. The noise might help Sayuri and them."

Sayuri murmured luck upon them, then turned to her comrades. "Where there is power, there must be machinery. Can anyone hear a kind of constant buzzing or unnatural whine?"

"My ears are not so tuned, but I might feel vibrations with my feet and hair," Autumn stepped forward.

Momo tipped his head and padded to the door left of the stairway.

I hear something moving that is not alive.

Autumn pressed her sensitive feet on the panels of the door, then stepped aside. "I think this is what you seek."

Sayuri cautiously lowered her hands. The glow faded and the dark left afterimages of light inside her eyes. She blinked to wash them away and cautiously pulled back the latch. Click. Creak. The hairs on her neck stood. But there was no light.

Boulder snuffled the air noisily. "No one," he grunted.

The open door funneled a sound toward them. The unmistakable hum of machinery.

"Come on!" Sayuri said excitedly.

"Bear goes first!" Boulder growled. "Bear's strongest. Sayuri might get hurt."

"No, let me," Autumn murmured. "I have eight legs and

every hair on my legs can feel movement around me. I can tap out the ground with more sensitivity than your rough paws can. Save your strength, Bear, for when we face the Patriarch."

"She's right," Sayuri said. "She is the best one for this job."

"Hmph!" Boulder snorted.

So the great spider went first, Sayuri and Boulder slightly behind and on either side, and Momo took the rear.

Sayuri did not call the light to her hands. If they were going to bring darkness to the whole city, she should hurry and get used to it. She trusted Autumn's senses to lead them, but the girl couldn't stop herself from holding a hand in front of her face.

The hum grew louder. Sayuri's heart thumped hard against her ribs. There must be someone guarding the room. And workers who kept the machine running. They inched more cautiously as the noise grew louder.

Then Sayuri saw a light escaping from a crack beneath a door. Shadows broke the light now and then, and she knew that creatures were moving around inside. The girl tapped the spider's back and Autumn stopped.

"We need to find out how many are inside the room," Sayuri whispered worriedly.

"I-I-I will go," said Dew, right next to Sayuri's ear. The girl gave a little jump. She had forgotten the toad was there!

"I-I-I will go. M-m-my skin can t-t-taste the air. I can count their scents."

"Okay," Sayuri nodded. "Just crawl under the door and

don't go further. It's bright in the room, and if you move they'll notice you. Be careful!" Sayuri kissed Dew on the nose and gently lowered her to the door. The brave toad wiggled through, and Sayuri and her comrades waited anxiously.

It felt like forever.

"What's taking her so long?" Sayuri whispered.

Patience, child.

"Bear breaks down the door?"

"No, hush," Autumn chimed.

Finally, Dew wiggled back and Sayuri scooped her up. Hugged her to her chest.

"S-s-sorry," Dew croaked. "I-I-I had trouble smelling them. Because they're f-f-faded."

"What do you mean?" Sayuri frowned. "They're not really there?"

"N-n-no, not like that. V-v-very little left of them. L-l-like the flowers after first frost."

"Could you tell if they had weapons?" Sayuri asked.

"D-d-don't worry. They're f-f-faded!"

Let us enter, child.

Sayuri took a deep breath. "Okay! I'm opening the door!" And she yanked back on the latch and they burst into the light.

36. THE AMPLIFICATION MACHINE

FOR A MOMENT, SAYURI WAS BLINDED BY THE SUDDEN GLARE and she stood in a daze. She blinked and blinked. The light was brilliant in the enormous room the size of a school gym. A strange humming emanated from the glittering back wall. It seemed to *pull* at Sayuri and she turned her face aside. Her companions, untroubled with the glaring light, roared past Sayuri. Boulder was a frightening sight; jaws wide open, his teeth yellow and sharp. Momo arched his back, fur standing on end. He looked three times his normal size. Autumn waved her long hairy legs about and that was enough. The creatures inside the room squeaked with terror and huddled together.

Sayuri blinked rapidly again. Shook her head. The creatures were hard to see. Dew was right. They were faded....

Two kappa, a large rat, and a huge snake stared in terror. Unlike the soldiers, their eyes weren't red. Did that mean they weren't his subjects? Sayuri rubbed her eyes, wondering if it was a trick of light. She could almost see right through them.

Their skin wasn't like the pale gleaming white of under-ground grubs. It was as if the material that made up their bodies was thinning into nothing. The creatures were almost transparent. They could harm no one.

Sayuri turned to the humming wall. The unnatural sound set her teeth on edge, like biting tin foil or the screech of nails being dragged across a chalkboard. Her fingers tingled, burned with the wrongness that filled the air.

The dazzlingly bright wall, Sayuri realized, was covered in mother-of-pearl! How many shells had it taken to cover the entire surface? Sayuri had only seen the forest, but there had to be an ocean somewhere. How heavy it must have been to carry so many abalone shells. And the work it must have taken to build the wall. Sayuri took a cautious step closer. The shells had been placed in a subtle pattern: the shape of an enormous spiral that bulged out slightly, like a vein beneath skin. And like a vein, it seemed to pulse with life, in time to the humming which filled the room.

The spiral was something the Old One had talked about. Was magic at work here? And how could the Patriarch use the same force to further his evil deeds?

A stone platform, the size of a small bed, was placed directly in front of the wall. Transparent tubes were attached to both ends of the stone "bed" and the tubes zigzagged on top of themselves like coiled intestines. They snaked up the entire wall, and Sayuri could see something flowing inside the hollow tubes. A glow of light pulsed in time with the humming of the wall as the substance was pulled upward, zigzagging through the passage. The transparent tubes drained into the mother-of-pearl wall close to the ceiling. The light that ran through the tubes must power the spiral in the wall!

The girl turned to the terrified creatures.

"We mean you no harm," Sayuri said gently. "Please tell us what this device does."

The two kappa glanced at each other, then stared at the snake. They shook their heads. The rat gnawed his lower lip with his big front teeth.

Sayuri crouched down. And the rat scampered toward the girl.

"No!" the kappa and the snake hissed. Their voices were faded too.

Sayuri extended her hand and the rat jumped into her palm. Nervously rubbed both hands over his nose and twitched his almost invisible whiskers.

"Thisss is the amplification room," the rat whispered. "Energy is amplified, made ssstronger, then it's used to power the whole cccity." The animal looked over both shoulders and curled tight into a small ball. As if to hide. "It is the power sssource for the dome as well."

"Ohhhhh!" wailed the other faded creatures. "The Patriarch will be angry. You should not have told. He said if we kept the motors running for five days, he would set us free! Now all is lost. He will make our lives worse living than dead!"

One of the kappa broke free from her faded companions. She looked wildly about as if she expected the Patriarch to step into the room. The other kappa tried to grab her wrist, but the first stumbled to the stone table.

"Nooo!" wailed the rat.

"Wha-?" Sayuri said, confused.

The desperate kappa crawled on the table and lay back flat against the surface. The stone around the kappa seemed to *lip* around the creature's body and a horrible sucking noise filled the air.

"Oh!" Sayuri gasped. "Stop her! Get her off!"

But the kappa, who had given up all hope, was drained past the point of recovery. The horrible sucking stone drank off every bit of living colour from the poor creature till there was nothing left except a transparent shell. The tubes that ran from the stone glowed even brighter with the life essence. Then the brittle shell of the drained kappa burst. All that was left was a tiny scattering of dust.

The remaining kappa and the snake wailed in thin voices.

"Bear will protect! Who is hurt!" Boulder snuffled the air in all directions.

"Child, tell us what you see," Autumn's voice rang out. The beautiful sound helped to break the evil spell in the air and Sayuri gasped for breath.

Peace, Momo murmured.

Sayuri lifted her hand so that the rat could perch on her free shoulder. Then she closed her eyes. Took three long breaths in and out until she had called calm back into her soul. She told her companions the evil workings of the stone table and what had happened to one of the poor kappa.

"What I don't understand is why you're still here," Sayuri said to the rat. "There are no guards to hold you. Why didn't you flee?"

"We are guarded by fear," the rat whispered, "and imprisoned by hope. The Patriarch promisssed our freedom if we could keep the ssstone fed for five days. Ssso we took turnss feeding the monsster and tearing each other away before the ssstone took everything. But every day, we are lesss than we were the day before." The rat shuddered.

"Guards brought us food so we would last longer. And they would sometimes have eyes they had plucked from those who succumbed to the Patriarch," the giant snake whispered. "The guards fed the eyes to the amplification machine. We didn't have to feed the stone as long on those days."

"Our eyes," Autumn said sadly. For all eight of hers had been stolen.

"The stone was first fed on the forest trees and plants the Patriarch had harvested. But the stone wanted flesh...." The remaining kappa shuddered.

"We can't just cut the power source and leave," the girl said grimly. "We must destroy this machine."

"Bear will smash it!" Boulder quivered with anger.

"Wait," Sayuri stroked the animal's head. "The Old One said 'cruelty calls cruelty.' If we wreak violence upon the stone, the stone might fight back."

"How can we destroy this evil without destruction?" Autumn chimed.

The great purple cat sat very still; only the tip of his tail flicked with his thoughts.

"Do you have an idea?" Sayuri asked the great cat.

The stone feeds, he mused. *What if it feeds on something that has no end...?*

Sayuri frowned. Was the cat playing one of his thinking games? She twisted her fingers together. The humming from the wall and the sucking stone fogged her mind.

"Something that has no end? Like what? Time? Or numbers?"

What if it feeds on something that never fills? The cat's tail flicked more quickly as he puzzled the problem. *What if we fed the stone with its own hunger?*

"Feed the stone with its own hunger?" Sayuri squeezed her eyes shut. Tried to imagine it. Hunger was always hungry and wanted food. If you fed the hunger with hunger, it would be a closed circuit instead of a one-way flow. Like she'd learned in school in science class, so very long ago. The hunger would get hungrier and try to consume more and more without ever getting full, until....

Yes!" Sayuri leapt. She felt toes scrabble on both her shoulders. "Sorry," she said to Dew and the rat. "All we need to do is rechannel the tubing from the wall back on to the top of the stone!"

"Slowly, child," Autumn said calmly. "Explain slowly."

Sayuri gulped, then inhaled slowly. Exhaled. "Momo said we should feed the stone with its own hunger. If we can break through the tubing, then we could turn the tubes back on to the surface of the stone table. The stone will be feeding on itself, on its own hunger in a continuous cycle. Its hunger will be fed by hunger, around and around, so much the stone will break down!"

More likely implode, Momo said drily.

"Implode! Implode!" Boulder swung his head about excitedly.

"We must hurry!" Sayuri remembered. "Blossom and the others must already be upstairs. Anything could be happening."

Sayuri gazed up at the transparent tubing. Shuddering, she reached out and touched the surface with her forefinger. The skin of the tube gave beneath the pressure. It wasn't solid at all! Frowning, she pressed with her finger again, as her eyes travelled up the length of the wall. Maybe, she thought, it not only looked like intestines, but it really *was* intestines! She jerked back her hand and shuddered. A glow surged in the place she had touched and she yelped with surprise. She wiped her tingling finger against her jeans. She gulped and stood straight. Intestines or not, the absorption stone had to be stopped.

THE CREATURES WORKED TOGETHER and Sayuri, now aided by the prisoners of the amplification room, had more eyes to help the blinded. They had a brief argument over where the tube should be cut down.

"As close to the bottom as possible," Sayuri suggested, gazing up at the slipperly height of the mother-of-pearl wall. "That'll be the easiest and quickest."

"But you s-s-said the tubing is filled with a glowing l-l-light," Dew croaked.

"Oh!" Sayuri kept on forgetting that Dew was on her shoulder. "Yes. The energy is being pulled upward slowly. The whole tubing is filled with the light."

"N-n-need to s-s-stop the energy s-s-source more quickly.

The light in the tubing will power the s-s-spiral even after we cut, if we cut from the bottom."

"What?" Sayuri asked impatiently.

"Yesssss," rat agreed. "The life force remaining in the tube will ffffeed the dome and keep the cccity lights lit for that much longer."

"We n-n-need the implosion as s-s-soon as possible," Dew explained.

And Blossom and the others await.

"How will we get up the wall?" Sayuri demanded. Hurry! Her heart pounded. Hurry up!

Momo and Autumn both touched the slick mother-of-pearl. Autumn tapped her sensitive hairy feet, finding minute crevasses. Her large heavy body started gracefully scaling the vertical wall.

"Ohhhhh!" the sighted creatures breathed in admiration.

"What's going on?! Bear wants to know!"

"Hush," Sayuri murmured. "Autumn is climbing up the wall."

"Bear's a good climber too," he bragged.

Sayuri hugged Boulder's neck fiercely. He was such a baby. Like her brother. "Yes," she smiled through wet eyes. "You're a good climber too. But you must save your strength for later, when we face the Patriarch."

Autumn walked up the wall like a weightless dancer. When she reached the top, she quickly webbed a sling to rest in, then dangled down a line.

"Someone must go up to cut through the tubes." Sayuri scanned her companions. Autumn was strong, but hoisting

Momo or Boulder was out of the question. Oh! She wished she'd brought a knife from the great dining hall! Sayuri gazed at her fingernails. Could she tear through the intestines? Were the walls of the tube fortified with some kind of protection?

"I will go," whispered the rat.

Sayuri awkwardly stared at the creature on her shoulder. "Are you sure?"

"I'm cccertain I can do it," the rodent nodded. The rat scampered up Autumn's line and was quickly at the top. The sound of gnawing joined the constant humming from the amplification wall. Everyone strained with their senses, held their breaths.

A great SPLOP! sounded as the tube the rat had gnawed burst away from the wall, whipping back and forth like an uncontrolled water hose. The rat clung on desperately as the tube flailed about like a thing alive. Golden light sprayed all over the room and dripped on to Sayuri's skin. She gasped, eyes wide, stared at her bare arms and saturated companions. "Is the stuff dangerous?" she squeaked.

The tube, finally empty, flopped on the ground. Rat weakly crawled off, panting.

"No," whispered the rat sadly. "It is only warm. We cannot be harmed by life force."

"Oh," Sayuri said in a small voice. Bit her lip. This terrible evil had gone on for far too long. "You rest, Rat. I will go." Sayuri set Dew on the ground. "Autumn, can you pull me up?"

"Tie the thread beneath your forelimbs," Autumn chimed. "But try holding your weight with your hands."

Sayuri gingerly grasped the spider's thread. It was fine, half the thickness of her pinky, but harder than steel and far more flexible. She tied a loop at the end of the line and stepped inside the circle. She raised the loop to her armpits, then gripped the thread where she had knotted it back on itself. "Okay!"

Sayuri shot up to the ceiling. "Stop!" she shouted.

"Ooops," Autumn giggled.

"Not funny," Sayuri muttered crossly.

Sayuri thought she could hear Momo snickering.

Autumn webbed another sling close to the remaining tube. Sayuri worked quickly. She bent her head and started chewing the pliant membrane. It was the same texture as balloons, but without the rubbery taste. Sayuri wrinkled her nose but didn't stop chewing. She tried not to imagine that she was chewing through intestines.

Sausages! she thought. She loved breakfast sausages and Jun had told her they were cased with intestines! That'd never bothered her before!

The skin started to give and a honey light seeped out, coating her hands. Sayuri wrapped one arm around the tube so it wouldn't spray wildly about the room. She chewed until her jaws ached and her face was glowing with spilled light. She was careful not to swallow the warmth that coated her lips. If the life and magic was drained from living creatures, their souls might have been trapped in the tubes as well.

She finally chewed through. The constant humming stopped. Golden liquid spilled all over her, but it was warm with life. And it was a liquid that somehow wasn't wet.

Autumn tied a new thread to the pipe and lowered it to the ground. Sayuri quickly followed and Autumn dropped down from the ceiling, knowing when to stop with the aid of her sensory hairs. The companions, who'd been waiting, raised a small cheer.

A horrifying suction slurped at the air. The tubes, empty of golden life and no longer attached to the amplification wall, sucked mindlessly for sustenance.

Sayuri cautiously gripped one of the limp tubes a good ten centimetres from the gaping hole. Rat wearily reached for the other tube. "Be careful," the girl warned. The suction pulled at her fingers, a numbing hollow ache that made her weary. Sayuri dragged the tube closer to the stone bed. The stone seemed to *reach* for her and she squeaked, dropped the tube onto the strange surface. The stone lipped around the tube like it was a giant straw.

"Let me, Rat," Sayuri cautioned. "I'll do it. You're weakened, so you might be pulled." Wearily, Sayuri placed the other tube onto the absorption stone. Two long tubes snaked from both ends of the bed and looped back into the top of the stone bed. The stone, feeding on itself, started to swell, the sides of the table bulging and shrinking. The sound of desperate suction rose louder and louder.

"We've got to get out of here!" Sayuri yelled. She lifted the toad and rat to her shoulders. The girl stumbled in the sudden darkness of the hallway, closely behind Autumn who led the way. They ran, lurched, groped through the darkness as the monstrous table started to scream.

37. THE SEARCH

FEAR FORCED THEM UP WINDING STAIRS, PANTING, GASPING, not even thinking that soldiers and guards must be about. They could hear the stone screaming, rising and growing, a bubble of sound expanding to the point of bursting.

They spilled out onto the main floor and Sayuri slammed the door behind her.

Filthy, sweaty, and stunned, they huddled in a small circle.

Something, thought Sayuri, we're supposed to do something. She stared stupidly. They were back in the main hall. She could see. Night pressed heavy in the long corridor and the small lights spaced evenly in small niches glowed a steady pale blue.

The power source hadn't been stopped!

"No!" Sayuri gasped. "It's impossible!"

What is it?

"The lights are still working!" Sayuri snarled.

"No," the rat whispered. "Our plan shhhould work.

There isss much energy running through a very large sssystem. It will take time for the remaining power to completely run out."

"What does Bear do now?" Boulder stood on his hind legs to sniff the air.

"We continue with the plan." Sayuri blinked nervously. What was the plan?! Ugh! What was wrong with her? She had to focus! Blossom! They were supposed to signal Blossom when the lights went out. "Light or dark, when the absorption machine implodes, there'll be panic. We can use it to face the Patriarch." Sayuri wondered if any of Blossom's people were hidden along the hallway. No guards anywhere. The Patriarch was overconfident. He must think that no one would rise against him in the center of his power.

"We must search out his quarters," Sayuri said grimly.

Boulder snuffled at the air. His nostrils flared in and out, as he turned a slow circle on his hind legs. "This way!" he pointed with his heavy paw. "Bear will never forget the way he smells!"

"N-n-nor I," whispered Dew fiercely into Sayuri's ear.

They scurried along the hallway, hearts pounding, senses stretched to the limit, waiting for the absorption machine to burst apart. The bear sniffed the floor, raising his head now and then to catch wisps of scent in the air. He turned through an open doorway, stairs rising up again. "This way!" Boulder grunted.

Sayuri turned to the faded snake and kappa. "You must stay here," she said. Cupped the rat from her shoulder and set him on the ground. "You are still weak from your ordeal.

Hide somewhere until the dome has broken, then tell all of the eyeless ones that it is safe to flee the city."

The snake and kappa bowed. The rat stared at the girl. "If you ever have need, I and my kind will alwaysss come. Call for Bright Leaf." The rat bowed low, then scampered down the hall.

Sayuri and her companions climbed up. The stairway opened into another hall, smaller than the one they had come from. An ornate golden door glittered under the pale blue lights and the bear sniffed silently, padded softly on his huge paws. He said nothing, only pointed at the door with his nose, nodded his blunt head.

From deep beneath the bowels of the Patriarch's fortress, an immense roar bellowed and swallowed itself at the same time, shaking the solid stone walls and the floor beneath their feet as the percussion rippled outward in all directions.

"Now!" Sayuri screamed.

"BRAAAAAAAAACK!" the toad croaked so loudly that Sayuri almost fell over.

They burst into the Patriarch's room as the distant thunder of Blossom and his companions roaring out of their hiding places filled the lower floors of the fortress.

38. REUNION

"WELL, WELL, WELL," A MELODIOUS VOICE SEEMED TO smile, "how entertaining you've proved to be. How very *industrious.*"

The Patriarch's room was lit brilliantly by a chandelier of cut glass. The facets angled perfectly so that light cascaded downward like water catching sunlight. Books lined two walls and the fox sat at a low desk, writing on a sheet of parchment. Ornately carved wood paneling decorated the wall behind. The stone floor was covered with a soft rug and Sayuri curled her icy filthy toes into the luxury. Soft as Momo's belly. The girl looked down. It wasn't rug. It was *fur.* How many creatures had he skinned to cover the whole floor?

"Child," the Patriarch said softly, "all my riches I would have shared with you."

"I would have nothing to do with you and your evil ways!" Sayuri spat.

The fox tipped back his head and laughed with genuine amusement. "The young are so earnest," he smiled. "So very moral." He set down his paintbrush and stood, clasping his unnaturally human hands behind his back. "You call my ways evil, yet what do you know of it? Do you know evil well enough to call it so? Do you imagine you are good?"

"Don't listen to him," Autumn said, the pure sounds of her bell-like voice breaking the growing spell of confusion.

The Patriarch frowned slightly, then lifted one hand and waved casually, as if he was turning away a plate of appetizers. Some strange sensation filled the air and Sayuri's fingers tingled painfully, desperately.

The great spider, the bear, and Momo sat stiffly in a row, their mouths sealed shut. The toad curled her toes into the cloth of Sayuri's T-shirt. The girl could feel how the creature pressed flat against her. The fox had not seen Dew. Or had, but had not thought her worthy of restraint. Sayuri whipped around and glared at her enemy.

The fox's nose was slightly wrinkled. "Such unseemly and messy company you keep. Do you keep them because you think they're *good?*"

"You call them unseemly, yet you are the one who maimed them! There is no question that you are evil!"

"Don't be tiresome," the Patriarch sighed. "What would a child know of difficult choices? I am part of the evolutionary process, but I am also a catalyst. Life moves slowly from day to day. Food, lessons, food, chores, food, sleep. That is a child's life. Exchange lessons for play, perhaps twice a week. The pattern repeats as you grow." The fox strolled back and forth, hands still clasped behind his back. "You become an adult. Food, work, food, work, sleep. This daily repetition, generation after generation, and what has been gained, hmmmm?"

"Y-you're wrong!" Sayuri spluttered. Blood pounding hot in her ears. "You say it like that, but there's more! People have dreams and hopes and they love and share! Their lives are important, even if you don't think so!"

Good, child, Momo murmured. *But calmly. Breathe. The creature wishes to goad you into making a mistake. He could strike you with magic but does not. Keep him talking. I will try to help. I cannot move, but he cannot hear my words.*

"Dreams! Hopes! Pah!" the fox snorted. "Does a human ask the ants and the beetles if they have hopes and dreams before destroying their homes to build his own? My vision is vast. I am not bound to the insect's details. I am pushing my world into a new existence. Power will feed power, and I will bind the many worlds into my own." The Patriarch smiled with all his teeth and his eyes glinted mischievously. "I would have you join me, child. You hold power, though I do not understand the source, since you come from a world with little magic. I'm intrigued. And I would rather have you join me than forcibly take your power for my own."

Sayuri took a step backward. A hand on her lips. "You're crazy," she whispered.

"Ah!" the Patriarch exclaimed. "Evil, crazy, what you call me matters little. They are just names for things you don't understand. What matters is who wins." The fox humbly lowered his head, then peeked upward. "And I always win." He whipped his face to the wood paneling behind the desk and clapped his hands twice, sharply.

A cleverly hidden door opened. A tousled black head of hair. A small child crawled into the room. The child stood up and smacked at the knees of his overalls, then brushed the dust off his hands.

"Keiji?" Sayuri's voice wobbled, hot tears filling her eyes.

"Yes," he answered politely. As if he was speaking to a stranger on the phone.

"I'm your sister," the girl gently explained, rubbing the back of her hand over her eyes. "I was looking all over for you."

"Oh," Keiji said. He stared at his fingernails, then glanced at the creatures sitting stiffly next Sayuri.

"We have to get home to Kimi and Jun," Sayuri softly explained. "Remember?"

"No." Keiji shrugged, almost apologetically.

Sayuri bit her lip.

The Patriarch didn't interrupt, just watched the exchange, an unreadable look in his eyes.

The girl opened her arms wide. "Can you come here, duckling?" she called, using her father's endearment.

Keiji frowned. Shook his head as if memory was a small insect flying about his head. He took a faltering step toward Sayuri, another, one more – then he clasped a hand over his heart and flinched, as if some invisible thing had yanked him backward with a chain.

"Oh!" the child gasped, then the dull look came back to his eyes. He hunkered near the Patriarch's feet.

"I'm sorry. He cannot stray too far from me. I've forged a chain with his memories, and we're quite attached, you might say," the fox laughed silently.

"Set him free," Sayuri said numbly. "My friends will lead him home, just set him free. And I will stay with you...."

No! Once you start obeying, it becomes harder and harder to listen to your own voice. He has no desire to keep your brother. He only wants you to go to him of your own accord. For only then is his victory over you complete.

"Yes," the Patriarch sighed, smiling with every single tooth. He took a step closer. "That's an obedient child."

"Sucker!" Sayuri taunted, thrusting out her chin. She turned around and wagged her butt back and forth. Then she laughed and laughed and the sound of her voice shook the chandelier, the pieces tinking against each other.

"What!" roared the fox, "you dare ridicule me?! Guards!" the Patriarch bellowed. "Guards!" He narrowed his eyes and licked his lips, sliding his unearthly thumbs over his fingers. "I tire of childish games," he hissed. "If you do not give me what I want, I have no qualms about taking it!"

In the outer hallway, a door crashed open and Sayuri shook with the reverberations. Then muffled voices shouted, ran down past their closed door until the noise was swallowed by the other end of the hall. Thudding feet tramped past in pursuit. No one entered the Patriarch's chambers.

"Well, well," the fox raised his eyebrows, "you surprise me."

"We have no fight with you," Sayuri said quietly. "We only wish to leave this place and return to our homes."

The Patriarch lifted his shoulders in a shrug, his palms facing upwards. "But how would I power the city? I must have my beautiful lights. So you see, the insects are still needed. I do apologize. Perhaps you'll rest more easily if I tell you it's for a good cause...."

The chandeliers flickered. A flutter of light like moth wings. Bright.

Darkness.

Sayuri's heart drummed in her ears. The room was dark. Where was Keiji? She could make out his form and those of her immobilized friends. It was not completely dark. The power had finally run out of the absorption machine, extinguishing all the artificial lights, but dawn was breaking and a greenish-grey light seeped through the window. Their blind companions had no advantages over the kappa soldiers. It was too late.

And if Sayuri could see, the Patriarch with his fox eyes could see even more.

"What have you done?" he asked in a quiet voice.

"The absorption machine is destroyed," Sayuri gasped. "We will leave now. We want no trouble."

The fox took a step toward the girl, his pale hands gleaming unnaturally in the dim room. "You have been nothing but trouble," the Patriarch smiled. His teeth glinted.

Hold steady, Momo soothed. *Just a little longer.*

"And now," the fox sadly shook his head, "I'll have to swallow your power against your will. I'm sorry I couldn't convince you to give it to me. Because it hurts dreadfully when it must be taken, hmmm?"

Sayuri trembled so hard that her thoughts were jumbled in her head. Helpless, wordless, she couldn't even call for help.

"Help," she whispered hoarsely.

"Ahhh, such a shame when a person must plead," the Patriarch beamed. Another step closer to the girl. She could smell his animal breath, but an older, decayed stench rose from the pit of his soul and the girl jerked her head away.

The fox lifted one hand and cupped Sayuri's chin. The touch of his fingers on her face filled the girl with rage.

"STOP!!!" she screamed, just as Dew's enormous toad voice blasted directly into the Patriarch's face. The fox stumbled backward, raising one hand to protect himself.

The Patriarch had lost his concentration. Momo, Boulder, and Autumn broke free from his spell and scrambled to their feet.

Then a strange creaking shudder rippled through the ceiling and Sayuri tipped back her head, raising her arm in case anything fell.

The ceiling was wrenched completely off!

39. THE GREAT FIGHT

"LITTLE BIRDIE! IS THAT YOU?" IN THE GROWING light of dawn, an enormous head peered into the exposed room and Sayuri gaped at a huge and fierce blue face.

"Great Blue Oni!" the girl squeaked.

Blue Oni turned his pitted and scarred face and yelled over his shoulder. "I FOUND HER! SHE'S STILL CHIRPING!"

Oh! A surge of hope warmed the girl's chest. Her eyes wet. Her vision in the baths! Old One had come! She had come with tanuki soldiers.

"We're saved!" she laughed, hopping up and down. "We've won!"

The Patriarch snarled and he spun around, scooped Keiji under his arm and slipped through the small door.

"No!" Sayuri screamed. She ran to the panel, but the door had disappeared.

She banged her fists against the wood until Momo pulled her away.

Stop it, the cat said distinctly. *You're wasting time.*

266

Sayuri snapped back. Ran to the center of the room. "Blue Oni!" she shouted. "Please lower us outside!"

"OKAY!" the oni placed his great dirty hand, palm upward, on the floor. Sayuri and Momo leapt on, Boulder and Autumn waiting for the second trip.

The streets of the city were filled with tanuki and kappa. The tanuki soldiers shouted with once voice when they saw Sayuri in the oni's hand. "Ganbare!" they roared as they clashed with the Patriarch's soldiers anew. And for all that the kappa outnumbered the proud tanuki, the green soldiers were pressed back, for they fought not with true loyalty and belief, but from fear of their leader.

Sayuri leapt off the oni's fingers and shouted her thanks. She wanted to shout encouragement to her tanuki friends, but she only whispered a blessing for their safety.

Her brother. The Patriarch had her brother.

Momo jumped lightly beside her as the girl frantically looked about. The gourd bumped against her hip as she ran, ducking beneath a spear and stumbling into an alley.

"He could be anywhere!" Sayuri shouted over the din of battle.

Search not for the fox, but for your brother.

Keiji, the girl thought. Keiji, she called, closing her eyes. She was soaring. High above the city, higher than the oni, she flew weightless as she cast her senses for her brother...there! By the fountain! The fountain she'd seen in the Old One's window so very long ago.

"They're at the fountain. In the city centre!"

"To your right!" Dew croaked in the girl's ear.

Sayuri jumped. She'd forgotten all about the poor thing again. The toad might have fallen off and she would never have known!

"I can catch the scent of water on my skin."

"Thank you!" Sayuri gasped, running already. "Momo!" she shouted.

Right behind you, the cat purred, *I can "see" from your thoughts where you put your feet and follow you.*

Sayuri didn't waste her breath answering. She ran even faster, the gourd swinging from side to side, her bare feet smacking the cobblestone road.

"Left, now!" Dew gasped. Clinging desperately with her toes.

Sayuri veered left and the small side street opened into a large square. A pretty stone fountain spurted water, and she could see the Patriarch's brocade jacket glinting in the bright morning sun, her brother still clasped beneath his arm. Keiji's arms and legs hung limply. Sayuri ran faster.

The Patriarch wasn't alone.

Another fox. A kappa.

Sayuri stumbled to a stop, panting heavily, Momo one step behind her. Sayuri stared from the Patriarch to Machigai and Echo. The kappa's eyes were still black. They hadn't been replaced with the Patriarch's red orbs.

"I'm so glad that you joined us," the older fox flicked his tail. He loosened his grip on Keiji and the boy slithered to the stones. Sayuri took a step toward him, but Momo lightly batted the back of her jeans to still her.

The Patriarch was pulling his hands together to triangulate his fingers and thumbs.

Sayuri's fingers tingled wildly, a burn that ran up her hands and into her forearms. The hairs on her neck and arms stood electric. Dew shifted uneasily, then leapt from the girl's shoulder to land on the rim of the fountain.

"It's not too late to stop," Echo soothed, her beautiful voice trickling coolly along their overheated senses.

Sayuri darted a look at her former friend. She didn't know whose side she was on. Don't assume, the girl reminded herself. Trust no one.

"Oh hoh, hoh, hoh!" Machigai laughed softly. Though he hadn't shifted into the form of the foxgirl. He cautiously walked behind the Patriarch so that now the creatures were spread wider than the old fox could see all at once. Momo, hearing Machigai's motion, followed his direction and Dew hopped over to make the circle complete.

The Patriarch faced only the girl.

Sayuri swallowed, a hard dry rock in her throat. How could she fight the fox? His powers were so great. And if Keiji was shackled to the Patriarch by his memories, what would happen if the chain suddenly snapped?

"That's right," the old fox smiled. "You would be wise not to resist me if you care for your brother."

The sound of fighting and shouting could be heard in the distance. Blue Oni's booming voice muttering and chuckling. The Old One's people would soon win, but what about Keiji?

"Come, Sayuri." The Patriarch's voice sounded so sweet the girl took an unwitting step closer. It was the first time he'd uttered her name and the sound pulled. "A part of you wants to know the pleasures of power. And I have so much to teach you. Listen to that voice. For what you think of as your good and my evil are in reality twins...."

Sayuri closed her eyes. If she took one step more, she would be lost. Lost in the swirl of desire for desire, her own need above all others, and it would taste so good. Because she wouldn't ever have to feel guilty....

"NO!" Echo screamed. Sayuri's eyes jerked open and she watched the world move in slow motion all around her. Echo, leaping across the square, seemed to float as if she was in outer space. The kappa dove, arching through the thick air, tackling the Patriarch. The hold he had over Sayuri's mind snapped.

Sayuri dropped to her knees.

Snarling, the Patriarch turned his glowing hands to blast Echo with a stream of red light.

"Echo!" Sayuri gasped.

The kappa sprawled on the cobblestones, her skin blanched of colour.

Machigai snarled and leapt on his great uncle, snapping, biting, the two foxes a blur of copper fur. They flickered in and out of forms both human and monstrous. Sayuri dodged their twisting bodies to reach for her brother who lay limply on the ground. His face was pale and his hair stuck wetly to his cold forehead. He muttered something and raised a hand to his chest. Sayuri slipped her arms beneath his neck and knees and carried him to where Echo lay.

The snarling voices of the foxes were horrible and Sayuri couldn't tell who was who, could only stare helplessly. Keiji cradled in her lap, she sat leaning against the fountain. She stroked Echo's cheek.

Momo stared blindly, following the fight with his thoughts and ears, but he could do nothing either. The cat tilted his head to one side, an ear tipped back, then gracefully leapt out of the square and down a narrow street.

Dew jumped into the fountain and disappeared beneath the spray of water.

Sayuri closed her eyes.

In the unsight, Sayuri saw a light begin to glow. Brighter and brighter, it was a mane of brilliant white hair. A broad weathered face formed within the glow and eyes glinted with the wisdom and laughter of a thousand lives. Sayuri unconsciously raised her hand. The Woman Who Watches! An unseen wind blew white hair over Yamanba's face and she faded, as another face began to form, a face so familiar Sayuri could only react with an ache in her chest, couldn't call out the name.

"Anyone give you a hard time just kick their butt!" the words rang inside Sayuri's head. Black eyeliner heavy on eyelids. Short cropped hair. Fading. And before the image of her mother disappeared, she heard Jun softly call out, "Duckling...."

Warm tears trickled down Sayuri's cheeks. Her hands were warm and she opened her eyes, stared at fingers that had formed a triangle on their own. A short gleaming katana of light hovered weightlessly between her fingers. Her mouth an "O" of wonder, Sayuri gingerly clasped the slightly curved grip of the sword. The blade dazzled the eye, the lines gracefully curving upward into a diagonal point. The cast of the light was peculiar. Echo had not one shadow, but two. And the second shadow was sitting up and watching Sayuri's actions. Keiji's face looked the same, but he was also a flower. The centre so bright she had to look away. And she saw a green stem growing from his heart. It was twined with a dark chain that was wrapped around the Patriarch's wrist.

Machigai and the Patriarch burst apart, and the foxes crouched low, panting and bleeding. The Patriarch spat out some fur and Sayuri stared, horrified, for Machigai was staggering, bleeding from his neck.

"No more!" Sayuri cried. And the panting foxes turned toward her.

The Patriarch grabbed the dark chain that was fixed to Keiji's heart and started to gather it up, one hand over the other, the unconscious boy dragged over the stones.

Yellow fire roared through Sayuri's body and blinded her vision, the katana a blaze of light. She leapt high, the sword held above her head, and swung with a scream, the blade of fire cutting through the Patriarch's wrists, the inhuman hands falling off like wooden stumps.

And as the light from the sword slowly faded, the green vine of memory snaked back to its home inside Keiji's heart.

The Patriarch gaped at his handless wrists. There was no blood.

Sayuri started shaking. Unclenched her hands as the weightless katana faded into tiny motes of light.

She lurched sideways and retched.

40. JUSTICE

"Your life spiral has taken many turns," an old voice creaked.

Sayuri numbly looked up. A withered old crone of a creature. Faded fur and great sagging breasts on a round belly. Eyes like her grandmother's.

"Old One!" Sayuri gasped. She ran to the aged tanuki and almost knocked her over. "I'm sorry. I'm so sorry," the girl gasped, shuddering with sobs.

"There, there," the Old One stroked her brittle claws through the girl's hair. "Why are you sorry, my girl?"

Sayuri turned to face the Patriarch, who sat on the ledge of the fountain. He dabbled his handless wrists in the water, a strange expression on his face. Keiji had curled up in deep sleep, the sun heating the stones and keeping him warm. Machigai sat on his haunches. His long tongue hung out.

"I-I-I could have done things differently. So much fighting...so many hurt." Sayuri dragged the heel of her palm over her eyes.

"You did what you had to do," the Old One said firmly. She gripped the girl's shoulder. "Not without consequences. But you made the best decisions you could in the circumstances you found yourself. That's the most anyone can ask for."

"My brother. I don't –" Sayuri gasped for air.

"Shhhh. Rest easy. Your brother is like one in a deep sleep. His memories are twining through his body and he will sleep like a bear in winter until he is whole."

"Oh," Sayuri sighed. He would be whole. She had found him and he would be okay. A strange anger flared briefly. For none of this would have happened if he hadn't gone after Momo so very long ago. But Sayuri let go of that too. And relief bloomed inside her. Keiji's face looked peaceful, his hand pressed loosely against his heart.

"The question is," a deep voice rang out, "what will you do now?"

Sayuri looked up. Momo was back! And the cat had brought someone with her.

A huge tanuki woman. She was a head taller than Sayuri, her arms and legs thick with muscle, flesh, and fur. Her chest was broad and her face sharp. Eyes dark and ageless as a starless night.

Sayuri gaped up at the powerful figure. She wondered if she ought to bow. "I don't know," the girl answered.

The tanuki woman strode toward Sayuri and gently clasped her paw on the girl's shoulder.

"Thank you, child," the powerful tanuki smiled. "You broke the spell that was cast upon me in the depths of Tanuki

Mountain. I had been asleep for one hundred tanuki ages and my soul had almost turned to stone when you left a small lamp of magic."

"Great Mother Tanuki," Sayuri's eyes rounded. "Was that really you in the tunnel behind the Blue Oni's cave?"

The Great Mother chuckled. "The cave used to be mine. What a stink Blue Oni has made of it! I followed the path of your passage and came to the Mountain's Blood Clan. The Old One sensed trouble and opened a window. I saw my old companion, Mischief. Though he calls himself the Patriarch now."

"He was your friend?!" Sayuri gasped.

"Yes," the Great Mother said mildly, "and a great player of Go."

"He tricked you and imprisoned you. He's killed countless innocent creatures!" Sayuri exclaimed.

Machigai limped to where Sayuri stood with her hands clenched into fists.

"Yes, he has." The Great Mother stared intently into the girl's eyes. "Would you do to him what he has done to others?"

Sayuri spun away, shivering. Stared at her sleeping brother. She suddenly felt cold and she rubbed her hands over her bare arms. "I don't know," she muttered fiercely. Caught sight of another figure still sprawled on the stones.

Echo! Echo had saved her life!

The girl stumbled to the fallen kappa and peered inside the bowl. Empty. She lifted the kappa, who was as light as her brother, and gently set her in the water. The Patriarch moved farther down along the curve of the fountain, but he didn't leave. He turned his back. Toad came swimming over to the girl and the kappa. She sniffed the kappa's skin and crawled up on the ledge.

"She is w-w-weak," Dew croaked. "She is like the faded ones. W-w-worse."

"No!" Sayuri clasped the kappa awkwardly to her chest. She couldn't die. After all that had happened. Everything endured. Echo couldn't die now. Sayuri held her friend tightly, as if she could pass some of her life into the kappa. Something pressed uncomfortably against her hip. The water gourd! Sayuri lifted Echo and propped her against the side of the fountain.

"Please help me," Sayuri called.

Machigai limped over to the kappa and leaned to hold her up. Momo sat on the other side, and Sayuri unstopped the gourd. A rich smell of minerals, blood, rose from the mouth of the hyotan. The body, Sayuri thought. The healing water smells of the body! With trembling hands she poured some of the precious liquid into Echo's bowl. The water stayed! They held the kappa upright and a trace of green blossomed beneath her skin, spreading throughout her body. Echo's eyelids fluttered. Blinked. Her dark eyes shiny and wet.

"Sayuri," the kappa whispered, like water over pebbles.

"Oh, Echo!" Sayuri clasped the slim green creature close, as if she would never let go. "I'm sorry I doubted. Thank you," the girl whispered fiercely. "It was you who let us out of our dungeon, wasn't it?"

Echo smiled weakly.

"Thank you," Sayuri hugged the kappa close.

Echo kissed Sayuri. "You have taught me much. Thank you for naming me when I could not name myself. Thank you for caring for me even when I was so weak as to succumb to the Patriarch. I am Fen of the Willow Valley."

Sayuri bowed awkwardly. "I am pleased to know you, Fen of the Willow Valley."

"Oh, hoh, hoh, hohhhh!" the foxgirl laughed. A grubby hand over her mouth.

Sayuri turned to the mischievous fox. "You stop that!" she scolded. "You've lost blood and you should save your energy."

The Old One shuffled to the fox and held up his chin. Clucked with concern. "This needs to be taken care of."

Sayuri left Echo in Momo's care and turned to the fox. She held the gourd in her hand and gave it a little shake. The slosh was lighter than before, but the girl raised the hyotan to pour some healing water over Machigai's throat.

The fox stopped the girl's arm with his dainty paw. "I think," he smiled gently, "you were saving that for something."

"No," Sayuri shook her head. "No. There's enough." She shook the fox's paw off her arm and poured the mineral-rich water over his torn throat.

"Ahhh," Machigai sighed.

Great Mother Tanuki sat next to the Patriarch, and they looked so casual, as if they'd been strolling on a sunny afternoon and had stopped for a small rest.

"That was quite a spell you cast upon me in the cave," Mother Tanuki shook her head.

"Yes, wasn't it?" the Patriarch smirked. "It cost dearly, that spell. I had to pay for it with my paws. Then I spelled new hands to grow, human hands, so that I could work a different magic. I'm not sure that was the most clever choice. But after the hands grew in, I couldn't exchange them. My magic changed in ways I hadn't imagined." The fox shrugged, staring at his bloodless stumps. "Perhaps the human child has done me a great service."

How could the Great Mother Tanuki treat the Patriarch like a friend? Sayuri scowled fiercely. Didn't murder count for anything in this place? Didn't they care that the criminal had maimed and destroyed?

What would you like to have done upon the Patriarch then? What do you think is just? Momo asked.

"In my world," Sayuri stated, "we punish criminals."

"How?" Dew croaked sleepily. Beads of water starting to dry on her pebbly skin.

"Well, we put them in prison. Don't you want justice? Look at you, Momo! You are blind because of the Patriarch!"

The Old One and The Great Mother gazed upon the girl with interest. The Patriarch dipped his wrists in the water again and circled his stumps around. The sight of it almost made Sayuri gag. Because she had been the one to maim him.

How will prison help the fox? How will prison change him?

"It might not change him," Sayuri granted, "but it keeps him from doing more harm! He loses his freedom as payment for his crimes. In my world, he'd be locked up until the day he died."

Would it not be better for all if he were healed? Then he

would be whole. And could start to "pay for his crimes," as you call it, by undoing the harms that he has wrought.

"And what about the dead?" Sayuri spat.

"That cannot be undone," the Old One finally spoke. "But someone healed will have the conscience to bear the weight of those deaths for the rest of his life." The ancient tanuki shook her grey muzzle sadly. "A terrible burden, and one that is borne every waking moment. No, healing is not such an easy thing."

Sayuri thought long. The sun was hot on her head and she shifted so that her shadow lay across her brother's restful face. The fountain behind them continued to spray and a light breeze blew a cool mist upon her cheek.

And what about me? Sayuri thought. What have I done? Your good and my evil are twins, the Patriarch had said. Was that why a fire burned so hot inside her chest?

Sayuri lifted the gourd. She pursed her lips to stop the flow, then trickled a few drops into her mouth. Swallowed. Coolness spread down her throat, into her belly, and seeped through every living cell. The girl sighed long and a heavy weight lifted from her shoulders and blew away. She shook the water gourd once more.

There was only enough left for one.

She stood up. The hardest steps she'd ever taken. She approached the Patriarch.

The fox looked up at the girl, squinting, for the sun was directly behind her head.

"Raise your arms," Sayuri said.

The Patriarch lifted his stumps from the fountain and

held them before him.

Sayuri breathed in deeply. Released. Poured the last of the healing water over the fox's wrists.

And as they all watched, fur began to grow, bones, muscles, simultaneously, a fast-motion film. The Patriarch's paws grew back, no longer human, but copper-furred and clawed with sharp black nails.

The Patriarch gazed upon his new paws, a whimsical look in his eyes. "How miraculous," he said softly, then patted the backs of Sayuri's hands in thanks. He stood upright for a moment, shrugging out of his beautiful blue jacket. When it fell to the ground, he dropped onto all fours. The fox click-clacked away down a side street until he disappeared.

"His healing begins," the Great Mother said sadly, "and his punishment has begun."

Hot salty tears filled Sayuri's eyes. She didn't know why. The empty gourd fell out of her hand and clattered on the stones, rolling to the side. Machigai pressed his cold nose into her palm and Sayuri smiled sadly.

41. A TIME TO HEAL

THE DAY WAS LONG WITH TOIL AND THE CARE OF THE injured. The Patriarch's kappa soldiers had been quickly subdued by the tanuki and the Blue Oni. The rest of the hot day was taken with turning the great dining hall into a hospital. The Old One and the Great Mother Tanuki wove spells of healing until they were exhausted. Sayuri had tried to call the magic back to her hands, but the familiar tingle was gone. She hadn't been injured, but exhaustion swamped every cell in her body. She made a nest for Keiji, who healed within deep sleep. She curled around her little brother and thought about nothing. And nothing had never felt better.

Fen of Willow Valley, who had been Echo, took care of the kappa soldiers. Sayuri had broken the Patriarch's hold over the creatures when she cut off his hands. The kappa's red eyes had dried in their sockets and dribbled out like sand. They were blind and filled with despair. Fen soothed them with her voice like water and spoke of hope and healing.

Word had spread about the great battle and creatures

came from afar with food and medicine. Blue Oni, with the help of Old One, shrunk in size until he was no taller than Sayuri and took control over the vast kitchens, ordering people about with his loud voice. His hearty broths of wild burdock, fish, miso, and greens filled bellies and gladdened hearts. Boulder, claiming to help the oni, stayed in the kitchen too. Autumn generously wove sheets and sheets of the strongest silk for bandages and blankets and Blossom turned out to be a gentle nurse. Dew disappeared to explore the fortress and Momo slept next to Sayuri in a large patch of sunlight.

Sayuri hadn't seen the Patriarch at all. It seemed no one had.

So the days passed with healing and rest.

Sayuri soaked in the central pool of the baths. Machigai had discovered the water was still hot and Sayuri had been overjoyed. "They must be natural hot springs!" she exclaimed. Those well enough started taking to the baths and the healing came faster.

Keiji began waking, though most of his days were still filled with sleep. One day, Sayuri took Keiji to the baths and kept him afloat with two hands beneath his back. The dark room was lit with small lamps that flickered shapes in the humidity. Keiji gazed at the twining mist with eyes bemused.

"Is this a dream?" Keiji asked.

"I don't know," Sayuri said softly. "If it is, it's pretty long."

Keiji laughed and closed his eyes.

"Do you remember what happened?" Sayuri asked gently.

Her brother nodded his head. "It's far away, though. Like a long time ago."

"That's good," Sayuri smiled. Wondered if Keiji would start forgetting this all happened when they got back home. And when he grew into adulthood, he would look back and shake his head at the imaginative boy he had been.

She'd never forget, Sayuri vowed. When they went back home....

"I want to go home," Keiji said. His eyes closed. His cheeks were red with the heat.

"Soon," Sayuri whispered. "When the time is right. Momo said he'd take us back to Yamanba's house in the mountains. Remember?"

"Yes," Keiji murmured, then fell asleep in his sister's arms.

Machigai paddled over, his sharp nose thrust into the air. "That cat would do well with a proper bath," the fox sniffed.

Sayuri laughed. Momo had breathed one draught of all the wetness and had stalked away, tail held straight up and down. Dew had approved of the moisture but not of the temperature. She'd started making plans for a cold pool in the empty room next door.

"I can hold your brother," Machigai offered. Sayuri smiled gratefully. The fox took her place and she glided backward, arms outstretched. The heat and water lifted her spirits and the steam beguiled. Sayuri stared at everything and nothing. The familiar feeling of the present faded away, her consciousness lifting outside her body. Her focus was not on what she saw but on what might be, and the wisps of moisture coalesced into an animal shape, an animal with a long pointed snout. The creature loping through the unnatural plains toward the city without a dome, something held in its jaws, a large basket....

Sayuri opened her eyes.

"What is it?" Machigai's ears were pointed directly at the girl, his eyes glinting.

"The 'Patriarch' is coming back." The girl jumped from the pool and dressed quickly. Held out a towel to carry her sleeping brother in. "Come on."

THEY HURRIED TO THE MAIN HALL and Sayuri handed Keiji to Blossom. The gruff tengu had taken to nursing with a great passion and bossily demanded that Autumn weave him new towels.

Old One and the Great Mother Tanuki worked patiently at the long dining table turned work table. Some tubing had been salvaged from the absorption room, and the two tanuki looked more like engineers as they drew out an elaborate plan.

"You know," the Great Mother mused, "a city isn't necessarily a bad idea. It could be a centre of study and the advancement of magic. This fortress could be a School of Higher Arts."

"Hmph," the Old One snorted. "Not a bad idea in theory. But a city needs power to be maintained. See what your old companion turned to."

"True," Great Mother mused, tapping a clawed finger against her furry chin. "If we used all our powers to keep the city running, we'd have none left to develop!"

Sayuri jumped up on a spare patch of the long table. Swung her legs thoughtfully, her body still flushed from the heat in the baths....

"The baths!" she shouted and Machigai leapt.

"Please!" he rolled his eyes. Paws clamped over his ears.

Sayuri ignored him, a smile spilling across her face. "The baths are hot because they tap into natural springs! You could dig deeper to hotter water and it could be used to power the city!"

Someone barked a muffled laugh. They looked up. The Patriarch stood in the doorway. His glossy fur was dull with dust and dehydration. His muzzle had aged in the days since his disappearance and the fur was whiter than the Old One's. He held a large basket in his jaws. The fox click-clacked closer to the table and carefully set down his load. The enormous basket was filled to the brim with dark fruit. Perfectly round and a purple almost black, they glittered in the lamplight. "A power source right beneath me the whole time and I never saw it." The fox smiled rather sadly at the girl. "You continue to amaze me."

Sayuri, feeling awkward, said nothing. She jumped from the table and crouched next to the basket, gently touching the orbs with a fingertip. The fruit felt slightly warm and moist.

"Don't eat them, child," the old fox murmured. "The See Berries I will magic into eyes for those I have blinded."

Sayuri jerked her hand back. For now the berries looked less like fruit and more like a basket of eyes.

"Iya, iya, iyaaaa," the Old One crooned. "See Berries, yes. That might do." She turned to the old fox and nodded approvingly. "You have journeyed far and fast to find these mountain berries."

"It is nothing." The old fox bowed with a gallant grace, then sat on his haunches, weariness settling into his bones. "I have thought long and hard while I ran over the lands I ordered to be destroyed. A great wrong I have done and the tasks facing me will take the remainder of my life. I would welcome an apprentice to pass my lore to and help me in my work." The old fox tilted his head at Machigai.

Machigai shimmered into the shape of the foxgirl, raising both hands to cover her giggling mouth. "I would be honoured, Patriarch."

The old fox raised a small paw. "I beg you, call me not by that name, for that one has wrought much damage. I would be pleased if you call me Haru, for though I am old, new life has grown, like spring come to winter."

"Haru," everyone murmured. "We are pleased to meet you."

"Bah!" the Old One snorted. "And I would have taken the fox home to my clan to live the pleasant life of a tanuki!

The foxgirl laughed, shimmered into the tatty tanuki shape he had assumed when he had played his great trick upon the Mountain's Blood Clan. He leapt to the ancient leader and licked her withered snout with his long pink tongue. The Old One pushed the tanuki-shaped fox away.

"Be off with you!" she grouched, though a smile spread across her face.

"You must rest first, Haru," the Great Mother commanded. "For the magic you propose will take much strength. Bathe, eat, and rest, and we will ready the maimed."

Haru bowed, then trotted to the baths, Machigai leaping lightly beside him.

Sayuri yawned enormously, and the Great Mother turned to her sternly.

"You must rest too," she scolded kindly. "You must build up your strength for the long journey home."

The girl kissed the old tanuki woman's cheeks. Blossom had settled Keiji back into the nest Sayuri had made in the sunniest corner of the room. Sayuri snuggled next to his warmth. No one had to tell her twice. Safe sleep was very sweet.

IT TOOK FIVE LONG DAYS for Haru to undo the harm the Patriarch had inflicted, but finally all the blind had been restored. Some of the animals were not ready to forgive what the Patriarch had done and muttered of revenge. Great Mother had to sing many songs of healing before they let their anger go. Momo, who had only had one green eye before the Patriarch blinded him, was pleased to have two new black ones. It took him several days to get used to depth perception again.

Many creatures began leaving the city. The kappa who had been soldiers left as soon as their eyes were restored, for they missed their marshy lands with a deep longing.

Sayuri watched them go, not marching in military columns, but in twos and threes, as kappa chose travel companions closest to their villages. Snakes, who preferred to travel alone, slithered off quietly, and rats and rabbits hopped off in larger groups.

Echo – no, Sayuri shook her head. Fen!

Fen dropped her cool hand to clasp Sayuri's warm one.

"And will you go too?" Sayuri whispered. They had not spent much time together, for Fen had been aiding her kin and Sayuri had been nursing her brother. And Sayuri had felt shy, for she had thought she knew Echo, but she had been wrong. And now she had no idea who Fen was.

"I will travel a little more with you, my friend," Fen smiled. "If you wish it."

Sayuri hugged the slim kappa fiercely. "There's nothing I'd wish for more!"

Keiji ran over, his eyes bright and a lavender fruit in his hand. Now that he was better, he ate constantly, and Sayuri beamed to see his hunger.

"Momo says we can start for home today!" he jumped excitedly. "He said he'd give me a ride when I got tired!" He bit into the sour fruit and spat out a green seed.

"Ugh!" Sayuri exclaimed. The boy ran off in search of the cat before she could scold him on his manners.

Sayuri had no personal items to pack. She'd searched for her worn sneakers, but had never been able to find them. So she'd continued with bare feet, wrapping them with cloths at night to ward off the cold.

Sayuri and Fen went to the kitchens in search of travel foods.

Blue Oni was bossing a tanuki and three rabbits as they chopped vegetables and washed tubers in giant tubs. The animals joked in front of his face, but the oni didn't seem to mind – he was enjoying himself so much his blue face was flushed purple. Boulder ground roasted sesame seeds into paste in a huge mortar, and the toasty mealy smell filled the air. The bear ducked glances at the oni and snuck tastes when he wasn't looking.

"We need dried travel food and water for our voyage. Will you be coming with us?" Sayuri asked. But she already knew the answer.

The blue ogre spun around and threw his thick forearms over the girl's shoulders.

"Little Birdie!" the ogre sobbed. "Blue Oni will miss you! Blue Oni is staying in this big kitchen!"

"Bear stays too," Boulder bobbed his head, licking seed paste from his paw. "Bear will winter here, then go back to the mountains in time for the Festival of the Dead."

Sayuri sighed. She would miss her friends. She hugged them tight and gathered the food into bundles to be carried on top of her shoulders. She left the Blue Oni sobbing in Boulder's arms.

GREAT MOTHER TANUKI, the Old One, Machigai, and Haru sat at the long work table in the old dining hall. Dew sat on top of the table, pointing her finger on a scroll. Autumn wove lengths of silken ropes. The mats laid out for the injured had been removed to smaller rooms, for only a few were left, and the large hall had been turned into a magic work room.

"We c-c-can re-route this natural tunnel here," the toad pointed, "and branch off smaller p-p-pipes to small steam engines, here, here, and here!" Dew hopped with excitement. "We c-c-can even develop a hot water magic amplification module! Who will help me?"

Autumn waved two hairy legs. "I will," she chimed. "You'll need a lot of ropes."

Haru chuckled. "First, I must replant the blasted lands with saplings and seeds. Then I too will help."

"I will send some young tanuki from my clan to aid you," the Old One nodded, "if you will train the brightest in the arts of magic and transformation."

"It would be a great honour," Haru bowed. The working of great magic and the burden of responsibility for the deaths of many were heavy upon the fox. He had aged tenfold since the great battle and he looked as ancient as the Old One.

"I will pursue the arts of healing," Machigai said. "I will begin research in the natural powers of plants. Blossom wishes to study the healer's craft and he will remain here also. There must be much unknown plant life in the mountains, further north where no foxes have travelled. I wish to see these wonders."

Sayuri threw her arm around the fox's neck. "Your life spiral takes you on a different path," she smiled sadly. "I'm going to miss you so much."

"You don't know when we'll meet." Machigai nosed Sayuri's belly until she giggled. "For you may yet again be called to our world. Or I may be called to yours. Wherever there is mischief, I'll be there."

"Promise?" Sayuri smiled.

"Promise." Machigai licked the girl's cheek with his long pink tongue.

Sayuri turned to the Great Mother. The wise tanuki's eyes

crinkled with warm affection. "Child," she crooned, combing the girl's hair with her black claws, "our people will sing many songs of the girl hero who wrought much magic in this world and saved many lives."

Sayuri flushed with embarrassment and pride. "You bestow honour upon me, Great Mother," the girl bowed. "I will tell our tale in my world, so that humans may know the courage and wisdom of your people."

Sayuri turned to Haru. The old fox tilted his head to one side. Sayuri stared, not knowing what to say. The old fox stared back.

"I have learned much," she whispered.

Silence.

"I, also. Thank you," the fox murmured. Haru turned aside and reached for something on the bench next to him. He held out two shoes, beautifully crafted from shiny blue brocade, the inside lined with soft down. "Don't worry," he winked, "I took the fur from the bear's belly when he slept! Come. Try them on."

Sayuri slipped into the warm slippers. They were beautiful and warm, and they fit perfectly, the bottoms finished with a protective seal.

"Thank you," Sayuri bowed.

"I am grateful you can accept my gift," Haru bowed in return.

"It is well," the Great Mother nodded.

Sayuri bent over to kiss Dew's nose. The toad smiled and kissed her back. Then the girl ran to the Old One and almost knocked her over with the force of her hug. "Grandmother," Sayuri sighed.

"Ahhhh, child," the Old One sniffed. "I will miss you like a grandchild. I stay a while longer here, to help my companions establish a School of Higher Arts and Healing. But I will carry you close to my heart. You and yours will forever be a member of the Mountain's Blood Clan. Your family here will always welcome you home."

Sayuri wept. Kissed the Old One's wrinkled face. She turned and stared at everyone's faces so she might remember them all just as they were.

She ran from the room.

42. BACK ON THE PATH

Sayuri, Fen, Momo, and Keiji left the city when the sun was half again past its zenith and halfway to the horizon. The four companions carried pouches of seeds: wildflowers, grasses, wingpods of maples, sticky burrs, and fruiting seeds also. They scattered small handfuls as they went in the hope that some would take root when the rains fell. Haru and the Old One's youngsters would plant saplings in the spring.

They walked steadily in the late afternoon sun. Fen was draped with a weightless, hooded silk cape Autumn had woven. Protected from the sun's drying rays, Fen walked with her eyes closed, hand clasped in Sayuri's firm grip. When Keiji became tired, Momo let the child ride upon his back until he was rested. Sayuri watched a trifle enviously.

I'm afraid not, Momo blinked.

Sayuri laughed at the cat's expression.

It took three days to walk out of the razed lands. When they entered the coolness of the woods, they marvelled at the sweet smell of growing things. Fen joyfully took off the silken cloths, relishing the moisture upon her skin. Birds chattered, ducking for insects, asking for the latest news from the Patriarch's domain. When they heard that the dome was destroyed and the Patriarch had taken a new name, swallows sent envoys to the learned crows in the mountains and the wise birds flew to the city.

"So many things are going to happen now," Sayuri said wistfully. "I wish I could see what becomes of the School. If I stayed here, I might learn magic arts too." She gazed into the crackling flames of their evening camp. There was a small pop! and Sayuri jumped. "There's no magic in the world I come from."

Momo had caught an enormous fish in a fast stream and they all lay with full stomachs, Keiji already fast asleep.

Fen glanced at the girl's moody face. The flames threw flickering shadows on her features. "Are you so sure?" the kappa asked gently. "Your powers are all your own. Perhaps your people have magic but have forgotten how to call it."

An image of Kimi staring blankly at her fingers came and went so fast that Sayuri gasped. Left her with a longing to see her mother that bordered on pain.

Fen laid a worried hand on Sayuri's arm, and the girl smiled at her friend's concern.

"I'm okay. And maybe you're right. Maybe there is magic still waiting to be called."

"I can't imagine any world without it," the kappa said. She placed another branch on the flames. "You sleep now, and I'll take the first watch."

"What for?" Sayuri asked. "The Patriarch is healed and we're safe in the forest."

"Sayuri," Fen shook her head, "the world is complex. We do not call danger, but sometimes danger seeks an audience. It is only wise to be cautious."

"Oh," Sayuri answered, feeling slightly foolish. Of course she hadn't cured the whole world! What a nut! "I'll take second watch," she said, then yawned. "Good night."

"Rest well, my friend," Fen whispered.

SO THEY WALKED THROUGH MEADOWS, marshes, and grove after grove of bamboo. Forests of deciduous trees turning slightly yellow along leaf tips. And still they walked, slower now, for the ground started to rise into hills and rounded mountains. The trees became taller and thicker, giants of a thousand years, the heavy perfume of pine and cedar sweetening the air.

Keiji stayed close to Momo, who told long tales of what had happened while the boy was a captive of the Patriarch. Sayuri could hear the cat's murmuring thoughts and her brother listened with great concentration. She didn't know if the child thought the cat was telling stories to amuse him or if he thought the stories real.

The moss grew thick and thicker still. Great carcasses of fallen timber made travel difficult. There were no rivers or streams, so Momo chose safe mushrooms to eat, warning the children never to pick them without an elder. The firm-fleshed, round-bodied mushrooms the great cat dug out from beneath the moss had the texture of firm tofu and the taste of chicken.

"Wow," Sayuri enthused, "Jun would love this! Low calories and a taste like chicken!"

"I miss Jun," Keiji whispered. Rubbing his face in Momo's fur. "I miss Kimi. I even miss the root cellar!"

"Hah!" Sayuri choked. "Root cellar! I forgot all about it!"

"Doesn't seem so scary, huh?" Keiji grinned.

"Woooooooooo," Sayuri moaned like a ghost.

And their laughter filled the pine-sweet air.

The sun set early in the mountain forest and the evenings grew chillier. Sayuri started to worry about her brother being warm enough.

"Fen," Sayuri asked as something occurred to her.

"Hmm?" the kappa answered, stepping silently over broken branches.

"Do kappa hibernate in the winter like toads and frogs?"

"Only the northern kin," Fen replied. "My people live farther south, where it's warm all year round. We have small cities too. With houses built on stilts in the water."

"Ohhhh," Sayuri sighed, "I would like to see your home."

"But not this journey." Fen smiled.

Sayuri grinned. "No. The next."

The girl blinked. Sniffed. Caught a faint smell of woodsmoke.

Yes, child. The Yamanba's hut is just over this rise. Momo purred.

"Oh!" Keiji gasped. "The Water of Possible!"

"Possibility," Sayuri murmured. "I forgot all about that."

"I must leave you now," Fen said sadly. "I cannot enter the Yamanba's house, because I was not called there."

"All by yourself?" Sayuri gulped. "But even you said there could be dangers! You can't travel home all by yourself."

Rest easy, Momo said. *When I have seen you safely into the Yamanba's hut, I will catch up to our friend and accompany her to her home. I have always wanted to see the floating cities of the kappa people.*

"Momo come home with Keiji!" The boy flung his arms around the cat's neck and wouldn't let go. "I saw you! You were sitting in the rocking chair. You can come with us!"

Shhhhhh, the great cat soothed. *I was called, just as you were. But that doesn't mean I am meant to stay in your world, nor you in ours. There are fine balances that keep our worlds rotating and we break the natural laws at great risk.*

"I don't care!" Keiji shouted. Then he burst into tears. Momo curled a paw around the weeping boy's shoulders and whispered gently with his thoughts.

"I'll never forget you," Sayuri said fiercely, staring at her green friend. Fen was crying and fat tears dripped down her face.

"You're wasting water," Sayuri hiccuped, laughing and crying at the same time. They hugged each other close, inhaling the scent of each other. Sayuri pulled back and dragged the back of her hand over her eyes.

"Here," she said, crouching down. She pulled the brocade slippers off her feet. Silky blue as the day they were given to her, the magic kept them free from wear and eternally soft. "It's all I have. I want you to have them." The girl thrust the slippers into her friend's hands.

"These are of special magic," Fen protested.

"Then they'd best stay here," Sayuri said firmly. "And I want you to keep them for me."

"I will," Fen whispered. She kissed Sayuri on both cheeks. "Safe passage home, my friend." And the kappa was gone. A blink of an eye. She'd vanished into the forest.

Sayuri stared into the trees.

"Farewell."

43. THE FINAL TEST

"Well, well." A huge brown face peered through the open sliding door, Yamanba's white hair spilling every which way. "You children have found your way back! What a great story you have travelled!"

"Yamanba!" they ran to the giant mountain woman. Yamanba scooped them up and kissed the tops of their heads.

"You have done well," she murmured with her deep voice. "I am very proud of you."

The children beamed as the mountain woman carried them inside to the warmth of her hearth.

"Well, cat," Yamanba snorted. "I thought you were too old for this business. And look at you. You come back with two eyes instead of one!"

Momo minced inside without a word. He sat in front of the fire and started grooming his back leg.

Sayuri and Keiji giggled.

A hearty broth bubbled from the great cooking pot hanging from the ceiling and the children's stomachs growled.

Yamanba laughed. "First eat. Rest. Then you will try the

Water once more."

"Yes," Sayuri nodded. "Yes, we will."

THEY ATE FROM THE YAMANBA'S COOKING POT as the giant mountain woman smoked from her long-handled pipe – the red ember circling in the air as she asked for the finer details of their great adventure.

"Aren't you the One Who Watches?" Sayuri asked.

Yamanba eyed her shrewdly. "Yes, child. That I am. But I watch many and can't watch as closely as I would like."

So Sayuri told her great tale, Keiji interrupting now and then to explain what happened to him while Sayuri wandered the forest and mountains.

Momo said nothing at all. Only slept so soundly he didn't even purr.

Finally, the telling was done and the children were full and rested.

Night was ripe.

"It is time," Yamanba said simply. And stood.

Momo rose to his paws, blinking his bright black eyes. *Children,* he purred, *our paths diverge for the moment.* He closed his eyes, raising his chin in a cat smile. *I will await the day when our paths cross again.*

Sayuri and Keiji threw their arms around the great cat's neck. Keiji sobbed and Sayuri wondered that he still had tears left to cry. Though she swiped quickly at the wetness in her own eyes.

"Thank you, Momo. For everything," Sayuri said fiercely.

Hmmmmm, Momo breathed.

Sayuri pulled Keiji away from their friend.

Momo blinked once more, flicked his tail, then leapt silently out the door. Keiji still gasped with after-shudders of tears, but he squeezed them back tightly when Sayuri clasped his hand.

"We're ready," Sayuri said.

THEY ENTERED THE ROOM where the large earthenware basin held the Water of Possibility. The lamp Yamanba held flicked long shadows on the walls. The liquid in the basin seemed to move, though nothing touched it, and the waters didn't reflect but pulled light inward.

The same rich moist smell was thick in the air, with the scent of decaying leaves, wet earth, and a tinge of sulfur.

Sayuri stared, her fingers tingling, glowing brighter and brighter. She glanced at her brother and he stared at the surface, mesmerized.

"Are you ready now to reach into the Water of Possibility, to receive both the good and the bad you carry within yourselves?" the mountain woman intoned. Her hair was wild and, in the flickering light of the lamp, expressions played across the giant woman's face, frightening, kindly, wicked, wise.

Sayuri squeezed Keiji's hand. She searched deep within her heart. And met strength.

"Yes," the children said softly.

"I am happy to know you." Yamanba smiled her wide-gapped teeth. She set down the lamp and was gone.

SAYURI STARED AT KEIJI'S FACE. He looked cautious but not frightened, and she was amazed at his fortitude. Couldn't believe he was the same brother who picked his nose and drove her wild. He still spoke in baby talk when he was upset, but maybe it didn't mean he was frightened like a baby. Maybe he was coping in his own way. Maybe, she thought, maybe I'm not the same sister.... She rubbed the top of her brother's head and he ducked out of her reach. Giggled.

"Okay? You ready?" Sayuri asked.

Keiji pressed his lips together. And nodded.

"Well," Sayuri advised, "breathe in deep. Like you're diving." And because the utter silence of the dark room called for formality, she lightly pressed her palms against her thighs and bowed at the Water. Keiji bowed too. "We are ready to receive," Sayuri uttered with great solemnity.

Silence rang in the air.

The children gripped tight, Sayuri's right hand in Keiji's left, their hearts tripping with hope and fear; they plunged their free hands into the mysterious liquid.

They were shocked. Neither hot, nor cool, the temperature of the Water was beyond their human senses. Only the feel of silk against their skin. Their eyes rounded, mouths "O's" of wonder, their arms reached deep, deeper than possible, whole galaxies, whole eons snaking past their fingertips.

Then, simultaneously, their fingers touched something tangible.

SOMETHING SO WONDERFUL, warm, and safe, they just knew. Their lips turned upward into glowing smiles. Their eyes soft. Sayuri and Keiji turned to each other and they laughed with wonder and joy. Gently clasped what their hands touched and raised to the surface.

IT WAS A GLOBE, THE SIZE OF TWO HEARTS. The surface looked like glass, but felt warm and yielding as skin. It gave beneath their trembling fingertips, warm as blood and slightly pulsing. The children were bathed in the glow the orb cast and they drew their faces close to the warm light that flickered with some inner movement....

Keiji and Sayuri gasped with joy. For what visions they saw! They gazed into the globe, each bringing with them their own longings. Sayuri heard her brother laughing just before she was pulled into a daylight bright, reflecting off waves in the brilliant ocean. Seagulls wheeled in the air, hoping for picnic leftovers. Sayuri Who Watches, watched Sayuri Who Swam. And the glorious warmth of the water! The salt held her floating as if she swam on air, and she glided, leapt, giddy with pleasure. Sayuri glanced toward the shore and saw her mother sitting beside her brother, eating onigiris and throwing bits of rice at the seagulls. Her father beside her, ducking beneath the surface to tug her feet. Sayuri dove in after, the scatter of brilliant fish, the light breaking in the water like gold....

...the flickering light faded, and all that was left was an orange ember deep within the orb.

"Ohhhhhhhh," the children sighed.

Sayuri and Keiji looked into each other's faces. Yes. That

was where they wanted to be. The heartsafe place. They looked longingly at the sphere, but the visions were gone, the orb a window and not a doorway. Sayuri tucked the now faintly glowing sphere down the front of her shirt for safekeeping. Keiji gave a little giggle and poked the roundness at his sister's tummy.

Grimly, they faced the Water of Possibility again.

"You know we have to do this," Sayuri said, resolutely.

"Jun says we should try to think of all options," Keiji suggested, attempting a nervous smile.

"Remember, at the beginning? Yamanba said that once we took the good, we had to receive the bad or the possible became impossible," Sayuri reminded.

"What if," Keiji looked about, "what if it's a trick?"

Sayuri gulped. She had considered that as well. Especially since Yamanba was gone. Wouldn't she be here to help them if she were truly a friend? Where were all their friends? Why was no one left to help them?

But no, that wasn't fair. Their paths were their own to face. And Yamanba had told them everything they needed to know. Hadn't she?

"I don't know," Sayuri muttered. "We have no way of knowing until it's too late." She sank to the ground, tired, miserable. She had felt so brave before.

Keiji crouched next to her, wrapping his arms around his knees.

Sayuri shivered. The wind outside swirled into the giant trees and she could hear them singing in whistling creaky voices. But inside the room where they waited, all was silent.

As if the very atoms of time had stilled.

Then the orb inside Sayuri's T-shirt began to glow. Brighter and brighter, it lit up from beneath the dirty cloth. It floated, bobbed, light as a bubble of soap. Slipped out of Sayuri's shirt to hang in the air above the basin. A small sun, it cast a warming glow and they bloomed beneath the gift. And under their feet! The soil moved. The nudge of dirt pushed aside by green shoots, seed husks dropping off sticky new buds as leaves spread wide, grew up and outward...the seedlings stretched, stems filled, bamboo groves shot from yellow-tipped spears, ferns, trees, and the room was no longer. It was a new forest and the perfume of growth was so sweet, the children danced in the heady air.

"Let's do it now!" Sayuri called out. "Let's do this when there's so much good around us!"

Keiji nodded. They clasped hands again, and plunged again, into the deep magic water.

The dark liquid rolled in the basin. Sayuri stared wide-eyed at Keiji's pale face. If they could, they would have jerked their hands from the Water, but they were drawn by some unknown force to choose that which they would rather never face....

AT THE SAME MOMENT, their fingertips brushed against something in the depth. Only, such fear and revulsion washed over them it was barely possible to breathe. Eyes wide with panic, they helplessly stared into each other's faces.

If only they could let go! If only — but they couldn't.

Because what they drew from the Waters came from themselves.

The horrible force compelled them. Their fingers clasped
and pulled something to the surface.

SAYURI GAPED. SHE HELD A HAND. A child's wet dirty hand,
and she drew the arm upward, a head breaking through the
surface of the water as if being born. Sayuri's heart thumped
in her chest, as the child started to lift her face, for Sayuri
didn't know what face her monster bore.

Sayuri staggered backward. Her mouth dropping with
shock. Horror.

The monster she had raised was herself.

Sayuri gulped, unsure, and the other Sayuri gulped at the
same time. What was the trick? Sayuri's heart thumped. How
could she neutralize any danger?

Fear meets fear. Welcome might call welcome. It had
worked when they had first been "chased" by Yamanba....
Sayuri slowly smiled and she was pleased, for the other Sayuri
smiled with her, but no, no! The girl's teeth shone too bright,
silver-pointed razors that overlapped, row upon row, in her
monstrous mouth, teeth that were meant to raze and destroy.

"No!" Sayuri screamed.

"Yesssssssshhh," the Sayuri monster seeped through her
murderous mouth and Sayuri turned her face away, retched,
for this monster had come out of herself...and the words of
the Patriarch came back to her, for he had said, your good
and my evil are twins.

All the times her heart had faltered. When she would have left her brother behind. When she had hated Echo. When she had abandoned Machigai.

When she would have killed the Patriarch in the name of justice.

These were Sayuri's also.

She wept.

"Let go of my sister!" Keiji shouted.

Sayuri opened her eyes. And saw. Superimposed on the monstrosity of her inner fear was the form of a clown. A funny-faced painted clown. Funny for her, but she knew it was her brother's worst fear. And that same brother was fighting, ripping the red ball nose from the clown, to save Sayuri's life. The clown lifted his arm to tap at the exposed flesh beneath and Sayuri burst out laughing.

The laughter broke apart the clutch of fear and hate inside her heart and her face blossomed.

The other Sayuri's jaw dropped open in surprise. Sayuri laughed even harder. She turned to the Sayuri Monster. Gazed fully upon who she was and who she could be. Opened her heart. Sayuri stretched out her arms and clasped the Sayuri Monster's body.

"I am you and you are me. I name you Sayuri and accept you."

The monster struggled in her arms, but Sayuri held tight, as the glowing orb above their heads grew brighter and brighter. The Water in the basin began to churn, faster and faster, a wind rising from the deeps, the forest, the green and growing, pulled in. The children felt the draw, not like a whirlpool, but the warm spiral flow of falling into sleep. Above them, the small sun was hot, brighter still, and the children shut their eyes to the incredible light.

THE LIGHT WENT OUT.

THEN, THROUGH CLOSED EYES, THEY FELT A CHANGE.

44. CHANGES

THEY OPENED THEIR EYES.

Above them a naked forty-watt bulb glowed in the root cellar. Sayuri held the end of the light string that she might have just pulled. The children stared at each other. Confused.

"What?" Sayuri said.

"Huh?" Keiji uttered. He looked down at his hand, because there was something in it. His fingers gripped a rubbery red ball, and on the end of it was a silver horn. He gave it a squeeze.

"Honk!"

They giggled.

"HONK! HONK!"

The children burst out laughing.

"What's so funny?" they heard their mom calling from the top of the stairs. "You kids finally got hungry enough to go to the root cellar?!"

"Kimi!" they yelled, dashing from the room, pounding

up the stairs.

The light in the kitchen seemed somehow overbright. Sayuri blinked and blinked.

Their mom hugged them, then laughed, "Wa! Ha! Ha!"

And for one brief moment, Sayuri seemed to see the face of the mountain woman superimposed on their mother's face.

"I'm sorry I'm late!" she boomed. "Did anything happen while I was gone?" Kimi stared at Sayuri's feet. "You should have shoes on when you go into the basement."

Everything felt so startling! The kitchen was bright and plastic bags full of groceries were spread all over the linoleum. Kimi's blue nail polish looked so unnatural! Sayuri slumped into the kitchen chair and stared at her bare feet. She stared at her hands, slowly turning her palms upward. The work-worn calluses were gone! Did that mean it had all been some kind of dream? But where did that leave her runners and socks? More importantly, would they affect the cosmic balance?

Sayuri giggled. Keiji glanced as his sister and giggled back.

No.

They had been there. Living Earth. Of this her heart was certain.

"You kids are up to something," Kimi wrinkled her nose.

"HONK! HONK!" Keiji squeezed his horn.

"Wa! Ha! Ha!" Kimi laughed. "Where'd you get that funny thing? Downstairs? You could put it on your bike."

The kitchen door burst open. Jun came inside, holding a

paper bag. He set his purchases on the table and Keiji dashed to him to be lifted up high in the air.

"Can we get a cat?" Keiji asked.

"Your asthma, duckling," his father reminded.

"I'm gonna be okay!" Keiji shouted, then laughed.

Sayuri watched as her mom put away the Japanese groceries she'd bought in the city.

There was a warmth deep inside her. Something had changed. Do I look older? Sayuri wondered. We were gone for so long. She looked at her brother, who was rubbing his face into Jun's neck.

"Your whiskers feel like a cat's tongue," her brother said.

"Have you been playing with strays?" Jun asked.

Sayuri burst out laughing. Then dragged her arm across her chest. Itchy! Her breasts were growing again.

"Do I smell something deep fried?!" Kimi sniffed, eyebrows raised.

Jun looked sheepishly at the bag on the table. "I suddenly had a craving for fish and chips," he confessed.

"Yay! I love fish and chips!" Keiji crowed, tearing open the bag.

Outside, the wind picked up and rattled panes of glass in the window. Sayuri looked up and for a brief moment the smiling face of a giant woman gazed upon her, a great cat blinked, and then the window was only glass.

"Kimi," Sayuri said slowly, "I want to take yoga lessons with you. Okay? It'll be good for your writing and good for my concentration."

Kimi raised her finely formed eyebrows. "Sure, ducky. I've

actually thought of that now and then."

"And I want to take rock wall climbing and orienteering, and Jun?" Sayuri grinned on the way up to the bathroom. She desperately wanted to brush her teeth! "Jun, you think we might consider a fish-only non-meat diet?"

"I'll look into it," Jun promised as Sayuri creaked up the stairs.

The old wooden boards screeched in protest and Sayuri giggled. To think that she'd been afraid of the house! She jogged into the washroom and ran bathwater as she cleaned her teeth. Sayuri brushed vigorously. It felt like she hadn't used a toothbrush for a month! When she was done, she stared into the mirror, watching steam rising from the tub behind her. The water roared like a waterfall. Sayuri closed her eyes. Where were Fen and Momo now? Did Yamanba watch over them? Was she watching over Sayuri?

"You see," she murmured, "we made it home."

THAT NIGHT, SUPPER WAS LATE AND LOUD. They joked and laughed, Jun telling funny stories from the hospital, Kimi sharing news about a film company wanting to turn one of her books into a movie. Keiji talked about how great it would be to have a cat, especially a cat that controlled mice with hantavirus.

Sayuri sat back and watched everyone, the miracle of their expressions, the emotions which played on their faces. How beautiful and remarkable they are she thought, her eyes dreamy.

"What's happened to you, tonight?" Kimi asked, her head

tilted to one side. "Are you feeling okay, ducky?"

Jun looked up from Keiji's impassioned speech about the cleanliness of cats and stared at Sayuri's face intently, as if he could measure her temperature just by looking.

"I'm just thinking," Sayuri murmured.

"It's off to bed for you," Jun said decisively. "You ought not go to Compet if you're not feeling well."

"Jun! I feel great!" Sayuri said indignantly. Then yawned enormously. Maybe going to bed wasn't a bad idea. But nothing would keep her from swimming tomorrow! She felt as if she could carve a whole second off her backstroke! She felt as if she could march up to Darryl and invite her over to see their house and her amazing loft room. And Sidney who'd made fun of her name. Maybe Sidney was unkind because she was scared of losing Darryl. Or maybe she was a jerk. Maybe Sayuri could invite Sidney over too, and see who she really was.

Kimi hopped off her chair and drew her arm around Sayuri's shoulder. Gazed at her daughter's face. Sayuri snuggled into Kimi's warm clasp and gazed back. And as Sayuri stared, she saw how her mother's pupils slowly dilated, as if Kimi was looking down a deep and dark well.

Far sight, Sayuri thought, her mouth slowly dropping. Kimi had the far sight too, and without really knowing. Was that why her mother wrote horror novels? Had she been to Living Earth before? Or somewhere else? For Momo had said that the One Who Watches had many gates to ward. And that their world was only one of many....

"Kimi," Sayuri murmured. "Mom. Come sleep in my

room tonight. I want to tell you some bedtime stories."

"Nothing would please me more," Kimi said solemnly, her eyes still far away.

"Me too!" Keiji cried. "I want to tell stories too!"

"I'd love to hear them," Jun cupped Keiji's face as if it was a flower.

"Let me tell you a story of a great purple cat called Momo," Keiji chattered as Jun led him to the bathroom.

AND WHEN THE HOUSE WAS FILLED WITH SLEEP, the stories that were told wove their strands like jewelled cobwebs. A girl slept beside her mother. The sky flew above their heads, dreams pulling stars from darkness to light.

DOWNSTAIRS, THE LIGHT WAS STILL ON IN THE ROOT CELLAR. It glowed warmly in the earthen room. That which was had changed in small ways. The concrete floor was no longer. Rich moist soil lay sweet and vibrant with potential. Then movement. Beneath the surface. A small nudge, nudging through aeons with the small magic of hope and compassion. A pale green shoot pushed through the dark dirt, twining upward from aged roots long thought dead. The verdant stem stretched upward, unfurling three small leaves. A warm wind brushed against the new growth, bringing with it the sweet scent of rain.

ACKNOWLEDGEMENTS

THE COVER OF A BOOK IS DECEPTIVE. It names the author(s) but not the many, many people who made the work possible. I believe that a published book is the artistic and political culmination of community, and I would like to honour the many people who made this novel possible.

My family is first. Thank you to Koji and Sae. Your questions and observations are daily revelations and your presence in my life is a remarkable gift: I do not know why I have been so blessed. And I am grateful. Thank you to my parents and grandmother, who raised a child who could become a writer. Tamotsu and my sisters, Naomi, Nozomi, and Ayumi: I appreciate your long-standing support, critiques, irreverence, and love. I could not have made it without you. A special thank you to sister/friend, Susanda Yee, for a late-night conversation about the narrow depiction of good vs. evil in popular culture. Your keen mind and thoughtful questions continue to challenge the limitations of my own ideas. And colleagues and dear friends who are there for me when the energy flags. Thank you Tamai Kobayashi, Larissa Lai, Aruna Srivastava, and Rita Wong. And a special thank you to Ashok Mathur for your always encouragement and setting up my time at the Leighton Studios!

Writing this book has given me the opportunity to reflect upon special teachers who've made a difference in my life, and I would like express my gratitude to them. Words you said, lessons you taught, rippled outward and affected me in positive ways. Thank you to Mr. Deny Ross, Mr. Walsh, Mrs. Alice Tarnava, Fred Wah, and Aritha van Herk.

I would also like to express my gratitude to all of the writers of children's books who depicted girls as heroes.

Coteau Books has been an amazing press. The level of support, sensitivity, and generosity has been more than a writer could ever hope for. It has been a joy to find a publisher that still reveals a soul. Thank you, Barbara Sapergia, for being a gentle yet astute editor. Your patience and commitment are truly inspirational and you asked the right questions in the right places.

I would also like to express my gratitude to The Alberta Foundation for the Arts, the Leighton Studios at the Banff Centre, and the Canada Council Millennium Fund for supporting this work.

THE SPIRAL IS A SYMBOL THAT ARISES IN MANY CULTURES throughout the world. I have been especially impressed by the significance of the spiral in Maori culture in Aotearoa. The depiction of the spiral, in this novel, has been influenced by my understanding of what it represents in Maori culture. It is my hope that I have not transgressed in working the symbol into this story and that the spirit in which I have written about it is acceptable.

Forms of the earth lodge were used in ancient Japanese cultures as well as First Nations cultures. The earth lodge depicted in this novel is based on Japanese and Klamath designs. The wigwam was used by many First Nations people throughout North America. I have not asked for permission from elders in representing the wigwam in this novel and I hope that my depiction has not been dishonourable.

The word "Yamanba" has been spliced from the correct spelling: Yama-uba. When pronounced out loud, the word "sounds" more like "yamanba" than the correct spelling looks like.

And, finally, I would like to extend my final appreciation to you, the reader.

Hiromi Goto
Calgary, August, 2001

Sources Consulted

Ede Miru Nihonno Rekishi, Shigeo Nishimura. Hukuonkan-Shoten, 1986.

The Tribal Living Book, David Levinson & David Sherwood, Johnson Books, 1984.

Where The Wild Things Are, Maurice Sendak, HarperCollins Publisher, First Trophy Edition, 1987.

ABOUT THE AUTHOR

H IROMI GOTO is an award-winning author whose 1994 novel *Chorus of Mushrooms* was the Best First Book for the Canada/Caribbean region of the Commonwealth Writers Prize and a co-winner of the Canada-Japan Book Award. Her short stories and critical writing have appeared in, among others, *MS* magazine and the Oxford University Press anthology *Making a Difference*.

Born in Japan, Hiromi Goto lives in Calgary and is an active member of the Canadian and Alberta literary communities. She works as a writing instructor, a culture and education advocate, and the mother of two.